Jack & Susan in 1913

Jack & Susan
in 1913

Michael McDowell

FELONY & MAYHEM PRESS • NEW YORK

All the characters and events portrayed in this work are fictitious.

JACK & SUSAN IN 1913

A Felony & Mayhem mystery

PRINTING HISTORY
First edition (Ballantine): 1986
Felony & Mayhem edition: 2012

ISBN: 978-1-937384-38-8

Manufactured in the United States of America

Printed on 100% recycled paper

Library of Congress Cataloging-in-Publication Data

McDowell, Michael, 1950-
Jack & Susan in 1913 / Michael McDowell. -- Felony & Mayhem
edition.
     pages cm
ISBN 978-1-937384-38-8
1. Nineteen tens--Fiction. 2. Motion picture industry--Fiction.
3. Mystery
fiction. 4. Love stories. I. Title.
PS3563.C35936J33 2012
813'.54--dc23
                          2012045487

For Ann Leigh

The icon above says you're holding a copy of a book in the Felony & Mayhem "Wild Card" category. We can't promise these will press particular buttons, but we do guarantee they will be unusual, well written, and worth a reader's time. If you enjoy this book, you may well like other "Wild Card" titles from Felony & Mayhem Press.

For more about these books, and other Felony & Mayhem titles, or to place an order, please visit our website at:

www.FelonyAndMayhem.com

Other "Wild Card" titles from

FELONY&MAYHEM

Jack & Susan in 1913

The Dramatis Personae of 1913:

JACK, a man of mystery, and a tinkerer who joined a profession that he didn't even know existed—

SUSAN, a beautiful actress who shows the new town of Hollywood a new trick or two—

HOSMER, Susan's other suitor, in work as well as romance a rival to the bumbling Jack—

And then *Tripod*, with three good legs and a wooden one, who "pad, pad, pad, taps" his way into Jack and Susan's hearts...

Part I

SUSAN

CHAPTER ONE

DAISY. *There are lots and lots of women taking care of themselves—putting up the bluff of being independent and happy who would be glad to live in a little flat and do their own work—just to be the nicest thing in the world to some man.*

KEITH. *That kind of a woman is a thing of the past.*

DAISY. *Oh no, they're not. They're lying around* thick. *The trouble is—a* woman *can't ask. Even if a man is— just at her hand—and she knows she could make him happy—she can't* tell *him—she can't open his eyes—she has to hide what might make things right for both of them. Because she's a woman.*

KEITH. *Oh—love doesn't cut much ice with a woman. Women are all* brain *nowadays.*

DAISY. *That's enough to use all the brains a woman's got— to make a home—to bring up children—and to keep a man's love.*

❈ ❈ ❈

One of the great difficulties about being an actress was being forced to speak the most appalling inanities. Of course, there were other difficulties:

Little work.

Long hours when there *was* work.

Scant pay.

Public opprobrium or, worse, public neglect.

The lechery of stage managers and the jealousy of sister actresses.

Susan Bright could endure those things. But it positively galled her to have to stand in front of an audience and play Daisy, a mooning nitwit of a female secretary. Daisy's ideas on the subject of female emancipation in the year of 1913 would have seemed conservative in the Garden of Eden.

Yet here was Susan, who had been of an independent nature all of her life, spewing this pabulum in front of several hundred strangers. During this little scene with the cretinous *jeune premier* she was supposed to be sappy in love with, Susan realized that the audience admired her for the very sentiments she despised. Those people on the other side of the footlights thought Daisy was absolutely right in wanting to give up everything for her man. While the play progressed, after her little exchange was over, Susan/Daisy seated herself on a couch far upstage to sew a button on a torn shirt.

She knew she ought to be more excited, for it was the opening performance of *He and She*. The play was a revival of a popular two-year-old domestic drama about a lady sculptor who finds herself in competition with her sculptor husband. There was a great deal of gassing and grousing about the role of the new woman in society, or woman in the new society, and it ended with the wife giving up her chance at artistic fame and fortune. *Of course.* Family came first.

In this tedious dramatic argument, Susan, as the repressed secretary, wore a starched white blouse and a skirt so tight she could scarcely walk across the stage. Susan's sleek black hair was pulled so tightly in a bun at the back of her neck that her eyes ached. Every time she opened her mouth, Daisy erupted into a piece of nonsense about woman's role and goal and reward in life being to take care of some man, no matter how much of an idiot, cad, or murderous ruffian he might be. Susan didn't complain—aloud—because it was work; in another week she would start to be paid for it.

Her last position on the New York stage had been, literally, behind the throne in some strange piece of business about Cleopatra. She'd waved a large palm frond rhythmically through two acts—even when Cleopatra wasn't on the throne. Her only pleasure in that role was in delivering the asp to the leading lady, who deserved a real reptile as much as any actress Susan had ever met.

She had decided that her present role would be worth the two payless weeks of rehearsal, thirteen hours a day—nine to noon, one to six, and eight to midnight— the uncomfortable, unflattering costume; the leading lady's patronizing civility; the stage director's amorous advances; and the inane babblings of her character. It was already worth it, in fact, in Susan's eyes, for her name was on the board at the front of the theater. That had never happened before. People buying tickets might look at the board, see the name "Susan Bright," and wonder, "What sort of actress is she?" There might even be a mention of her in the papers, for although Susan despised Daisy, Susan meant to make Daisy believable and likable.

The play wound its way toward its tedious, improbable end, and it was a blessing that Susan had so little to do in the last few scenes. She sat in the green room and read the serial adventure in *McClure's Ladies Magazine* while her fellow actors, also awaiting the curtain call, played whist. Audience response was polite but not overly enthusiastic, and the *jeune premier* whispered ruefully, "Ten days." Susan happily detected an increase in the applause when she stepped forward for her solo curtsy, and in the third row on the aisle was a tall, clean-shaven man who was clapping madly. He would have stood up out of his seat to continue the ovation, but his jacket caught on the arm of the chair and prevented him. Susan would have liked to believe that this gentleman was the dramatic critic for the *Sun*, but she was still too clearheaded for that. Weariness competed with excitement in Susan's system, but on account of the two rehearsals earlier in the day, weariness won out. She dragged herself down the worn wooden steps toward the basement of the theater.

Susan shared a dressing room with one Ida Conquest. This actress had attained a certain notoriety for being the Aeroplane Girl in the *Follies of 1912*, and her photograph in aviatrix costume had sold many thousands of copies. Ida was playing the "forthright" girl in *He and She*, the one who *doesn't* think that a woman should give up everything for her man's satisfaction. Susan would have been much more comfortable in that part, and anyway, Ida didn't appreciate the role. Ida was against women's suffrage because she felt that "girls suffered quite enough already, thank you very much." She was a young lady who, in general, did her thinking on the installment plan.

The dressing room was about the size of a closet, and Susan's body here and there bore little bruises where she'd come into sudden contact with clothes hooks on the walls. "Not enough room to swing a cat by the tail," Ida said, at least three times a day, and whenever Susan inadvertently elbowed her.

"I glanced out the window on the way down," said Susan. "It's still snowing."

It was the early part of January, and winter's early darkness made Susan blue. She saw little of the daylight. Theaters are always dark, and the few windows built into them are in out-of-the-way corridors and open on to air shafts. The dim light that shines through them always seems grimy. For actors, daylight is like a pleasure vaguely and fondly recalled from a country childhood.

Ida Conquest gazed at herself in the mirror. Even in this dank, dingy hole at the bottom of the New Columbia Theatre, somewhere below West Thirty-eighth Street; even with her powdered countenance lighted by a fitful gas flame; even in a costume that looked quite splendid at a distance of thirty feet, but appeared tawdry and dirty close up—Ida Conquest was a dazzling beauty. She was buxom, with a tiny waist, and well-turned calves. Her dimpled cheeks, tiny mouth and vast blue eyes were framed by yellow curls.

Susan Bright was the physical opposite of Ida Conquest. Whereas Ida was of short stature and a pleasing roundness, Susan Bright was tall and tended toward angularity. As a child, Susan's mother had declared that her daughter had "no end of neck," and even now Susan tended to wear the sorts of collars that disguised that feature. Whereas Ida's complexion was all creams and blushing pinks, with naturally golden hair and brows nearly invisible, Susan had a complexion that was a uniform, almost marble-white. No matter how uncomfortable Susan was, she didn't blush becomingly—as Ida did. Susan's hair was black, and it shone nearly blue in certain lights. Her eyes were black as well, and in those you could read Susan's soul—which was often more of an inconvenience than not. Susan's soul sometimes had interesting but not very complimentary things to say about other people.

Susan had always suffered in comparison to women like Ida Conquest. But she was about to have her revenge. She had noted of late a change in styles, for women's bodies are just as much subject to fashion as hats or the length and silhouette of skirts. Susan scarcely dared to believe it, but she had noted in magazines devoted to women and their dress a tendency away from the Ida Conquest ideal of beauty, and toward a Susan Bright type of form and coloring. It was no longer de rigueur to be buxom, with a small waist and massive hips; a much slenderer form was splendid for the new tight skirts. Susan had once audibly gasped when she saw a drawing, in *Ladies Home Journal*, of a fashionable woman with a neck *longer* than her own. If the change happened quickly enough, it might be that Susan's beauty would actually eclipse that of Ida Conquest—though nothing, it had to be admitted, would compensate for the advancing years of an unmarried woman. At the age of twenty-seven Susan Bright would have been regarded as a spinster in any but theatrical circles. In theatrical circles, an unmarried woman of twenty-seven was assumed to be kept.

Susan was not kept. If she were, she ruefully admitted to herself, she'd be living in considerably better style than she was now.

Sometimes she wondered just what her future was to be. An endless succession of roles only a little better—if that—than her present one? The same dreary two rooms on West Sixtieth Street? Maybe even union with some aging *jeune premier*, simply because an easy, slipshod marriage was a less unthinkable condition than that of being always alone. But such morose thoughts occurred to Susan only when she was packed in tight with Ida Conquest in their damp unheated closet far below the level of the street. Or when she examined her purse each morning, and found ever less cash inside it—knowing that her scanty inheritance was little by little dwindling away in the bank account down on Wall Street.

That small inheritance and the indifference of distant relatives had allowed Susan to leave her hometown in Connecticut just before her twenty-fourth birthday and take up residence in New York. She had been the "star" of several amateur theatrical productions there in Winter River, and several times she had even been hired by traveling companies for bit parts. The praise of friends and even the managers of these companies was no guarantee of success in the city, and life had been hard for Susan Bright in the last three years. Her success was meager: five plays—about fourteen weeks of work altogether—in all that time. Despite the dismal projections of the *jeune premier*, Susan hoped for good notices and a long run.

Some actresses—such as the actress who had her elbow in Susan's ribs this very moment—had meteoric rises. Ida Conquest hadn't been on the stage for more than six months. Before that she had been a clerk at a ribbon store on Canal Street. Then she was "discovered." Susan knew in her heart that Ida would go on to an even bigger role in another play just as soon as this one was finished. Ida had that kind of luck. Susan would slog along in her theatrical career, step by wearying step, and perhaps never achieve the success that was undoubtedly going to fall into Ida's lap.

"Would you like to go out for a sandwich and cup of coffee?" Susan asked her companion. She was half-ashamed of the thoughts she'd entertained about Ida. After all, it wasn't Ida's fault she had been born beneath a conjunction of lucky stars.

"Lord no," returned Ida with vigor—as if the idea of eating simply and cheaply were mad, unpatriotic, and salacious. "I've got a gentleman waiting for me at the door. We'll be motoring over to that hotel on Fifth Avenue, what's it called? The expensive one? Sherry's. Sherry's is very dear. I'm going to have oysters. Oysters always make my complexion very pink."

"So does champagne," said Susan.

"How would you know how champagne tasted?" returned Ida casually.

"I've tasted it," said Susan but it was a lie and Ida knew it—and Susan knew Ida knew it.

"Maybe someday when you get a part that lets you wear some *real* clothes, maybe you'll attract somebody in the balcony—someone who can't see you too close up, I mean—and maybe he'll send you flowers and candy and ask you out to a restaurant where the champagne is already ordered." Ida's tone suggested that this was a possibility about as likely as Susan's starting out for California in a covered wagon at dawn the next day. "It could—*possibly*—happen."

"Ida, I'm very happy tonight, and I don't need champagne or flowers or candy to make me any happier."

"So you'll run home alone to that dreary little flat and lie down in your narrow little bed and stare at the cracks in the ceiling and think how lucky you are to have a role in *He and She*. And you'll wonder, 'What would they think of me back in Jersey now?' Ain't I hitting that nail square on its head?"

"Connecticut," said Susan ruefully. But in other respects, although Susan certainly wouldn't admit it aloud, Ida was right. And some of Susan's happiness dissolved and puddled on the stone floor of the dressing room when she thought of her dreary flat, her narrow cot, and the Florida-shaped cracks in her ceiling. "Come," she said loudly, answering a double knock on the door.

It was the doorman's daughter, who ran little errands in the theater. She was holding a square envelope, for which Ida automatically held out her hand.

"For Miss Bright," said the sad, pinched girl, who'd gotten a coating of dusty snow on her shoulders when she passed an open air-shaft window on her way down.

Ida threw down the chamois cloth she'd been rubbing her nose with, fell back against her chair in apparent astonishment, and turned a disbelieving gaze on Susan. "For *you*?"

Susan smiled, and took the note as if she were long-accustomed to receiving them. Only admirers sent such notes; it was Susan's first.

"Perhaps he mistook you for me," said Ida thoughtfully as the errand girl pulled shut the dressing room door. "Perhaps he thinks that *you* are Ida Conquest."

"No," said Susan. "I don't believe that's it at all." Actually, that's exactly what she did believe.

She opened the letter and read:

My dear Miss Bright,
I vastly admired your performance as Daisy tonight, and predict a glowing future for you on the boards of our many theaters. It would be a great honor if you would allow me to escort you to supper tonight. I will wait at the stage entrance for your reply.

With admiration and hope,
I remain,
Yours,
JAY AUSTIN

Susan suspected that Mr. Austin was the gentleman in the third row who had ripped his jacket while applauding her.

CHAPTER TWO

"IT'S CODE," said Ida definitely, when she'd read the note.

"Code?"

"He's planning something wicked. I guess you know what I mean by *that*."

"It seems quite straightforward to me," returned Susan, a little hotly. She certainly did know what Ida meant by *something wicked*.

"*Supper* is the code word. Supper means *something very wicked*. It means 'that which makes a woman fonder and a man more careless.' If ever I saw an invitation to a bedroom, this is it. The thing's clear as ice."

Susan was dubious. Ida was not known for her generous heart, and it might be that she was simply trying to spoil Susan's simple pleasure in the admiring note. On the other hand, why would a woman with as many admirers as Ida Conquest bother about depriving

Susan of one gentleman caller? Susan didn't know what to think.

"This is the scrawl of a fossil," added Ida, tossing the note aside.

That was jealousy.

"I'm going to see what he looks like," said Susan.

"Sixty if he's a day. Two things on his mind. One of them is his digestion."

Susan sighed. It was hard work being a single woman in New York. It would have been very pleasant to think of having supper with that young man in the third row. His face had been somewhat shadowed, and the footlights had been bright in her eyes, but she *thought* he was handsome.

"You're going to be disappointed," Ida warned her.

❧ ❧ ❧

A quarter of an hour later, protected against the snow by a cape, a wide-brimmed black hat, gloves, and boots, Susan headed for the front doors of the New Columbia Theater. The box-office keeper unlocked one of the doors for her. The snow that had been falling since morning was inches deep in those places where it had not already been swept up or trampled down. It was falling harder now, and the wind blew it horizontally across the glowing patches of streetlamps.

Holding the cape closed at her neck and lowering her head so that the brim of her hat shadowed her face, Susan crept to the corner of the building. She peered into the blind alleyway where the stage door was located.

A solitary man stood there at the concrete stoop.

He was not the man in the third row. That much Susan could tell from just his silhouette. The man in the theater, madly applauding, had been young and slender, and this man was definitely middle-aged and corpulent.

Perhaps sensing her presence he turned, and his face was illumined by the electric light beside the door.

Jay Austin was, in accordance with Ida's prediction, sixtyish. Moreover his complexion was red—probably from sharing too many bottles of champagne with young actresses.

Even from that distance of a dozen yards, and at night, in a driving snow, Susan could also tell that Mr. Austin was indeed the sort of gentleman to employ code words in notes sent backstage.

So Ida had been jealous—but Ida had also been right.

With a sigh, Susan Bright turned away into the snow.

Back at the entrance to the theater she ran into the show's stage director, and several of the actors. This group was retiring to a small neighborhood restaurant to wait for the reviews, with a bottle or two or three of wine, and they asked Susan to join them. Without knowing exactly why she did so, she declined the invitation.

When this group had ambled out of sight, she pulled the veil of her hat over her face, just in case Mr. Jay Austin should come out of the alleyway. Susan crossed Eighth Avenue and looked up and down. She had decided that if she found a taxicab, she'd take it. With the moderate hope of several weeks of employment—she would be getting in excess of thirty dollars a week—she could afford the fifty-cent extravagance.

The streets were now filling up with snow considerably faster than the municipal authorities could remove it, and no taxicabs were to be seen. She could either walk home—twenty-two blocks—or she could walk to the subway station at Times Square. She decided that the subway was by far the wiser idea.

With Times Square as her goal, Susan headed straight across residential Thirty-eighth Street toward Seventh Avenue where she would turn north at the Hotel York. It was still a long walk through the driving snow, alone at so late an hour, a prey to footpads or likely to be mistaken for a prostitute.

Just then a small white dog—a wire-haired terrier—bounded down the sidewalk toward her, yapping ferociously, and diving into small snowbanks at the base of the streetlamps as if he thought rats might have taken refuge inside. The dog was obviously as delighted with the weather as Susan was inconvenienced by it, and that gave her a little perspective on the gloominess of her disposition. After all, this should be a night of celebration—an opening night, the possibility of weeks of work, a purse that was going to swell instead of shrink. Susan could not help wishing that Mr. Jay Austin had proved to be someone her own age, or perhaps a little older, comfortably situated, unmarried, and not predicating a friendship on her making certain amorous concessions. It was a great mistake on the part of the lay public, Susan thought, to imagine that theater people were any less lonely than the rest of humanity.

"Here, boy," she cried with a snap of her fingers.

The dog ran up and leapt into the air, playfully snapping at her hand.

She caught him out of the air and hugged him and tossed him into a fluffy snowbank.

The dog burrowed down, shot back up again in a different place, ran around Susan three times, and leapt into the air again.

This play continued up the street as Susan made her way toward Seventh Avenue. If the collarless dog was a stray, then at least he was a happy stray.

At this late hour and in this weather the few people she passed were men, but she did not see their faces, they were so bundled against the driving snow. She knew that after they'd passed, they turned around and looked at her—a lone young woman on the snowy street at this hour. But Susan hurried along, laughing, with the white terrier.

As she rounded the Hotel York Susan became certain that she was being followed.

Just a feeling at first, confirmed a moment later by the noise of crunching snow in the silent city behind her.

The dog, tossed into yet another snowbank, this time came up growling.

Susan quickly reached down and snatched up the animal. She shook the clumped snow off him; he was now all teeth and hot doggy breath. He dug his claws into the front of her cape, and climbed up her shoulder, snarling and growling at whoever followed.

Probably it was just another lonely soul like her, stranded in the snowy night, with no intention more sinister than getting home as quickly as possible.

The dog scraped and clawed, evidently with the intention of attacking the person who was steadily lessening the distance between them, but Susan held him tight. The dog was a weapon, and she didn't want those ferocious jaws out of her hands.

The dog scraped, and barked, and clawed—and finally began to howl in his frustration. Susan moved along as quickly as she could, without seeming to run, without risking a fall on the slippery snow. She watched for cabs, for policemen, for sympathetic passersby. She was alone on the dark streets of Manhattan in a snowstorm, with a recalcitrant dog, and a dogged pursuer.

As she was crossing Thirty-ninth Street, the man stopped her with a hand on her shoulder.

The surprise of his touch loosened her grip on the terrier, and the dog flew over her shoulder and clawed his way through the air.

"Oh, Lord!" cried the attacker in a hoarse croaking voice, "Miss Bright—get him off!"

Susan turned, a bit less alarmed, but now confused. The man who'd been following her lay in the middle of the street—fortunately empty of traffic—keeping the terrier at bay with his feet.

"How do you know my name?" Susan asked, but just then she recognized her pursuer as the tall man in the third row and she knew the answer.

"I sent you a note this—"

"Yes, Mr. Austin. I looked for you—"

She grabbed up the terrier and held him close to her tightly to prevent him from making any further attack on her admirer.

"I waited for you outside the stage door. When you didn't—"

"Oh, I didn't see you. There was a fat man—"

"—waiting for Miss Conquest. She told me that you had already left, so I—"

"But I hadn't—"

They didn't seem to be able to finish a sentence properly, but it *was* a bit difficult to carry on a normal conversation, given the circumstances. On top of the fact that Mr. Austin was having some difficulty getting to his feet, and Susan was having even more difficulty in controlling the dog, from the croaking sound of Mr. Austin's voice, he seemed to be on the verge of coming down with the grippe. Lying for long in a snowy street wasn't going to help that very much.

But at least it was happily apparent to both that some sort of unintentional error had been made.

Mr. Jay Austin finally pulled himself to a standing position by grasping the fender of a parked automobile, took a breath and said, "You ought not be out alone, Miss Bright. May I see you safely to your home?"

The terrier, as if understanding this speech and objecting to it strenuously, made one more valiant lunge in the attempt to implant his sharp teeth into the man.

"Yes you may, Mr. Austin."

It was very aggravating to Susan that she still couldn't properly see his face. The snow was thick, the street was dark, the brim of his hat shadowed much of his visage, but she saw enough to allow her to hope that he was really quite handsome.

"You have a very rambunctious canine there," he remarked ruefully.

Susan thought he would have taken her arm, had it not been for the dog. She would have put the dog down, but she was certain it would attack again. So they headed toward Times Square, a few feet apart, chatting as best they could in the intervals between threatening snarls and frigid gusts of snowy wind.

He had waited for half an hour at the stage door, and must have been there when she peeked into the alley. But because he was not standing in the light, they decided, or hidden by the overfed form of the man who was waiting for Ida, Susan had simply not seen him. He had finally given up hope and emerged from the alley when he saw a female figure, alone, cross Eighth Avenue and then disappear into the darkness. He'd followed hesitantly at first, unsure of her identity, but caught her profile when she'd once turned in the lamplight and lifted her veil—and now here he was.

"Your performance was entrancing."

"You were in the third row. On the aisle."

"You saw me!" he exclaimed.

"I saw you rip your jacket."

"Now I've ripped my trousers as well. It's just as well that it's so dark out."

Susan fretted a bit as they walked. It was the middle of the night, she had accepted the company of a stranger, *and* she was an actress—would he expect more? Would he demand it? How could she show her interest in him without leading him to think that she often accepted this sort of attention—and much more—from gentlemen who waited at the stage door? It was difficult for a woman to meet a man on anything like equal footing, and now Susan's years of independence seemed to melt beneath this daunting difficulty.

She was often lonely, and tall gentlemen who could afford third-row aisle seats—and who admired her acting to boot—were not easily come by. With that thought in mind, despite the weather, the wriggling dog in her arms, and the possibility that Mr. Austin was coming down with pneumonia, Susan deliberately walked past the entrance to the

Times Square subway station and continued uptown, as if it had been her intention all along to walk all the way home.

Broadway would have been more direct, but Seventh Avenue was a quieter and longer route. Though recently many commercial buildings and hotels had sprung up in this area, there were still a number of brownstone houses that remained private residences. Despite the pleasure of the tall gentleman's company, Susan was pleased that they were now quite close to her home—it was nearly one in the morning, the snow showed no sign of letting up, and the dog in her arms had not ceased his efforts to fly at Mr. Austin's aching throat. She'd tried to put him down once, but snatched him up again as quickly as he'd torn the cuff from Mr. Austin's right trouser leg.

Despite the lateness of the hour, there was more traffic in this area of the city, and several taxicabs now passed, making their cautious slow way through the slippery streets. Mr. Austin offered to fetch one of these for Susan, but she had declined: "I'm so near home..."

They were about to cross Fifty-eighth Street, when a long covered touring car came crunching toward them through the snow, its yellow headlamps creating cones of yellow light through the swirling precipitation. The automobile stopped near them and for several moments Mr. Austin and Susan were caught in the yellow glare. A chauffeur emerged, opened the rear door of the car, and a large man, wrapped in a vast dark fur coat, got out and started up the steps of the house on the corner.

"The Russian consul's home," said Mr. Austin, stopping at the curb, "and unless I am very much mistaken, that is the consul himself. I imagine he is quite used to weather like this."

"How do you know—" began Susan, but her speech was abruptly cut off in surprise. For from around the corner lurched a scrawny, bearded man wearing a thin overcoat and heavy boots. Staggering forward through the snow, he shouted something in a strange language.

Coming to a stop almost next to Mr. Austin and Susan, the man produced from beneath his overcoat an object about the shape and size of a large melon, which he appeared to be ready to hurl at the man Mr. Austin had identified as the Russian consul.

At that moment, the dog made another lunge at Mr. Austin, and Susan's companion lost his footing.

His legs flew out from beneath him, and he slid forward, colliding heavily with the bearded man.

The melonlike object flew straight up in the air, hovered there a moment, and then began to drop straight down.

Two things occurred to Susan as this was happening.

The first: The bearded man in the thin coat and the boots was an anarchist.

The second: The melonlike object that was spinning down through the air toward her was a bomb.

Its glowing fuse described a perfect parabolic spiral through the snow-laden air.

CHAPTER THREE

JAY AUSTIN HAD barely regained his footing on the sidewalk, when he saw the danger presented by the bomb. Without a moment's hesitation, he threw himself bodily on to Susan, crushing her down into a soft bank of snow at the curb.

Protecting me, she thought, and then all thought—of the anarchist, of the falling bomb, of the dog squeezing out of her grasp, and of Mr. Austin's selfless behavior—were flashed away by an explosion—an explosion of pain in her right leg, a pain of an intensity she'd never felt before.

Mr. Austin had completely covered her body with his, pressing her into the cold snow.

"Oooooff," he said, and she felt him flinch when the anarchist's bomb struck him a glancing blow in the small of the back.

She turned her head, brushing one cheek against the snow, and the other against the rough wool of her protector's overcoat. She saw the sinister black device roll into the snow, where the fuse fizzled into nothing more than a stub of black charcoal.

"Please let me up," Susan whispered—whispered because he was so heavy atop her, it was hard to get breath into her lungs. "The bomb didn't go off."

Mr. Austin raised himself and rolled over on his side away from Susan. He stood up, grabbed the bomb, and hurled it down the street as if it were a ball in a game of tenpins.

All this occurred in a matter of seconds. Susan, still lying in the snow, saw the Russian consul hurry up the stairs of his residence—experience probably having taught him not to wait around in order to satisfy his curiosity about certain altercations in the street.

At the same time, the chauffeur blew a shrill whistle, and called out imprecations and threats against the bearded anarchist, who had turned and was headed down the avenue at a trot.

"Anarchists!" shouted the chauffeur. "Anarchists!"

Windows began to be raised along both sides of the street.

The white terrier stood near Susan's feet, looking indecisive. He seemed to be trying to decide whether to attack Mr. Austin again or to run after the anarchist.

He whined.

Susan threw out an arm and pointed down the block. "That one."

The terrier barked happily, and at once dashed off in pursuit. At the corner of Fifty-seventh Street he caught up with the would-be bomb-thrower. Seeing his chance, the dog leapt on to the hood of a Pope Hartford touring car parked in front of the Osborne Apartments and then hurled himself on to the anarchist's head.

The man screamed, and tried to shake the animal off.

The dog clawed and barked and bit, tearing at the anarchist's face and neck.

Blinded, the anarchist stumbled to the right, knocking into a streetlamp. Then he stumbled to the left, slipping on a patch of ice.

Just as the anarchist at last succeeded in clawing the dog loose from his head, a police van approached the corner of Fifty-seventh Street—not with its siren on, but just on a routine middle-of-the-night beat. The anarchist held the dog aloft, screeching imprecations at it in Russian, then flung it into the street, right into the path of the oncoming vehicle.

Flailing helplessly, the little terrier tumbled end-over-end through the swirling snow and landed a couple of yards in front of the van.

The driver, seeing what had happened, instantly pulled the brake lever, causing the tires to skid on the snow and the vehicle to spin out of control. The animal tried to scramble to safety, but in another moment was caught beneath one of the turning wheels of the van.

The dog let out a howling yelp, but that pitiful scream was overridden by another—and a human one at that—as the anarchist, blinded by his own blood that had been scraped out of his forehead and scalp by the dog, was also struck by the out-of-control vehicle. With a terrible grinding, the anarchist's legs and midsection were crushed against the lamppost; the impact of the collision was so great that the lamppost cracked in two and fell into the street across the roof of a taxicab.

As the police clambered out of their van and surrounded their unintended victim, Mr. Austin arrived on the scene and ran out into the street and grabbed up the battered but still-breathing dog. He walked back up the avenue to where Susan Bright still lay in the snow.

The dog whimpered in Jay Austin's arms, and his attempts to bite the man were pitifully ineffectual.

"I think he's broken his leg," said Mr. Austin sadly, and held out a hand to help Susan to her feet.

But she merely waved away the proffered assistance with a gesture of disgust. "So have I," she said with dismal certitude.

❀ ❀ ❀

> Susan Bright, a young actress new to our stage (at least I cannot recall having seen her before), played the part of the heroine's sister-in-law, and played it extremely well. She is a good, reliable, and interesting actress, with a certain amount of personality, and I should say that she will be a useful addition to our list of leading ladies—or perhaps I should make that "stars." She lacks the original methods of a great actress, but has all the qualities of a good one. These are nice and comforting things to possess, and Susan Bright will be seen again—let us hope, in a more becoming frock.

She didn't have the heart to read any more of the reviews, though the stage manager, who visited her in the ward at Bellevue Hospital, assured her that they were all very good. It was just her luck that on the night that promised to be the beginning of a long and prosperous career, she should suffer a broken leg.

And not only was her leg broken, but she'd learned that one of Ida Conquest's friends took over the part of Daisy the following evening, and from all reports, was irredeemably dreadful. For her two weeks of intensive rehearsal, for all her hopes, and for all her plans, Susan received exactly seven dollars and twenty-five cents, a pro rata salary for one evening's performance—a sum that was immediately consumed by the first night in the hospital.

What good were handsome reviews when you lay in bed with a broken leg? The doctor *hoped* she wouldn't limp for more than six months, but of course you never could tell in cases like this.

"Cases like what?" Susan demanded.

"Broken legs," said the doctor, unhelpfully.

After he'd done with the police, Mr. Austin came to the hospital, but Susan wouldn't see him. She knew that the accident had not been his fault—that he really had been trying to save her life—but still, she could not help but feel that it was on his account that she had lost her part in *He and She*. In fact, if the limp were permanent, Susan would no longer have any future at all on the stage. Maybe Bernhardt could do it on a wooden leg, but it was an unwritten law among theater managers that ingenues needed their limbs intact.

Mr. Austin sent flowers. Mr. Austin sent her notes. Mr. Austin went to her doctor and said that he would be responsible for all charges incurred by Miss Bright's confinement in the hospital.

Susan blushed with shame when she heard this, and hastened to inform the doctor that *she* would pay all the fees. Single women did not accept money from strange gentlemen.

Susan fretted in the hospital. The days were long and tedious. The old woman in the bed on one side of her was alternately nonsensically garrulous and comatose. The young woman in the bed to her other side insisted on Susan's reading aloud to her all the serial stories out of the past year of *Cosmopolitan* magazine. Susan got her fill of the improbable inanities of such sagas as "Virginia of the Air Lanes."

She estimated that this stay in the hospital, which the doctor said would be about two weeks, would cost her about one hundred dollars, which represented exactly two-thirds of her scanty Wall Street cache. That left her less than sixty dollars to live on for the next two months—the amount of time, the doctor also said, she would have to spend at home recuperating.

Fifty dollars was not enough. It would give her a weekly allowance of about six dollars, and her rent was three dollars a week. That left three dollars for such incidentals as food, firewood, clothing, and transportation. Then, even supposing that she did make do on this fifty dollars *and* that her leg healed properly and with miraculous swiftness, what then?

To live she'd be absolutely dependent on her income, and stage jobs were not easy to come by. It had, after all, been a long while between the fan-waving of Cleopatra and the syrupy love-swooning of *He and She*. Why, oh why hadn't she simply gone home directly after the opening of the play? Why had she ever read the note that Mr. Austin had sent her? Why hadn't she listened to Ida's warnings? Why hadn't she allowed that unfortunate dog to drive her admirer away?

It wasn't his fault, she knew that. But when Susan conjured up and execrated Malign Fate, Malign Fate possessed Mr. Austin's shadowy features and hoarse voice.

Yet even with her constant refusals to see him when he visited the hospital—at least every other day—Susan was somehow disappointed when she received a final-sounding letter from him.

January 20, 1913

My dear Miss Bright,
I know that you will not be displeased to hear that I am going away from this city. My financial guardian and advisor has interests in Chicago, and has asked me to oversee some difficult transfers of properties and holdings. If I had any hope that I might be of use to you, I would refuse to go, but as my presence here provides you no comfort, and seems only to irk you, I have acquiesced to his wishes. I start west this evening. If I may ever be of assistance to you in any fashion, please do not hesitate to write to me in care of the American Exchange National Bank, No. 37 Wall Street.

Sincerely yours,
Jay Austin.

It was with a heavy heart that Susan Bright returned, in a taxicab, to her apartment building—the somewhat grandiosely named Fenwick—on West Sixtieth Street.

It was with great discomfort and difficulty that she trudged up the stairs to her rooms on the fourth floor. The plaster cast on her right leg was heavy and stiff, and threw her off-balance. The cast was completely hidden by her long skirt, but she wobbled along like a cripple—the object of pity of passersby on the street. Even before she'd reached home, she'd decided she would try to make trips down to the street as infrequently as possible.

It was with no hope in her heart that she anticipated twelve weeks in those two rooms on the fourth floor, looking out at the street for hours on end. While her purse dwindled, and her leg healed, life would pass her by more fleetingly than ever.

But then, with her key in the lock of the door, it was with considerable surprise that she heard a high-pitched bark of a dog on the other side.

Her heart sank with the conviction that she'd been turned out of her home; that some party willing to pay a higher rent had taken over.

She turned the key, twisted the knob, and steeled herself to greet unfamiliar faces, see different furniture.

Where would she go now? Where—

The furniture was the same, dustier than she usually allowed it to get, but the same.

No one was there.

No one, that is, except a small white terrier, which despite the wooden leg strapped to its hindquarters, managed to leap into the air at her in the open doorway.

She grabbed him and held him close. The dog squirmed and slathered away happily at the tears that welled in Susan's eyes.

CHAPTER FOUR

SUSAN BRIGHT (fourth-floor front) had a down-stairs neighbor, Hosmer Collamore (third-floor back). Mr. Collamore worked as a moving picture cameraman at the Cosmic Film Company, situated in a warehouse near Madison Square. Often, in the past, Susan and Hosmer had found themselves leaving the building together, or traversing the hallways at the same time. The apartment building's only telephone was outside the door of Hosmer's room, so when Susan received calls, it was Hosmer's habit to alert her with a rap at the door. In short, they had always enjoyed what was called an apartment house intimacy, but Susan suspected that Hosmer would have been pleased to make it as deep and real an intimacy as the other dwellers of the building undoubtedly suspected it was.

Late in the afternoon of her arrival home, Susan sat at her open door, listening for the sound of her neighbors coming in from work. When she heard a masculine tread on the floor below, she called out, "Mr. Collamore? Hosmer?"

"Miss Bright? Susan?"

Apartment house intimacy wavered between polite and familiar forms of address, but after a few minutes, conversation generally evolved into the latter.

Hosmer Collamore presented himself forthwith. He actually kissed Susan's hand in welcoming her back. His smile was full of melancholy sympathy and interest in her injury.

Hosmer was darkly handsome, though not much taller than Susan herself. His cheek was swarthy and he wore a thick black mustache that he combed and treated with a sweet-smelling pomade. His hair was nearly as black as Susan's, though his was wavy. But most striking were his dark brown eyes, with lashes so thick and black that they almost looked as if they were blackened with kohl. He was spruce and neat, and although a West Sixtieth Street address generally indicated a modest income, Hosmer always dressed in the style of the quite well-to-do. The impression that Hosmer made on Susan was probably not as masculine, not as positive, and not as alluring as he would have liked to imagine.

Susan held the terrier in her arms, lest he attack Hosmer, but the dog squirmed loose and flew toward the cameraman. Susan opened her mouth to scream, but to her amazement Hosmer just laughed and picked up the dog—and presented his face to be licked.

The dog barked in obvious affection, and dug his wooden leg into—and through the seam of—Hosmer's waistcoat pocket.

"This dog, Hosmer. Have you any idea how he came to be in my apartment?"

"I put him here," said Hosmer. He had lived on Manhattan Island some years now. His accent, however, clung to its Brooklyn roots.

"But—"

"How did I come by this particular animal, you mean to ask?"

"Yes?"

"A couple of days ago a policeman brought him by and said he belonged to the young lady on the fourth floor. He already knew you were in the hospital."

Susan shook her head, auguring that this animal had found its way back to her through the unacknowledged agency of Jay Austin.

The dog's missing leg made her think hard about her own injury, and she now fully realized that hers could have been considerably worse. After all, her cast would eventually come off, and there *might* not be a limp. But this poor animal would scrape along for the rest of his life on three legs and a tapered wooden stick. *Pad pad pad tap. Pad pad pad tap.*

"What do you call him?" asked Susan.

Hosmer laughed. "What do *you* call him? He is your dog, I presume."

Susan shrugged. Hosmer's occupation as a cameraman occurred to her and she said, "With only three legs I suppose his name must be Tripod."

❉ ❉ ❉

Near-total invalidism was not a pleasant state for Susan Bright. She was used to activity—even if it was usually not much more than going from theater to theater throughout the city trying to find work. But Tripod proved to be great company, for he was an intelligent—if volatile—dog. And Hosmer visited every morning before he went off to work, and dropped by every afternoon when he returned. Susan was grateful for these visits, for sometimes Hosmer was the only human being she spoke to in the course of the day. He ran errands for her as well, so that she was not often put to the necessity of going out. This was a good thing, for she'd been told that the more time she spent in bed, the sooner she'd be up and out of it. She borrowed stacks of magazines from Mrs. Jadd across the hall—*McClure's, McCalls, Cosmopolitan, Woman's Home Companion, The Modern Priscilla*—and read them cover to cover.

Two weeks passed, and Susan grew proficient with the use of her crutches. She was now able to scurry about her two rooms with energy and dexterity that almost matched Tripod's. The weather was wretched and streets were piled with snow one day and awash with slush the next. She did not venture out. The possibility of filling her cast with frigid water was unpleasant indeed. Meanwhile her small money supply dwindled. The hospital and doctor's fees were higher than she'd anticipated, nearly one hundred and twenty dollars, and that had left her only forty—and that forty had rapidly dwindled to twenty-five, and now, in the first week of February, was down to eleven dollars and twenty-three cents.

If Susan had been prone to misery, she now would have been miserable indeed. Her whole life felt crippled. Even her dog didn't have a full complement of limbs.

Pad pad pad tap. That was Tripod.

Slap clunk. Slap clunk. That was Susan Bright, with a worn slipper on one foot and a thirty-pound cast on the other.

Her entire life was confined to the narrow circumference of two rooms on West Sixtieth Street, with a frigid rain beating against the window and the landlady hanging about the front stoop, just waiting for the tenth of the month so she could come up the stairs and knock on the door of fourth-floor front and demand twelve dollars—which Susan Bright didn't have.

Pad pad pad tap.

Slap clunk. Slap clunk.

She had received another letter from Mr. Austin, postmarked Chicago. He had urged her to call upon his bankers in Wall Street should she find herself short of funds. He asked permission to continue to write to her. He begged for a reply, even if it were only a postal card with the single word "Yes" on it.

Susan sent back a post card with a tinted picture of Ida Conquest as the Aeroplane Girl. On the half of the card reserved for messages, Susan penned the single word "No."

Susan Bright hadn't done what she'd done for all these years, and struggled as she'd struggled, to give up all her hard-bought pride and independence to the casual generosity of a stranger. Oddly, the nearer Susan got to destitution, the stronger her resolve never to take Mr. Austin up on his offer.

So she heard no more from her admirer in Chicago, but the two letters from him lay unfolded in the top drawer of her dresser, and sometimes she would inadvertently catch sight of them.

❋ ❋ ❋

One day, which had offered the prospect of being no different from all the rest, ended with a surprise for Susan. At half-past six came Hosmer's expected and characteristic knock at the door.

She swung herself to the door on her crutches, opened it and was astonished to see that Hosmer was not alone. Standing beside him, in an outfit that would have made her seem quite at home on the stage of a variety hall doing a turn entitled, "The Glorification of Girl," was Ida Conquest. Her black-and-white striped dress had huge gold cuff buttons, and was adorned with a "beauty pin" the size of a lemon. Both wrists were draped with gold bangles, and she wore a black hat decorated with not only a white feather, but also with a hatpin with a butterfly cap. Susan remembered Ida had once been a ribbon clerk, and now she looked like a ribbon clerk's apotheosis of feminine allure.

Ida Conquest was the last person in the world from whom Susan had expected a visit.

Ida gazed over Susan's shoulder into the apartment with a hard eye, then she glanced at Hosmer Collamore with an equally stony gaze as if to convey a message to Susan on the order of, *This is a conductor, not a companion,* then she dropped her disapproving gaze to Tripod, who was scratching his chin with the tip of his wooden leg. Then she said, with the lisp that reviewers managed to find at once charming and incomprehensible, "I've heard your limp is quite the most pathetic thing in New York."

"Won't you come in, Ida?"

There is only one course to take with people like Ida Conquest, and that is to treat them with absolute civility and courtesy, no matter how much you'd like to fly at them with a fistful of sharp objects.

Susan would not ask how Ida, who preferred her masculine company to be moneyed and well-placed even before they were handsome, had come to be with Hosmer. Susan had at first supposed that the two had simply met outside her door, but Hosmer's gloating smile said plainly enough that he had succeeded scraping acquaintance with the Aeroplane Girl.

"Won't you take a chair?" Susan said politely to her guests.

"Thank you. I'll stand by the window," Ida said, in a manner suggesting that being splashed with cold rainwater was preferable to possible contamination by Susan's upholstery.

"Ida has agreed to appear in several Cosmic Film productions," said Hosmer giddily.

Susan glanced sharply at Ida. Ida turned away, perhaps to conceal a blush. When she turned back, she amended, "Under the *most* favorable terms of course."

Acting in moving pictures was considered a comedown for stage actors; it was thought of as nothing but a caricature of *real* acting. Gentlemen and ladies of the stage who had lost their voices through accident or disease were excused, but an actor who left the legitimate boards for the grimy moving-picture factories relinquished not only self-respect but the sympathy of other thespians. Better to hack along in a third-rate touring company on the Omaha-Kansas City-Peoria circuit than to prostitute oneself in front of a grinding camera, an opinion Susan had often heard Ida express.

"*He and She* closed," said Ida.

"So I read."

"And Mr. Fane pursued me with stupendous offers."

"Junius Fane is president of the Cosmic Film Company," explained Hosmer.

"Mr. Fane thinks that my face and talents are ideally suited for moving pictures," said Ida. "Mr. Fane promises me also that I will be very rich. I am to be known as the 'Cosmic Star.'"

"Ida's photograph will appear in the next number of the *Clipper*," said Hosmer, referring to New York's preeminent sporting and theatrical paper. It was read principally by gentlemen smoking cigars in barbershops, and gentlemen smoking cigars at the races.

Susan was amused not only by Ida's meretricious change of opinion on the subject of the moving pictures, but also on Hosmer's evident infatuation with the new Cosmic Star. It had been obvious to Susan in recent weeks that Hosmer had been forming an attachment to her, and she'd rather dreaded the time when she would have to call a halt to *that*. But now she could see that her place in Mr. Collamore's shallow affections had been usurped by Ida Conquest.

"Ida takes wonderfully," said Hosmer.

"Takes?"

"She looks splendid on celluloid, I mean. That's what I mean by 'she takes wonderfully.'"

"Will the Cosmic Star take tea?" Susan asked.

"Yes," replied Ida. "I will."

Slap clunk went Susan to her little cubbyhole of a kitchen where a tiny gas flame could warm a pan of water after perhaps a quarter of an hour of diligent effort.

The good tea was on the top shelf, out of harm's way, and Susan couldn't very well reach it.

"Tripod," she called.

Pad pad pad tap came Tripod to the kitchen. Susan snapped her fingers and the dog leapt into her arms. Susan held the dog aloft and Tripod snagged the small canister in his teeth.

Ida and Hosmer remained just long enough to be served their tea, though not to drink it.

"It's terrible to think you won't never find work again," Ida said. "Not on the stage anyhow. And not anywhere else where people will have to look at your gimp leg. What *will* you do, do you think, Suss?"

Suss rhymed with caboose, and Susan hated it when anyone called her by that detestable nickname. Glancing at Hosmer, she realized with a sinking feeling that he would probably call her by that repulsive syllable forever after.

"I'll manage," said Susan brightly. "I've gotten along pretty well up till today, and I don't foresee that tomorrow will be much different."

Oh, but tomorrow looked fairly bleak when Susan closed the door on the Cosmic Star and her worshipful astronomer. Because tomorrow the rent came due, and Susan was short thirty-seven cents. Thirty-seven cents was very little when it was a surplus, but when you lacked that sum, it could seem to be a very great deal of money indeed.

Even supposing that—in this extremity—she took to her crutches and went out on the street and begged in the name of her broken leg and her dog's infirmity and got the thirty-seven cents to make up the difference, what would happen after that?

Firewood, and even cheap tea, and the electricity that burned feebly inside the tiny glass globes in the wall sconces—these weren't things that came to West Sixtieth Street without payment.

Susan knew what happened to young women in 1913 who found themselves without work, without income, without relatives to apply to for assistance. The timid applied for charity, but were turned away because their clothes were too fine. So they pawned their clothes, and then were too ashamed to be seen on the street. The industrious and honest took in sewing and ruined their eyes. All these got by on less food than formerly, and on no pleasure at all. The brazen and the forward (and, probably, more intelligent) young women became—what was that dreadful phrase?—*nymphs du pave*. But women who made their living on the streets at the very least could dress warmly and have enough to eat. There was a great deal to be said for not starving or freezing to death. Perhaps there would come a time when the unfortunate and the destitute were not simply swept into the gutters of the city streets, when provision was made for the homeless, for those unable to find work, for the permanently invalided. But that time was not now, and Susan knew that without assistance, she *would* sink.

She found herself oddly curious about which path she would take in her downward descent and spent most of the night restlessly pacing the room.

Slap clunk. Slap clunk. Slap clunk. Slap clunk.

Bed to the window, and window back to the bed.

Slap clunk. Slap clunk. Slap clunk.

Stirring up the embers in the dying fire. How much did embers go for these days?

Slap clunk. Slap clunk.

Staring out the window at the darkened city.

Tripod growled in his sleep, warning away imaginary enemies.

Destitution was no phantasm of the mind.

Slap clunk.

CHAPTER FIVE

Having slept for little more than an hour, Susan awoke with a start, sitting up in bed with eyes wide and staring. She worked to dispel a nightmare in which her landlady knocked at the door and demanded the monthly twelve-dollar rent. In her black dream, Susan came up thirty-seven cents short of the sum required.

But it was no dream.

Feverish with anxiety, Susan rose from bed and tried to perform her daily routine. Washing, dressing, laying out a butcher's bone for Tripod. But nothing seemed to go right. She'd go to the bureau, and a few moments later end up at the window, with no memory of why she was supposed to have gone to the bureau.

Slap clunk. Slap clunk.

Tripod, too, was eager to go out. It was Susan's custom simply to open the hall door, and let the dog maneuver his way down—it was no easy task for a three-legged dog to descend four flights of steep stairs. At the front door, he'd wait for someone coming in or going out to open the door for him. He'd be gone for about a quarter of an hour. On returning, he'd wait patiently outside until, again, someone came in or went out. Four flights going up was even more difficult, and poor Tripod would be winded and weak by the time he scratched at Susan's door again.

Susan reflected that not all dogs were as intelligent as Tripod. In fact, in her experience, she had known some dogs that were downright stupid.

But this morning, the tenth of February, with the rent due, Susan was distracted, and Tripod had to whine at the door to get her attention.

"Oh, Tripod, I apologize!" Susan cried, and hurried to the door to let the dog out. She pulled the door open and Tripod hurried out into the hallway. But before Susan even got the door all the way closed she heard the dog growl, then bark—and then a ferocious tearing of cloth.

"Get down! Get down!" a masculine voice cried out.

Susan peered out into the hallway. There near the stairs was Tripod, tearing away at the trouser cuff of a tall, bearded man who was backed up against the wall. Susan had never seen the man before.

"Tripod! Stop! Stop that right now."

The cuff in the dog's teeth remained attached by a thread. Tripod gave one last tug, and it sheared away. Satisfied, the dog began his hobbling, sliding descent down the stairs.

"I *am* sorry," said Susan to the man. He was about her age, though the beard made it hard to tell for sure.

"Your dog?" he asked in a not particularly friendly tone of voice.

"Yes. Tripod *is* excitable. He didn't bite you, did he? Please come inside and let me—"

"Do you know what time it is?" the man asked suddenly—and ferociously.

"Half-past seven? I heard bells a little while—"

"It is a quarter past *six* in the morning," he said, stepping inside the room. "And you live in these apartments?"

"Yes..."

"Madam, your husband has the heaviest tread of any known mortal. I did not so much mind that he kept me up until four-thirty this morning while he paced the room. But when he got up again only half an hour ago, I thought that I *must* speak to him. So if you would kindly—" He nodded his head toward the bedchamber in back.

"I'm not married—" She saw a flicker of surprise cross the bearded man's features, and she hastened to add, "That was me. I. And I'm sorry that—"

"That was your tread?"

She lifted the hem of her robe to reveal her cast. "I suppose you're the new tenant—directly below me?"

"Yes," he replied, "and though probably I have no right to ask you to give up walking, I *beg* you to walk either all night, or else all morning—but not both."

"Of course," said Susan quickly. "Mr.—"

"Beaumont," said the gentleman. "My name is Jack Beaumont."

"Mr. Beaumont, please let me repair your cuff. Tripod is sometimes—"

"—rambunctious," said Mr. Beaumont.

Susan noticed, in the greater light afforded by the apartment windows, that Mr. Beaumont's clothing was far from brand-new and quite threadbare. It was clean, but worn carelessly. Perhaps he'd just thrown on whatever came to hand when he'd decided to mount the stairs for his complaint, and what came to hand was not the best his wardrobe had to offer.

"Please don't think about it," said Jack Beaumont, and with that he simply walked out the door.

She listened to his heavy tread as he made his way down the stairs.

❄ ❄ ❄

Mrs. McCalken, the landlady of the Fenwick, was a generously proportioned woman of indeterminate middle age. She had pitted skin, a red nose, a fat neck, and half a dozen teeth of assorted sizes and colors. She was pleasant in such a way as to make you wish that she were more standoffish. She generally made the rounds of the building twice on rent day, first at noontime, and then again in the evening, so as to be sure to catch all her tenants in.

Which is to say that Susan had approximately five hours in which to scrape up thirty-seven cents.

She decided to do what all young women in her position did when faced with a shortage of funds.

She'd pawn all her jewels.

All her jewels consisted of a gold bracelet that had belonged to her grandmother, and a diamond ring with a stone so small it ceased to sparkle if so much as a mote of soot fell on to it.

As she dressed to go out, Tripod scratched at the door. The dog, still bearing the woolen trophy of Jack Beaumont's trouser cuff in his mouth, trotted in and Susan rather impatiently snatched the fabric from those grinning, self-satisfied jaws.

"Just for that, you won't go out with me," said Susan, excited by the prospect of a trip downtown. *She's been visiting First Avenue* was euphemistic green-room tattle— for on lower First Avenue was a cluster of pawnshops. She'd been out so little lately that she was happy for even so melancholy an errand as this.

But Tripod looked so forlorn as she was pulling on her cape that Susan relented. "All right, you can go too."

The animal struggled out from underneath the table where he'd crept, and flung himself through the air at Susan in his happiness.

He dashed against her, nearly knocking her over, and when he came away, she saw that he had a small pink envelope in his mouth.

Susan looked at it a moment in perplexity, and then realized that the envelope must have been protruding from the pocket of her cape, which had been hanging on the back of the door.

The pink envelope smelled half of Tripod, and half of a perfume of violets.

Inside were five one-hundred-dollar treasury notes.

CHAPTER SIX

M‍Y DEAR MISS Bright,

I know that I am acting directly contrary to your wishes in writing to you once more, but I wanted to tell you that you would never hear from me again. Having found Chicago a congenial city in every respect, I have decided to settle here. I do not anticipate any return to New York.

My memory of the inadvertent injury done to you still makes me quake in mortification and remorse. And even though you have refused to accept any recompense whatever from me so that I might atone, in some small measure, for your discomfort—physical and mental—I am taking the liberty of enclosing a sum of cash. There is no way for you to return this money, as I have refrained from giving you my address. My account in Wall Street has been closed. If you still

do not wish to have even this much reminder of
our unfortunate encounter, I beg you to give the
money to some worthy charity.

In painful regret, Miss Bright,
Of What Might Have Been,
I remain,
Most Sincerely,
Your Humble Servant,
Jay Austin

Tripod jumped into Susan's arms, and together they
danced happily about the room—until they were interrupted by a loud thumping sound from below.

Susan suddenly remembered Mr. Beaumont. He was
evidently knocking against his ceiling with the handle of
the broom or some other such object.

She immediately stopped dancing, but her excitement
still sought release. She threw open the window, pushed her
face into the cold air, and produced one brief, loud, happy
scream. Then she leaned farther out and craned to see as
much of the city as she could. This was precious little—a bit
of the street, a slice of river, the tops of a few trees, and a great
deal of wall. But brilliant February sunshine beamed down
upon everything, and New York seemed a brighter, cleaner,
and more promising place than it had seemed in weeks.

❀ ❀ ❀

Mrs. McCalken arrived shortly after noon, and never had
Susan counted out money as happily as she did then. To
have paid her rent and still be possessed of four hundred
ninety-nine dollars and sixty-three cents seemed more
riches than any mortal deserved.

Except of course that it wasn't hers; she had no right to
it, and conscience demanded that she return it as quickly

as possible. She would be penniless again, but under no circumstances could she keep the money.

The appearance of the envelope in the pocket of her cape had at first seemed a mystery. But it quickly became apparent to Susan that Ida Conquest had left it there on her visit the day before.

Jay Austin would have known Ida, from *He and She*, gotten in touch with her and persuaded her to assist him in this deed.

The quickest way to find Jay Austin, and return his money, was through Ida, who made it a point to keep track of rich young men.

Adjuring Tripod to remain inside, Susan took one of her crutches and hobbled down to the telephone on the third-floor landing. She lifted the receiver and asked to be connected with the Cosmic Film Company.

The Fenwick Apartments' telephone was on a private exchange servicing that portion of the city west of Central Park, and the Cosmic Film Company was on a much larger commercial exchange downtown, so it was some moments before the operator could make the proper switchings. As Susan waited, she noticed that the door of Mr. Beaumont's apartment was cracked open, and that his bearded face was peering out at her.

"When does your cast come off?" he asked in a low voice.

"Mr. Beaumont," she said, "I *promise*—no more dancing."

"Thank you," said Jack Beaumont curtly, and shut the door with a bang.

On the other end the telephone rang, and a high-pitched voice—that of a boy, Susan thought—intoned drearily, "Cosmic Film Company."

"Could you please call Miss Ida Conquest to the phone?" asked Susan.

"Couldn't," replied the boy. "She's getting shot."

"I beg your pardon?"

"Shot. They're shooting her now."

"Then might I speak to Mr. Hosmer Collamore?" It really was impossible to speak into this machine with any semblance of ease. One's voice always sounded strained and formal, and Susan like many others had never quite been convinced that it wasn't all some form of prestidigitation foisted off on a gullible public in order to collect monthly fees. This dreary child was really in the next room, speaking to her through a hole in the wall. There might come a time when people became really accustomed to this sort of thing, but Susan doubted she'd live long enough to see it.

"Colley's the one shooting her," said the boy in a voice that was now disgusted as well as dreary.

"Then would you please ask Miss Conquest to phone me when she's free? My name is Susan Bright and my number is River Zero-Six-Three-Zero."

After giving a sigh a martyr might make as the pyre is lighted, the boy announced he would have to go find a pencil. When he came back he demanded that everything be repeated, then spelled, then repeated again.

Susan was told, grudgingly, that the shooting would be over in approximately ten minutes—or maybe thirty— and that Miss Conquest would be given the message. Rather than struggling back up to her room, Susan decided that she would simply sit on the steps there and wait for the telephone to ring.

Basking in the warmth—temporary though it was— of the thirty dollars she had impulsively placed in her pocket, Susan looked out a grimy window to the dingy garden. Despite the sunlight, the leafless tree in one corner looked stark and dejected.

"Did your dog drive you out of your apartment?" a man's voice asked from behind her.

Susan turned quickly. There stood Mr. Beaumont, holding a crate filled with trash which he was evidently about to take downstairs to the street.

"No, no, Mr. Beaumont, I was only waiting for the telephone to ring."

He nodded silently and then proceeded down the stairs with his heavy tread. Susan thought what a shame it was that he wore a beard, that he was so gruff and unfriendly, and that he couldn't afford better clothes. It would have been pleasant to have a handsome, cordial, well-dressed gentleman living just below her. Actually, Hosmer Collamore fit that description, but Hosmer wasn't what Susan wanted.

She wondered what Mr. Beaumont did for a living that enabled him to be at home in the middle of the day; every other male above the age of six left the building by eight o'clock every weekday morning. He wore soft-collared shirts, which meant he had no job outside the house; and by his carriage and his speech she knew that he was not a laborer. Peering around, she noticed he had left the door of his apartment ajar, and curiosity got the better of her.

Certain that she'd be able to hear him when he started back up the stairs, Susan moved quietly to the door and pushed it open.

She had expected to find the rooms of a single gentleman who wore threadbare clothes to be scantily furnished, with unmistakable, shabby indications of a lack of superfluous wealth. Certainly, despite his careful wardrobe, the furnishings in Hosmer Collamore's apartments were not remarkable, and this was also true of the room in which Susan now stood. There was an old patched divan pushed against one wall, a rag rug in the center of the painted floor, a long table against the blind wall, a shorter table beneath the windows, and a Swift's Premium calendar hanging from the molding. A wire extension from one of the wall sconces had been draped to the center of the ceiling, and a large bare fixture hung down which appeared capable of positively flooding the room with light in the evening.

But if the furnishings were not unusual, the other objects in the room were. For everywhere in the room—spread, stacked, piled, and pyramided on newspaper and scraps of dirty cloth—were pieces of machinery. All of it black and metallic, all of it oozing grease or oil. It was impossible to tell if this jumble of wheels and cogs and levers actually belonged to one large machine or to a hundred smaller ones. On the tables were small wooden boxes filled with nuts and bolts, screws, nails, and small tools. Larger tools were arranged beneath the two tables. Several work aprons, each stained with the sort of black machine grease that permeated the air, hung on nails on one wall.

Mr. Beaumont, she decided, was a tinkerer.

To Susan's eyes, it appeared that he was more adept at taking things apart than he was at putting them back together, though she didn't want to judge him so harshly on so short an...acquaintance.

Standing in the middle of the room looking around—with one ear cocked for the sound of Mr. Beaumont's returning footfalls—she wondered if she dared risk a peek into the bedroom.

No, she decided. That would be unredeemable snooping. After all, the door to this room *had* been open, while the bedroom door was most emphatically shut and—

She heard a step on the stairs—but not from below. Instead, it came from above—the step of her across-the-hall neighbor, Mrs. Jadd, on her way out shopping. As usual, Mrs. Jadd was accompanied by her twin five-year-old daughters. Susan moved quickly to the door, but found that it was too late to slip out, Mrs. Jadd and her children already having got halfway down the stairs from above. The woman was of a suspicious nature, and, as it was, credited Susan with enjoying the very worst sort of intimacy with Hosmer Collamore. Susan certainly did not wish Mrs. Jadd to see her emerging from Mr. Beaumont's rooms. She carefully eased the door of the room shut, and held it closed as she heard the little entourage pass by and turn down the next flight of stairs. It was easy to mark their progress, for Mrs. Jadd invariably repeated to her shrinking children a litany of the perils of the city streets.

When Susan could no longer hear the woman's voice—she was talking about a little boy whose body had been separated into four different pieces just on the next block because he let go of his mother's hand and ran out into the street into the path of an automobile driven by a drunken mechanic—Susan quietly and carefully opened the door.

"Pardon me," said Mr. Beaumont, standing directly in front of her, "I must be on the wrong floor. I thought this was my room."

CHAPTER SEVEN

"OH, MR. BEAUMONT," exclaimed Susan, "a sparrow flew in your window, and I was chasing it out when the wind blew the door shut."

"Then this *is* my room, and not yours."

"Yes of course, I—"

"I understand perfectly," said Mr. Beaumont, and it was apparent to Susan that his understanding *was* perfect. He did not believe a word she'd said.

Out in the hall, the phone rang.

"Perhaps that's the call you're waiting for," said Mr. Beaumont, and Susan scuttled out of the room as quickly and as unobtrusively as a thirty-pound cast and acute embarrassment would allow her.

The door was slammed shut behind her.

"Suss?" inquired the voice on the other end of the line.

"Ida?"

"Mr. Fane don't like us to have calls."

"I'm sorry, but I had to thank you."

Ida made no reply to this. Susan understood that Ida was following Mr. Austin's instructions not to acknowledge her part in delivering the money.

"You were very kind to assist Mr. Austin," Susan went on hesitantly, "but of course I could never accept his money."

"Did something heavy fall on your chapeau?" asked Ida after a moment.

"You know what I'm talking about?"

"Sure," said Ida composedly.

"What's his address then?"

"Whose?"

"Mr. Austin's. I want to find him."

"Have you tried an insane asylum?" Ida asked, in a tone which suggested that Susan might well be acquainted with such a place.

Susan realized there was no help to be got from Ida on this point. "All right, Ida, I know you must have made your promises. And I thank you, but I don't thank him. You understand that, don't you?"

"Oh, perfectly," Ida concurred. "Clear as mud."

"And thank you again. I know you meant well."

"Always do," said Ida imperturbably. "Have to scat, Suss, they're calling me." Abruptly, she broke the connection.

Susan returned to her room and, despite the fact that Mr. Austin's note had said the account was closed, she penned a letter to the bank in Wall Street, and dispatched it by messenger—a dirty little boy who played hookey from school every day, and loitered about on West Sixtieth Street in hope of obtaining a dime and carfare for just such random errands as this. She got back an immediate reply, with the expected news that Mr. Austin no longer had an account there, and the disappointing addendum that there was no forwarding address.

She momentarily considered putting the bills into an envelope addressed, "Mr. Jay Austin, General Delivery,

Chicago, Illinois," but then realized how foolhardy a move that would be. Instead, she simply wrote out a receipt:

> Received of Mr. Jay Austin, the sum of $500 (five hundred dollars), on February 10th, 1913, which sum is payable on demand, with added interest of three and one-half percent per annum.
> (Signed) Susan Bright

Susan wasn't quite sure that the form was regular, having had no experience whatever in taking out loans, but it *seemed* quite proper to her.

The next morning, Susan hobbled downstairs with Tripod on a leash and walked around the corner to a branch office of the Bank of New York. She opened a savings account with four hundred and fifty dollars, hoping that she would never be forced to touch another penny of Jay Austin's money and further, that someday she'd be able to replace the missing fifty dollars. On the way home she dropped the envelope containing the one-sided loan agreement into a postal box. Even if she didn't consider it really hers, Susan felt better knowing that she had such a comfortable sum in an interest-bearing account.

❊ ❊ ❊

That evening, about seven o'clock, Hosmer Collamore stopped by Susan's room to bring Tripod some scraps of meat he'd picked up at the butcher's, and to tell Susan about Ida's triumphs before the camera.

"We're doing this splendid drawing-room drama," said Hosmer, "and Ida is a secretary who stays up all night in order to help her sister finish a ball gown. The next day at work she falls asleep at her desk after everyone else has gone home and when she wakes up she overhears a group of ruffians planning a bank robbery. She calls her boss, but before he can inform the police the ruffians capture him and so it's up to Ida—and her boss's rich and handsome son—to foil the bank robbery, only the boss's son is shot trying to protect Ida from the gang's bullets. She is then kidnapped and taken to a farmhouse in New Jersey, where her purity and innocence convinces the old man who's guarding her to allow her to escape. She returns to New York and there's a breathless rescue on the top of a building, and the boss's son calls out for her in his delirium and his life won't be saved unless he marries her, so he does."

"What happens to the ruffians?" asked Susan, who saw several holes in the story.

"Oh, Ida throws them off the top of the building. It's a two-reeler. In twenty-eight minutes you can tell a lot more story than you can in just fourteen."

"I guess you can," said Susan uncertainly.

"Cosmic is in the forefront," said Hosmer proudly, "because we're hardly doing one-reelers anymore. People want more for their nickels. They're tired of pictures ending just minutes after they've begun. They want real life, and they want *stars*."

"Like Ida?"

"Yes," Hosmer agreed anxiously. "Ida will be the greatest of them all. Wouldn't you like to visit the studio and see her at work, Suss?"

"Please call me Susan, Hosmer."

"At the studio they call me Colley," said Hosmer, "and everybody seems to have a nickname there. But won't you visit us? And watch Ida be shot?"

"I'd love to come sometime," said Susan, "but..." She raised her skirt, revealing a little bit of her plaster cast.

"But you get around very well with your crutches. Please do come tomorrow. I've invited Mr. Beaumont as well, and I'm sure that he wouldn't mind escorting you, if you're—"

"Mr. Beaumont?"

"Yes, he's—"

"I know very well who he is. But why did you invite him, Hosmer? He is not—from what I can tell—a very friendly person."

"He's been quite pleasant to me," said Hosmer, surprised. "He's offered me cigars—even though I don't smoke. And last evening he asked if I wouldn't go with him to the theater. And I went. We saw the new Irish play, *Peg o' My Heart*. He asked about you, in fact."

"About me?"

"He asked who lived in the room above him, is what I mean to say."

"I fail to see what business it is of his."

"He asked your story, your history—not snooping-like, but casual," Hosmer hastened to add.

"And what did you tell him?"

"Told him you'd been splendid in *He and She* and other things, and about how you'd broken your leg—saving the life of the Russian consul. He seemed very impressed by that."

"What do you know about *him*?"

"He's an inventor, he says. Can't make much money at it, by the look of his clothes." Here Hosmer preened just a little, taking pride in what sartorial elegance a man *might* achieve on limited means.

"Where does he come from?"

"Upstate," he said. "Elmira."

"And why did he come here?"

"To be nearer the people who pay money for inventions, I suppose. He may be poor now, but in a few years, if he's able to invent something that will make people happier than they are now, well, then, I suppose he could make himself very rich. Just as you could be very rich once you're able to go back on the stage," he added with a little of the deliberate flattery of old—*of old* being the time before he'd transferred his affections to Ida Conquest.

"And just as Ida will become very rich as the Cosmic star," said Susan with a smile, having more confidence in Ida's dramatic future than in her own. Hosmer readily agreed to this assessment.

❋ ❋ ❋

Having finally said yes to Hosmer's invitation to visit his studio, and to do so in the company of Mr. Beaumont, Susan was up and about early the next morning. Somehow Tripod seemed to understand that he was about to be left home alone, and he became quite distressed. He fawned and wheedled, and when this didn't work, he barked threateningly. When this also failed, he climbed on to a chair and gazed forlornly out the window, appearing to suggest that he would throw himself out if Susan did not take him along on her expedition. Susan dragged the chair away from the window, and Tripod skulked into the bedroom.

But as soon as she opened the hallway door, out the dog ran, barking and happy—as if he assumed that she had been playing a joke on him all the while. When she closed the door behind her, however, Tripod began a ferocious barking, and from the thumps against the door, Susan knew that he was repeatedly flinging himself against the wooden panels.

She went down the stairs, slowly and clumsily maneuvering with both crutches beneath her left arm.

Mr. Beaumont was waiting outside his door, ready to go.

"The dog alerted me," he explained, not as sourly as she'd expected.

"Mr. Beaumont," said Susan, "I fear I'm going to be such an impediment—"

"Nonsense," he said with a shrug, and a little more than five minutes later they were down three more flights of stairs, standing at the front door.

She smiled at him tentatively. "Perhaps we simply got off on the wrong footing—"

He smiled, and blushed more deeply than even Hosmer Collamore did at the extremity of his embarrassment. "Yes, of course—" he began, then tugged at his collar as to allow a little of the blood that suffused his face to spill back down into his body. He really was quite handsome, Susan decided, and in contrast to the thinning of his hair, his beard was quite lush and covered a great expanse of cheek and chin. There was even a certain endearing clumsiness in his movements that she hadn't noticed before. When he tried to help her out the front door, he succeeded only in getting one of her crutches caught, and then—in releasing it—kicking it down into the street.

"Let's call a cab," said Susan, "or else we'll be all day getting down there. I have the money here," she added quickly, to spare him the embarrassment of thinking that perhaps he could ill afford such extravagance. She had already figured out the probable tariff: thirty cents for the first half-mile, ten cents for each quarter-mile after that. A trip of approximately three miles, doubtless with some waiting time, came to one dollar and thirty cents plus a ten-cent gratuity to the driver. Which is to say, forty percent of her weekly allowance to herself—an extravagance indeed. Would there be any time, Susan wondered, when she wouldn't have to labor over such melancholy calculations?

Jack Beaumont thought for a moment about Susan's decision to pay for the cab, then nodded. He loped around the corner to Columbus Avenue in search of a vehicle that was free. Susan did not allow herself to be disappointed that Mr. Beaumont did not insist on paying himself. She was certain that he was as financially strapped as she.

The day was bright for February. It was also warm for February, and all the snow that had lingered for weeks had melted. Everything was quite dirty with soot from the coal fires that burned throughout the city, but it had been so long since Susan had gone on an excursion for pleasure that she was not disposed to find fault with anything that the sky above or the ground beneath had to offer her today.

A few minutes later a cab swung around the corner and came to a stop in front of the Fenwick. Mr. Beaumont climbed out to help Susan inside. This was no easy task, owing to an inconvenient combination of the height of the cab door, the weight of Susan's cast, and the length of her skirt. But at last it was accomplished when Mr. Beaumont simply put his strong hands about her waist and lifted her inside, then climbed in behind her. He picked up the speaker tube and instructed the driver to take them to number 27 West Twenty-seventh Street.

On the way Susan tried not to think of the extravagance of this cab, but turned in the seat so that she could peer out the back flap of the closed compartment, which Mr. Beaumont gallantly held open for her. It seemed as if she had never seen a crowd before, so entranced was she by the sheer numbers of people on the streets. She had never considered Seventh Avenue to be particularly splendid, but today she thought there was no street in the world to match it. At least she held that opinion until the cab turned on Forty-fourth Street, and then continued on down Fifth Avenue. For *nothing* was more splendid than that.

"You've been hiding away in that room too long," Mr. Beaumont said, a trifle hesitantly, as if afraid that he might have made too personal a remark.

"Sometimes I think I'm going mad up there," Susan admitted, still gazing out the back flap. "That's why you hear me pacing so. That's why I sometimes find myself doing a tarantella at eight in the morning—"

"—with a three-legged dog for a partner?" Mr. Beaumont said with a laugh, then blushed again.

"I'm entirely mad," said Susan. "And I do thank you for allowing me to come along today. I'm not sure—in fact, I know I wouldn't have ventured so far away from home—"

She broke off, for that admission made her sound like such a timid creature! The fact was that her hibernation had nothing to do with fear or an unwillingness to exert herself. Now she felt as if for the past several weeks she had been a pathetic, trapped creature, imprisoned not by a broken leg but by depression and a lack of self-confidence. The thought made her ashamed, even though she knew that one couldn't be strong *all* the time.

She felt happy today, and seeing so many people all about who quite demonstrably *got by* in life suggested to Susan that she would be able to get by as well. But what was she to do with herself? And where was her life to go? The question wasn't one that was going to melt like January snow.

CHAPTER EIGHT

SUSAN'S EXPECTATIONS concerning the appearance of the Cosmic Film Company were not fulfilled. She'd assumed, rather laughably, she guessed, that moving pictures were made in a theater. But the building at 27 West Twenty-seventh Street was much more like a factory, plain and brick. It did not possess posters outside the entrance, only a small placard announcing that on the third, fourth, and fifth floors were located the premises of the Cosmic Film Company. No marble foyer with gilt and mirrors and crimson carpeting greeted them inside, but only a grimy granite entranceway and a growling elevator, the door to which Mr. Beaumont held open for her.

They rose to the third floor and emerged into a large low room that was quite reminiscent of a factory, with a strong odor of chemicals. Men in long dirty white aprons ran about in a general air of barely controlled frenzy. One of these men stopped long enough to stare at them in a way that plainly asked their business. "We're here to see Mr. Collamore," said Mr. Beaumont.

The man stuck out an upraised thumb, which signified *up*. Susan and Mr. Beaumont got back into the elevator.

"Shall we try four?" Susan suggested.

On the fourth floor was clearly the business end of the operation, for here telephones were ringing—five of them on a single desk, behind which sat a sullen young boy. Susan was certain it was he who had been so rude to her the previous day. Messenger boys in blue uniforms waited about, apparently for canisters of film to be taken out to the various theaters, while several harried-looking young women clattered away at typewriters. Two fat men stood in one corner in close conversation, punctuating their exchange with lighted cigars. Obviously they were the most important people in the room, since they were the only ones not working.

"Mr. Collamore," said Jack to the boy at the telephone desk.

He wordlessly held up a hand with all his fingers splayed. Fifth floor.

The fifth floor was at the top of the building, and there skylights were set at a height of over thirty feet. As a result, the space was filled with intense sunlight. The room was, in its way, as active as the floors below, but here there was a difference. Susan was acquainted with the back-stage area of a legitimate theater, so she was not surprised to see bits of scenery about: drawing-room interiors, stone walls, great bushes in tiny pots, corners of city buildings, doorways of rustic cottages, and flats and canvases representing a seashore, a majestic mountain chain, a field of growing cotton.

The sense of being in a factory was enhanced, not lessened, by her perception of how moving pictures were made here. The only thing that looked the same to her as in the legitimate theater were the actors going through their scenes—but in what a peculiar fashion!

In one corner was a couple spooning in a rowboat set in a tin tub of water hardly larger than the boat itself, and the passing scenery unrolled behind them on a painted canvas. Only ten feet away a desperate struggle ensued in what looked like an opium den, with a dissolute woman defending her lover against the police, the latter having just broken through a pasteboard door with axes and shotguns. And ten feet away on the other side a quadrille was being performed, in old-fashioned costumes, to the tune of "Daddy Wouldn't Buy Me a Bow-Wow" played on an accordion just out of camera range by a very young girl with a shriveled leg.

In front of each of these varied scenes were the strange moving-picture cameras. They looked rather like big boxes with a tube at the front and a handle at the side. Behind each camera hunched a young man, earnestly turning the crank and watching the action through some sort of viewer. Susan recognized the man filming the opium den scene as Hosmer Collamore, and after a moment she picked out Ida Conquest as the lady in the yellow panniers and powdered wig at the center of the quadrille.

Besides the cameraman, each scene had a kind of stage director, shouting directions at the players, and a musician, to set the mood of the piece. Above the music and the shouted commands of the directors and the improvised dialogue of the players, was the hissing of the massive arc lamps that supplemented the daylight coming through the glass roof. In another portion of the room, carpenters built more sets and painters worked on various canvases. Everything was noise and confusion. It was a wonder to Susan that the actors could concentrate at all, or convey with any conviction the sense that they were trapped in an opium den deep beneath a city street.

"Miss Nethersole," called out the director to the wanton lady in the opium den, "please, when you faint, will you simply fall to the floor? Do not fall on to the couch, even though it is softer. I want you on the floor.

Mr. Westermeade, please do not step on Miss Nethersole's head as you are murdering Mr. Perks. Mr. Perks, please die quickly today, we've not yet gone into three reels. So would you mind—oh, no—stop the action."

He'd been interrupted by Hosmer, who'd suddenly stopped turning the crank on his camera. Something appeared to have gone wrong with the instrument. The director threw up his hands and turned away with a sigh of disgust.

Miss Nethersole got up off the floor and lay down on the divan, while Mr. Perks—one of the policemen—sat at the end and tickled her bare feet. Mr. Westermeade, the dissolute lady's dissolute lover, took out a harmonica and softly played an old Stephen Foster melody. The other actors wandered off toward a table laden with plates of food and an urn of coffee.

The other two scenes, on either side, went on uninterrupted.

"Who are you?" the stage director suddenly demanded of Susan and Mr. Beaumont, whom he'd nearly wandered into.

"We are friends of Mr. Collamore," said Mr. Beaumont, "and he asked us to visit him today."

"Well, there he is, having just ruined that entire act, so that the whole thing will have to be done over. Props!" the stage director called out suddenly, "get us a new door and reload those pistols."

Susan and Mr. Beaumont went over to Hosmer, who had pulled open the side of the camera, exposing the film inside.

"I lost it," he said with a grimace.

"Let me see," said Mr. Beaumont, peering into the workings of the camera. "Do you know what happened?"

"The film slipped from the sprockets and jammed," said Hosmer dismally. "This is the second time this week. The first time it was during the filming of a burning building down on Houston Street. No props man to set *that* one up again."

Mr. Beaumont turned the camera on its side so that light from above spilled into the interior. "Hosmer," he asked, "do you happen to have an old camera like this one around? One with the same parts?"

Hosmer glanced at Susan and said, "You see, Suss, I told you he was a tinkerer." With that Hosmer hurried away toward the other side of the enormous room.

"Suss?" Mr. Beaumont inquired with raised brows.

"No," she replied, "Susan, Susan, Susan. Never Suss."

"I promise I will never call you Suss if you will call me Jack," said Mr. Beaumont. He turned away, toward the rowboat scene, but not before Susan caught yet another blush mounting his cheeks. The reddening skin actually seemed to turn his beard darker.

After a few minutes, Hosmer returned, carrying two battered cameras, one over each shoulder. "Trust men," he explained mysteriously, putting the cameras down.

"Trust men?" echoed Jack, tugging at the side plate of one of the beat-up cameras.

"The Trust men are hooligans hired by the Patents Trust—the nine companies who control all the motion picture patents. They try to break up independent operations like ours, because they feel we're infringing on 'em. Come in at night, expose our film, smash our cameras, tear our canvas." Hosmer shook his head ruefully. "I got hit on the head once, and they're promising to do more soon. This is their work, these cameras."

"Why don't you just go to work for a company with patents instead, then?" asked Jack simply. He'd borrowed a screwdriver from a passing workman and was prying loose a geared wheel on the inside of the camera.

"Because they're boring stick-in-the-muds," said Hosmer. "They're still going to be doing one-reelers in 1933. Lord, Tom Edison is still filming on a rooftop over in New Jersey, and when it rains everybody has to run inside. The Patents are like a velocipede with dented wheels, and the independents are like a big red sixty-horsepower automobile."

This last sounded to Susan very much like something that Hosmer had heard or read somewhere rather than something he came up with on the spur of the moment.

"Also," Hosmer admitted after a moment, "the independents pay better. They pay the players better, and they pay their cameramen better, and pretty soon—"

"Pretty soon what?" asked Jack, handing back the first camera. "This one's no good," he added parenthetically, and took the second one and began work on that.

"Pretty soon," said Hosmer, "the independents are going to be on top, and the Trust will be coming to us for help and advice. I think it's probably happening already."

By this time, the quadrille was finished and the actors were told to take a break while the setting was being altered. Ida Conquest, after spending some moments talking with the director, wandered over to the little group gathered about the broken cameras.

Ida pulled her wig off and beat it against the side of her massive costume. White powder billowed into the air and a fair amount of it was deposited on Susan's skirt.

"Lord, Suss," she said, "is that you? On two feet?"

Jack Beaumont glanced up over the top of the camera at Ida briefly, but then he went back to his business.

Susan was surprised that she felt a little inward murmur of relief at Jack's apparent indifference to Ida's considerable physical charms. Conquest wasn't that girl's name so much as it was the way she lived her life.

"Yes," said Susan to Ida, "I'm fascinated by this entire business. I watched you, Ida, and it seemed to me you were quite splendid."

"It's a wonderful part," Ida admitted. "One I've been aching for ever since I was tapped for the *Follies*."

"Miss Conquest is playing Martha Washington," said Hosmer.

"It's a historical episode," said Ida complacently. "That was the wedding dance you saw. Next we're doing the scene where General Lafayette asks me to go back to France and be a countess and Mr. Washington comes in and I pretend the reason the general is on his knees is that he is showing me a picture of his little boys back home and then when Mr. Washington leaves I tell the general I can never go with him to France because number one, I am married, and number two, I have eighteen children of my own and couldn't leave them behind. I have this stemmy blue frock and wear flowing ribbons down my back."

Susan and Jack exchanged repressed smiles.

"Miss Conquest appears very elegant and refined on celluloid," said Hosmer. "Next week, we will all go to the theater and see her."

"So soon?" said Susan.

"We shoot this week, and on Saturday and Sunday the film will be developed, printed, and put together in proper sequence. On Monday copies will be made, and on Tuesday they will be delivered to the New York theaters and will go by mail to every theater in the country where Cosmic pictures are shown. Next week, all of Kansas City will be talking of nothing but Miss Conquest, the new Cosmic star, in her role as the mother of our nation."

"I don't doubt it for a moment," said Susan, and in her heart she did rather believe it.

"Hosmer," said Jack, holding up a narrow toothed wheel, "here was your problem. This crack here." He twisted the wheel between his hands, and a tiny gap could be seen in the metal. "Once in a while, when your rhythm in turning the crank was off, the film dragged on this, the sprockets got out of alignment, and the whole business was gone. I've switched wheels, and from now on the thing ought to go right."

Delighted, Hosmer thanked Mr. Beaumont profusely, then loaded the exposed film in the repaired camera and ran it quickly through without a hitch, proving that the job had been done properly. While doing this, Hosmer introduced Miss Conquest to Mr. Beaumont. Ida smiled a quick, cold smile. Cold and quick was all that was due, in her estimation, to a mere mechanic, friend of Mr. Collamore's or not.

The stage director returned, still not in a pleasant frame of mind. He said to Hosmer, "If you're quite finished with your friends, Colley—"

"My friend here fixed the camera, Mr. Fane. I'm sure it won't give us any more trouble."

The director's expression instantly changed to one of surprise, and then it deepened into satisfaction. "Thank you," he said politely to Jack. "I take it you are mechanically adept?"

"Yes," replied Jack. "And in fact, if you wouldn't mind, I'd like to work on a couple of these smashed-up jobs and see what I can do with them."

"By all means," said Mr. Fane magnanimously. "By all means take away as much broken machinery as you please, Mr.—"

"Beaumont."

"I'll bring them uptown this evening," Hosmer offered.

"Yes," said Mr. Fane blandly, already walking away. "Now Colley—"

Hosmer hurried after the man, and Jack looked about the Cosmic factory. "Have you seen enough?" he asked.

"Yes," said Susan, and then added in a quiet voice, "did you ever hear such nonsense as that 'historical episode'?"

"No," he laughed, "I never did."

"I could do better than that," said Susan.

"Then give it a try," said Jack. "I think Hosmer told me Mr. Fane pays twenty dollars apiece for his picture stories."

CHAPTER NINE

As JACK TURNED and started to lead Susan back toward the elevator, she suddenly said, "Oh, just a moment, please. I'd like to have a look at this." She was gazing in the direction of the spooners in the rowboat in the tin tub.

Susan recognized the actor—a great, funny fat man called Manfred Mixon. Susan had seen enough of the countless Cosmic productions to realize that this was yet another comic epic in which an impecunious Mixon wooed a spinster for her money. With only slight variations, that seemed to be the plot of every one of his improbable farces, and the endings were of two sorts: he was driven out of the woman's life ignominiously, or he ended up chained to her at a wedding ceremony, wondering if he really had got the better of the bargain.

"I could *certainly* write one of these," Susan said, casually picking up the typewritten scenario that lay face up on the director's table. The cameraman, the director, the actors, and all the others were paying attention only to what was going on in the scene. Turning a little in order to use Jack as a shield, Susan folded the pages, slipped them into her wrist bag, then began hobbling slowly away toward the elevator.

"Wouldn't it have been easier simply to ask for one?" Jack asked when they were out of earshot.

"They might not have given it to me," replied Susan, surprised at herself. For in one lightning-bolt moment she had suddenly understood how she could get money, despite a broken leg, despite vagaries of the theater and despite theatrical producers' prejudices against ingenues with decided limps. She would write a scenario for the Cosmic Film Company. And to do that, she needed only to see how such things were done, and toward that end she had purloined the typewritten scenario—an act less of desperation than inescapable logic.

"Is there anything else you'd like to steal before we have lunch?" Jack asked with mild amusement as they stood waiting for the elevator.

Susan sighed. "A typewriting machine would be a great blessing, I suppose, but—"

"But your bag is too small," said Jack, pulling open the door of the elevator. "I happen to own a typewriting machine. I took one apart once to see how the thing worked, and then put it back together again. We need only to steal you a manual of instruction."

❊ ❊ ❊

"I insist," said Jack. "I allowed you—against my better judgment—to pay for the taxicab, so you must allow me to buy lunch."

"Just a dairy bar, please," said Susan, thinking not of her appetite, which was large, but rather of Jack Beaumont's budget, which was obviously not.

Around the corner from the Cosmic Film Company's offices they found a tiny restaurant catering to the meager stomachs and purses of secretaries and typewriters in this quarter of New York. Since Jack and Susan hadn't even such regular employment as *that*, such a place seemed not beneath their dignity. Susan seated herself at a little round marble-topped table at the front window, and in a few minutes Jack brought her a sandwich and a cup of coffee and sat down beside her. He'd taken the same for himself, and Susan had the satisfaction of knowing that, even if they decided to have dessert pie, Jack would not have spent more than thirty cents altogether.

"Tell me what else Hosmer told you," said Susan eagerly, as soon as Jack had sat down. He appeared tall and awkward in this place that seemed to be frequented exclusively by bustling working girls.

"What about?" he asked, mystified by her question.

"Scenarios, of course." She had already taken the folded pages from her bag, spread them out on the table, and was reading them through with great concentration. As she read, she had less and less doubt that she would be able to produce something at least as good—and possibly a great deal better.

Jack took a bite of his sandwich thoughtfully, and after a moment recalled, "Hosmer said that Mr. Fane produces about three two-reel pictures a week as well as a couple of one-reelers for theaters that still want to show them. He says Fane can't get enough good scenarios to suit him, and sometimes he just makes them up as he goes along."

"And he actually pays—" prompted Susan.

"I think he said twenty dollars for a two-reeler. I might have got that wrong," Jack warned, "but—"

"But even if it were only ten—"

Jack glanced away, blushed, and said hesitantly, "Am I right in assuming that you are not exactly—"

"'Replete with pecuniary emoluments'?" Susan said with a laugh. "You might say that, Mr. Beaumont. You might even say, as Miss Conquest undoubtedly would, that I am just about 'stone broke.' Even if Mr. Fane paid only ten dollars, that is more money than I am likely to make on the legitimate stage with a broken leg."

"But once your leg is mended—" Jack protested.

"Once my leg is mended, I am likely to be walking the rialto with most of the other actors in the city."

"Walking the rialto?"

"Unemployed."

"Oh," said Jack, taking another bite of his sandwich. Even his neck turned red when he blushed, Susan noticed. Looking at him this closely she saw also that his eyes were not the blue she'd first thought them, but rather a startling gray.

"So you see," she said, "I will consider ten dollars to be a perfectly adequate recompense."

Jack opened his mouth to speak, but evidently then thought better of it. He took a sip of coffee instead, but choked on it. Susan slapped him hard on the back a number of times and he finally recovered himself.

"I know what you were going to say," said Susan. "That I shouldn't get my hopes up. I know that. I've had a lifetime of disappointments, because nine times out of ten, my hopes were 'dashed against the stony walls of circumstance.' That's the problem with actors, you know—they're always quoting lines from bad plays they were in. I quote terrible speeches and I still get my hopes up. I'm afraid my hopes are up now, and it doesn't do a bit of good in the world for you to tell me they ought not to be. Wasn't that what you were going to say?"

"Yes," Jack admitted quickly, fearing his choking attack would return if he said more.

Susan smiled, and then asked—with a tentativeness that was rare with her—"Would you really like to be of some help to me?"

Jack nodded, not trusting himself to more speech.

"Then you can spend a few hours with me this afternoon—in the nickelodeon?"

❀ ❀ ❀

It was by no means difficult to find a theater exhibiting moving pictures, even in this neighborhood that was mostly devoted to business. Three doors down from the little restaurant where they'd eaten was Parker's nickelodeon, and though Jack suggested that they might find a much more up-to-date and grander place on Broadway or Sixth Avenue, Susan said, "I don't want to see the best, I'm interested in seeing the ordinary." So she paid her nickel entrance fee, and insisted on paying Jack's as well.

Parker's was an old-fashioned place, having been in business at this location for almost a decade. It was just one long narrow room with a stained canvas sheet secured to the wall at the end; on this the moving pictures were projected. Rows of cane-seated chairs were arranged on either side of a narrow aisle, and a dejected looking man with a wracking cough played music on a spavined piano directly below the screen. There weren't more than a dozen patrons in the place when Susan and Jack entered, and all of them were bunched down front on the right— more interested in the warmth of a stove in the corner than in what was being projected onto the canvas.

What was showing was a jittery travelogue that purported to be authentic scenes of the Casbah in Fez, though the faces of the natives looked as if they'd been dyed with berry juice rather than burned by the Moroccan sun. Jack and Susan sat in the back with their coats drawn tightly about them. It was colder inside the theater than it had been on the street.

After the phony-looking travelogue came several equally inauthentic-looking newsreels, then two dismal vaudeville skits, and then at last an installment—somewhere in the middle of the story—of the serial, "The Adventures of Kathlyn." Kathlyn was a singularly naive young woman who got herself into one scrape after another, and seemed to have a penchant—strange for such a wide-eyed innocent from the country—of falling into the clutches of the most dangerous criminals on the North American continent. Susan entertained a little fantasy of Ida Conquest playing the part of Kathlyn as she watched Kathlyn get tossed off the edge of a precipice, locked in a bank safe with a bomb suspended from her neck, hypnotized into the desire for assassinating the governor of Illinois.

Parker's being a Patents Trust theater, there was no feature at all, only a couple of two-reelers, no longer than the one serial. The first was a bit of melodramatic nonsense called *The Siren's Serenade* in which a husband with a fake mustache was tempted to leave his wife for a woman he met on board an ocean liner, but true love conquered in the end when the wife, employing a *nom de stateroom*, somehow appeared on the boat and won her husband's love anew. The siren drowned when she washed overboard during a storm. The second feature, *Boarding House Barney*, was purportedly a comedy, though no one in it was funny, and its portrayal of so universally known a situation as a paying boarder bore no remote relation to reality.

"Let's find an independent theater," Susan suggested as they emerged into the February sunlight. "And one showing Cosmic films, if we can."

"Your cast and crutches," Jack protested gently, but Susan waved away this concern for her discomfort.

With purpose and hope in her breast, Susan felt better than she had for weeks—better, in fact, since the night when that idiot Jay Austin had thrown himself on top of her in the snow. It was true that her feet were sore, her arms ached with the unaccustomed exercise of the crutches, and some sort of grit had got into her cast and was making her mending leg itch madly, but Susan had no intention of going home *yet*.

Jack went into a druggist's shop, entered a phone booth, and called the Cosmic studio to find out at what nickelodeons they might see Mr. Mixon's latest essay in comedy. He was told that this could be seen at an establishment called the Paragon, which was located at Sixth Avenue and Forty-third Street. This saved them a deal of trouble and walking about, and they were able to take the Sixth Avenue elevated straight up to Forty-second Street.

The Paragon's presentation, from the independent film companies, was a much more enjoyable bill than the first they'd seen. It began with a travelogue of the splendors of California, then was followed—in considerable contrast—by a newsreel of local disasters, including a fire in a Brooklyn factory. Next came a comedy short involving a man in blackface and wedding clothes being chased through City Hall Park by a large group of women in blackface and wedding gowns. Then Jack and Susan were mystified by an episode of *The Purple Mask*, which climaxed with the detective-hero locked in a steamer trunk which was then hurled off the Brooklyn Bridge. And, at the last, came *Nobbin's Nuptials*, the Cosmic two-reeler featuring Manfred Mixon playing the owner of a livery stable intent on wedding the mayor's widow. There were comic wooing scenes, a comic costume ball, a comic horse race, and, at the end, a comic wedding.

Susan and Jack laughed, and laughed heartily, for Manfred Mixon was indeed an accomplished comedian. When it was over, Susan placed a hand on Jack's arm and said, "May I ask you one more favor?"

"Of course," said Jack.

"Could we sit through it once more?"

The second time through, Susan watched with a sharp critical eye, and took notes on some scraps of paper that Jack found in his jacket pocket.

❈ ❈ ❈

When Jack Beaumont knocked on Susan's door that evening, Tripod seemed to know who it was, and began hurling himself at the door with a ferocious barking. Susan dragged the dog into the bedroom and shut the door.

Jack brought in a Densmore typewriting machine and placed it on Susan's table.

"It looks quite new!" she exclaimed.

"Well, I cleaned it up a bit," he admitted with a blush, which Susan again found immensely charming. "But I don't know anything about the way typewriting is done. I'm told it's a little like playing the piano, but I don't know how to do that either. I came across a ream of paper, too."

"Thank you so very much," said Susan earnestly, looking at the machine with ill-concealed excitement. Not that she had any great love for new-fangled gadgetry, but because this was the instrument that might change her fortune. Since they had left the Paragon late that afternoon, she'd thought of nothing else.

"Jack, I'd ask you to stay—"

"But you want to get right at it, I presume."

"Yes. In fact, I've already started." She shyly touched the top of several sheets of yellow paper with handwriting scrawled all over them.

"May I—"

"Oh, no! Not till it's done. But then I'm going to want your sincere opinion."

"I'll be happy to give it," said Jack. "But wouldn't Hosmer be a better judge, since he is in the business?"

"No, no," said Susan. "I don't want Hosmer to know I'm doing this. I don't want anyone to know—in case I fail," she added with brave candor.

"But you've told me," said Jack.

"You're my sole confidant in this, and I rely on your discretion."

"I'm honored," said Jack. "But I'm sure that once Mr. Fane has seen your scenario—"

"Oh, we mustn't talk about it or we'll jinx it."

After Jack left, Susan let Tripod out of the bedroom, boiled a pot of coffee, and set out a bowl of Oysterettes on a table beside her chair. Then with her cast arranged as comfortably as possible on an ottoman, and with a small blanket thrown over her lap and the dog squeezed in beside her, Susan began writing a new story for Manfred Mixon. She stared at the black square of window for a long while, scribbled furiously for a few minutes, stared at the blackness some more, rearranged the blanket, scribbled some more, listened to the voices coming through the thin walls of the apartment building, and scribbled on through the night.

CHAPTER TEN

Mr. Hopwood's Harem
by
SARAH LIGHT

S CENE 1.

Harry Hopwood (Mr. Mixon) runs a ramshackle boardinghouse in a small town in New Jersey. Hopwood has a full complement of guests, each more unpleasant than the other, and he has his apron full trying to take care of them at breakfast every morning. Each morning is a series of disasters. In the kitchen Mr. Hopwood is an inexperienced cook, and at the breakfast table Mr. Hopwood is an indifferent serving girl, despite fetching feminine costume. The guests revolt and riot, and more of them defect to the widow Filkins's boardinghouse.

Scene 2.
Mrs. Filkins's boardinghouse is in complete and noble contrast to that of Mr. Hopwood. It is the height of gentility. Her guests, even those defected from Mr. Hopwood's establishment, are uniformly genteel and well behaved, creating a place of order and good breeding.

Scene 3.
Mr. Hopwood is left with only one boarder—a cantankerous old gentleman who hasn't paid his rent for three months, and affects an illness in order not to be tossed out on his ear. Then a fresh worry: The pompous town banker arrives with a warrant of foreclosure. Mr. Hopwood gets an idea. The way out of his difficulties is to merge with Mrs. Filkins. After all, he is fat and she is thin; he is impecunious and she has money salted away; he has no idea of how to run a boardinghouse and she was born to the job.

Scene 4.
In Mrs. Filkins's parlor, Mr. Hopwood declares his love to the widow and proposes marriage. But at this tender moment the widow Filkins's young nephew, a scamp of a boy, pops Mr. Hopwood in the eye with a bean shooter. In chasing the boy about the parlor, Hopwood manages to wreck the sofa, and ends up rolled in the draperies, a goldfish bowl over his head. He is ejected by Mrs. Filkins, and told never again to darken her door.

Scene 5.
The end of Mr. Hopwood's hopes has driven him insane. With wild hair and a frenzied countenance, he sets fire to his own boardinghouse. The cantankerous old invalid suddenly proves

himself quite spry and rushes out at the sight of smoke and flames. A sudden rain shower puts out the fire, but Mr. Hopwood, still mad, takes a pistol and rushes off into a nearby forest with the intention of ending it all.

Scene 6.
In the forest, a group of chorus girls on a picnic from the city are being menaced by two hooligans intent on stealing jewelry and kisses. Mr. Hopwood arrives on the scene, still in a frenzy and, only half aware of what he's doing, frightens the ruffians away. The chorus girls fall on Mr. Hopwood as their rescuer, and prevent him from carrying out his plan of suicide. They listen to his tale of woe with great sympathy.

Scene 7.
The girls have installed themselves in Mr. Hopwood's boardinghouse. Not only do they perform the duties of cooks, maids, and serving girls, but they are also guests. Soon, there is a line of gentlemen outside the house, waiting for rooms in this most interesting of establishments. In the parlor, the pompous banker is soothed with the blandishments of the chorus girls, and there is no longer any danger of foreclosure.

Scene 8.
Mrs. Filkins's house is now almost empty, and she sits at her vast dining table alone with an old deaf woman—the very last of her guests. When Mrs. Filkins's nephew upsets a plate on the sideboard, Mrs. Filkins slaps him. Mr. Hopwood is announced, and Mrs. Filkins meets her competitor. Mr. Hopwood proposes that the

two establishments be united, and Mrs. Filkins happily accepts his proposal of marriage.

Scene 9.
Mr. Hopwood and Mrs. Filkins are married, with the chorus girls acting as bridesmaids. At the end of the ceremony, all the chorus girls are paired with handsome young gentlemen of the town—not excepting the pompous banker and the cantankerous old gentleman—while Mr. Hopwood begins to wonder if he did not get the worst of the deal with scrawny Mrs. Filkins.

"I think it's quite wonderful," Jack said admiringly, early the next morning.

"Oh, do you really?" cried Susan happily, spinning around in a blue flannelette kimono. "Are you telling me the truth?"

Jack nodded solemnly, as if mere words were inadequate to express the depth of his admiration for this new masterpiece of moving-picture scenario.

"I'm so glad," said Susan. "I was up till past three, and there were times I wanted dreadfully to pace the room. That's what writers do, I'm told, when they're lacking inspiration. I didn't because I was afraid of disturbing you."

"As it happened, you wouldn't have disturbed me," Jack laughed. "I also was up half the night."

"Oh, yes?"

"Hosmer brought home some of the cameras that were broken by the Trust ruffians, and I played with them. Took them apart to see how they worked—and didn't work. When I get involved with something like that, I don't much notice the time."

"I like writing scenarios ever so much more than conning lines," said Susan. "Memorizing lines," she said by way of clarification, when it was apparent that Jack hadn't understood the theatrical jargon.

"Do you think you have it in you to write any more of these?"

"Oh, loads. But I don't want to be 'numerating the barnyard fowl.' Don't forget, Mr. Fane hasn't seen this yet—and he won't see it till I've typewritten it. And remember I have to figure out how that machine works."

Typewriting the scenario proved as much of a chore as composing the thing had been. Susan found out the rude mechanics quickly enough, as there were only a limited number of ways for the paper to fit, and the keyboard was clearly marked. But remembering where the letters were, and getting up any sort of rhythm was difficult, and the laborious erasure of errors was a trial of petty aggravation. Not till one o'clock that afternoon was the thing done—and though a bit smudged and crumpled, it was legible, and done in the same form as the one she'd stolen the day before.

Susan had never felt such elation. Writing, she'd discovered, was different from stage acting—where one is at the mercy of a text (usually asinine), a director (often incompetent), fellow actors (invariably jealous), and an audience (generally unsympathetic). But this scenario, simple and straightforward, was an unqualified product of her mind, and it would rise or fall by merit alone.

She stomped hard three times on the floor with her cast foot. In a few moments, she heard Jack's tread hurrying up the stairs.

"I'm finished with it," she said, opening the door.

He made a movement as if to grab her up in her elation, but then he held back. His arms seemed to quiver for a moment at his sides, and then were still. She wished he had gathered her up. There were definitely times when a young woman needed a friendly embrace, and this was one of them.

She threw herself into his arms, but the motion was so unexpected to him, and her weight so unexpectedly heavy because of the plaster around her leg, that they both staggered backward into the hallway...just as Mrs. Jadd and her two timorous daughters were emerging for the day's shopping.

Mrs. Jadd grabbed her two children and spun them around so that they would not be witness to such wickedness. And just across the hall!

Jack blushed so that Susan half-feared his eyes would fill up with blood, but she only laughed, and dragged him back inside. She smilingly closed the door in Mrs. Jadd's scandalized face.

"Oh dear," Susan laughed, "I'm afraid we've just been branded. But I don't care, I'm so excited, so happy—"

Jack looked over the typewritten sheets. "Why did you put the name as Sarah Light?"

"Just in case..."

Jack nodded in understanding. In case she failed. "Now," he asked, changing the subject, "how do you intend to get this to Mr. Fane?"

Susan thought for a moment. "I shouldn't like to mail it, for it might be mislaid, or never get to him. And I wouldn't entrust it to Hosmer, for if Mr. Fane thinks no better of Hosmer than he indicated yesterday, he may be prejudiced against anything that Hosmer brings him. It might be best if I simply took it myself, and asked for an interview with Mr. Fane. Though—"

"I could take it," said Jack.

"You?"

"I have an appointment with Mr. Fane in only a couple of hours. I'm going to talk to him about an improvement I have in mind for his cameras—all that work I was doing last night. And I'll be happy to show him your scenario, say that it is the product of a friend of mine, and see what he says."

❀ ❀ ❀

Susan waited on tenterhooks in Jack's absence that afternoon, and though she knew it nonsense, she still labored under the conviction that Mr. Fane's yes or no would determine the course of the rest of her life. She was not given to great enthusiasms, with the exception of her one great decision to move from Winter River to New York to become an actress. Since then, nothing had fired her determination and her hope as much as this essay into the peculiar field of writing stories for moving pictures.

Actually, she thought she'd done her work well on the vehicle for Mr. Mixon. It was exactly like all his other moving-picture comedies. It didn't require very much in the way of outdoor scenes or camera tricks. Most of the work could easily be mounted and filmed in the West Twenty-seventh Street studio. The scenario provided ample opportunity for Mr. Mixon to do the business he liked so well—he invariably wrecked a room in the course of each of his features, invariably appeared at least once dressed as a woman, and invariably smashed a piece of furniture by sitting down or leaning too hard on it. Susan's only real innovation was the inclusion of the chorus girls, but she thought that this was an inspired idea—the trotting-out of a great number of snappily dressed, pretty girls did wonders for the most dreadful plays on the stage. Why should it not do the same for moving-picture features?

After enumerating to herself all these felicities of her composition, Susan dropped into an instant blue funk, thinking, *Oh I'm such a little fool to think that Mr. Fane will pay twenty dollars for three typewritten pages that I, with no experience whatever, wrote in the course of a single night.*

In a sudden state of nerves, Susan took a brush, a pailful of water, some Fairbanks Gold Dust cleansing powder, and scrubbed at everything that could be attacked with impunity. When she was done with that, she danced with Tripod, humming "She's My Lady of the Nile." Then she sat down and scanned the last half-dozen issues of *The Modern Priscilla*, hoping that maybe one of the articles or stories would suggest an idea for her next scenario.

But then she threw even that aside, and clapped her hands. Tripod flew up from the floor into her arms, and Susan hugged him close. "Oh, Tripod," she cried in exasperation, "*when* is he coming back?"

At that very moment, Tripod barked and began to wail. He struggled out of Susan's arms on to the top of the chair. From there, he hurled himself at the door to the hallway.

Jack Beaumont was back—Jack, with her fate in his hands.

CHAPTER ELEVEN

SHE FLUNG open the door.

Tripod rushed out and leapt at Jack's throat, but only caught his teeth in the thick woolen scarf around Jack's neck.

Tripod swung like a pendulum, his teeth embedded in the end of the scarf.

"Tripod is really the smartest dog I ever knew," said Susan, "but I do think he's taken an undeserving disliking to you."

"Of that I'm convinced," said Jack, unwinding his scarf. This seemed the only way of separating himself from the growling terrier.

When Tripod was safely, though not quietly, sequestered in the bedroom, Susan sat on the edge of a chair. "You saw Mr. Fane?" she asked, trying unsuccessfully to disguise her anxiety.

Jack nodded slowly.

"And you showed him the scenario?"

Jack nodded again.

"And he promised to read it?"

Once more.

"And he will phone me if he decides to buy it?" Jack hesitated. "I don't understand," said Susan.

"He said there was no need to wait for his phone call."

Susan dropped into the chair where she'd written the scenario the night before. Suddenly she was very tired, and realized how little sleep she'd gotten, and how much energy she'd expended in her excitement. Her leg itched madly inside the cast. She wanted to go to sleep for a long time. Till her leg was healed, till she had another role on the stage, till this long period of penury and helplessness was past, and by some unknown means her dreary life was flooded with light and gold.

Something dropped into her lap.

"The reason you needn't wait for his phone call," explained Jack, "is that he bought it on the spot."

Susan stared at the long white envelope in her lap. With trembling fingers she picked it up, pulled out the flap and peered inside.

"Greenies," said Jack.

Wonderingly, Susan counted: seven five-dollar notes.

"But this is more than—"

Jack shrugged. "I told you I wasn't certain it was twenty dollars. Do you want to send back the extra fifteen? I'm sure the Cosmic Film Company will be pleased to receive it."

Susan took a long breath and with eyes wide as saucers, counted the bills again. It seemed scarcely possible that they were hers.

"Are you at all interested in what else Mr. Fane had to say?"

"Oh, I'm sorry. Of course! It's just that I'm—tell me everything, please!"

"Well, he said the scenario was perfect for the company and for Mr. Mixon, and he wondered if Miss Light hadn't written for the moving pictures before."

"What did you say?"

"I said you hadn't. Then he asked who you were, and I told him you were a friend, who for the moment wished her identity to remain a secret. He said he didn't care if your name was Apple Brown Betty and you looked like the missing link, as long as you could give him another like this."

"Another one!"

"As soon as possible—another two-reeler for Mr. Mixon and, if you can come up with something appropriate, a two-reeler for Miss Conquest. Something in which she gets to give up everything for her man and wear pretty frocks, he suggested."

Susan leaned back in the chair, stunned. Laughing, Jack leaned down, took hold of her cast, and lifted her leg carefully on to the ottoman.

"Is it really this easy?" Susan asked softly.

"You provided Mr. Fane with what he needed," said Jack. "He paid you for your trouble and your talent, and now he's asking you to repeat the performance. That's what business is all about—or so I'm told, for I must say it never seems to go in so straightforward a manner for me."

Jack's tone reminded Susan that the main reason for his visit to Mr. Fane had not been made to proffer the Manfred Mixon scenario. "Did you speak to Mr. Fane about your ideas for his cameras?"

"Yes," said Jack, leaning against the table opposite her. His legs really did seem most absurdly long. "He thought they were very interesting, and felt that I should go forward with my experiments." Jack smiled a melancholy smile.

"But he didn't give you any money," said Susan.

"No. But he said he'd be happy to see how I was progressing at any time."

"I'm sorry," said Susan. "You know, I don't really know what it is you're doing with those cameras." It was difficult to center her attention on Jack's project, when what she really wanted to do was jump into the air, spin around, and clutch seven five-dollar bills to her breast in an agony of relief, pride, and hope. Nevertheless, she gazed at him with what she hoped was interest on her face.

"I've thought of a small device to go *inside* the camera. You know how sometimes the moving pictures are jerky?"

"They are always jerky," said Susan with perhaps more enthusiasm than she strictly felt about this technical matter. "And I've always wondered why someone didn't do something about it."

"Well, once I'd looked inside the cameras, I realized what the trouble was. What's needed is something that will steady the film as it passes behind the lens—something that will make the speed absolutely uniform, which it isn't now. If I were to come up with something like that, it would be an improvement for every camera in the moving-picture business."

"It sounds simple," said Susan, "but I'm sure it's not."

"So what I would like to do is develop the device, patent it, sell it to all the moving-picture companies, and retire from tinkering on a fabulous income. But I make a living now making small repairs, such as on your type-writing machine. That takes all my time, and I've none left over for the work that might bring in real money."

Without thinking what she was doing, Susan took two of her precious five-dollar bills and proffered them to Jack.

He held up his hands. "Oh no, please, I won't."

"Why not?"

"Because that is your hard-earned money."

"But it's more than I need."

Jack shook his head. "No. I won't take money from you. I'm not destitute, and I'm young and strong and my constitution will be able to stand a few late nights of work. While the rest of the city is asleep, you'll be up here going *scribble, scribble, scribble* on your next scenario, and I'll be down below, *grind-*, *grind-*, *grind*ing away at some broken moving-picture camera. So you can pace and dance and act out all the parts to your heart's content without fear of keeping me from sleep."

"You're certain you won't take the money?"

"Positive. It would make me ashamed."

❀ ❀ ❀

For the next weeks Susan was in heaven. She could think of no other situation that would compare to her present one. She sat all day in the great comfortable chair in her sitting room, with her mending leg propped up on the ottoman and Tripod squeezed in beside her. She wrote and wrote and wrote. While she dressed, bathed, and prepared her little meals, her imagination was in another place. She daydreamed as she had not daydreamed since she was a little girl staring at the dusty road that led out of Winter River and wondering where it would take her. She dreamed now of impossibly sweet romances, improbably comic weddings, and exciting adventures fraught with danger to the hero. She even imagined a beautiful young woman, kidnapped, sequestered, and threatened in a lonely house in a forbidding landscape. But the difference between her childhood imaginings and these sweeping fancies was that these would bring Susan money, if she was able to dream them in enough detail, and could put that detail on to paper, and get that paper into the hands of Mr. Junius Fane of the Cosmic Film Company in time.

Susan first wrote another comedy for Manfred Mixon, and was a bit chagrined that it was so close in its outline to the first one, but that appeared to be exactly what Mr. Fane wanted, and Jack brought back another envelope, and once again it contained thirty-five dollars. From being in a position of wondering where the next meal was coming from, Susan was now in the happy position of wondering whether it was wise to keep so much money about the house.

Next she went to work on a romance in which Ida Conquest figured as a well-bred orphan deprived of her fortune by an unscrupulous guardian, who intended to marry her off to a degenerate English aristocrat. Just when the hour seems blackest, Ida is carried off by her chauffeur, whom she'd once scorned as beneath her. She falls in love with the man despite his lowly station, and gives up all in order to marry him for true love. On the wedding day—with the guardian and the profligate aristocrat in the custody of the police—an astonished Ida discovers that the chauffeur is actually a rich cousin (through marriage) who was keeping an eye on his beautiful relative, whom he has loved since they were children.

The story was more romantic than probable, of course, but the whole thing could be filmed on the premises of the Cosmic studio, and Ida would get to wear any number of splendid gowns.

Susan, fearing she was taking advantage of the good nature of her neighbor, begged Jack to seek the services of the neighborhood errand boy for the delivery of the scenario to the Cosmic studios. Jack said he would not hear of it. For one thing it was far too valuable a document to be entrusted to such an unreliable courier; for another, he liked staying in touch with Mr. Fane, and it gave him pleasure to field the man's probings into the true identity of the wonderful and mysterious Sarah Light.

So Susan let Jack go, though she had some misgivings about this third scenario. The Mixon comedies were so formulaic that it would have been difficult *not* to produce something useful, but a romantic scenario was entirely different. Perhaps she hadn't the knack for it.

But Jack returned with a third envelope—again with seven five-dollar notes inside.

"Mr. Fane says that he has never read the work of anyone with such a grasp of what was needed by a film company working on a small budget and a tight schedule. He says that Miss Sarah Light would be welcome at any time on the premises, and that he would even be pleased to treat her to luncheon. But he says that if she prefers to remain distant from the operation he is eager to respect that as well."

"I see no reason to keep up the pretense," said Susan. "Now that he's taken three of my stories."

Jack made no reply, but instead looked at Susan with a hesitant expression.

"What is it?" she asked. "Is there something I don't know? Is there a reason for this to remain secret?"

"I think perhaps there is..."

"Then tell me, please," she said, a touch of concern in her voice.

He shook his head. "Despite your infirmity, could I persuade you to accompany me on a short walk?"

"Why, yes you may, Mr. Beaumont," she said, now very curious. "I feel that with over a hundred dollars' income in the past week, I can afford a bit of recreation. Besides, I feel the exercise would do me good."

She could get along now inside the apartment on just one crutch, but she still felt safer outside with both. It was nearly three o'clock on a gray and blustery afternoon, and Jack, making small talk, suggested they head in the direction of Columbus Circle.

The wide circular intersection was filled with traffic— automobile, horse-drawn, and pedestrian—all day long, and around it were ranged restaurants, theaters, and clothing emporia. At the corner of Sixtieth Street and Broadway, Jack paused. Susan, unable to contain her curiosity, said, "Could you please tell me the destination and purpose of this excursion?"

"This is our destination, as a matter of fact," said Jack.

Susan looked around, and saw nothing but the old Circle Theater, which three years ago had gone from being a legitimate theater to one exhibiting moving pictures.

It was more expensive than the nickelodeons, charging twenty-five cents for the best seats, but it showed very much the same programs. And then Susan looked up at the theatre's marquee. She gave a small lurch and grabbed for Jack Beaumont's arm as she read:

HOPWOOD'S HAREM
A Cosmic Film Company Production
featuring
That Favorite Fat and Funny Fellow
Manfred Mixon

Susan hardly saw the travelogue, the newsreel, or the one-reel comedy that preceded *Hopwood's Harem*. She was so nervous and excited that Jack laid a hand on her arm, as if he feared that she might get up and begin pacing the theater aisles. His hand was warm on the sleeve of her blouse, and she thought alternately of his touch, and the astonishing fact that she was sitting in a moving-picture theater a scant block and a half from her home, about to witness her own story translated into celluloid pictures.

She had no thought that what she'd written was in any way equivalent to a *real* play—even to such a piece of sentimental tripe as *He and She*. It had to be true—didn't it?—that the worst legitimate play ever mounted on a creaking stage was inherently superior to the most ambitious screen drama. Be that as it may, Susan was as full of pride in her production as if what she'd written was about to be mounted on the stage of the Eltinge or the Shubert theater.

When it came time for *Hopwood's Harem*, Susan grasped Jack's hand in excitement and fear and squeezed it tight.

A filigree-bordered announcement appeared on the screen, displaying the title and Mr. Mixon's name and caricatured face—exactly the same as all the other Manfred Mixon photoplays. Next appeared a second card bearing the names of the other players in the piece, headed by the inscription: "The Cosmic Players." And after that came a third card, which read:

This Photo-Drama
was written expressly
for the
Cosmic Film Company
by a
Young Lady in High Society
Who Wishes
Her Identity to be Kept Secret
Owing to the Possible Censure
of Her Parents and Friends

Susan turned and stared at Jack in the semidarkness: "What on earth did you tell Mr. Fane about me?"

CHAPTER TWELVE

OUTSIDE THE THEATER again, Susan stared about her as if she'd been dropped at Columbus Circle directly from the Argentine pampas. Everything was now different in her life. Until now, she had never really quite believed that the words she had sat in her chair writing would actually be translated into real moving pictures, and that complete strangers would then gather in darkened rooms and pass judgment on their worth. The audience in the Circle Theater seemed to have been favorably impressed, it was true—but what if they had hissed? How would Susan have felt then?

"Are you not feeling well?" Jack asked.

"Thank you," said Susan uncertainly, "perhaps if we could..."

Directly on Columbus Circle was Faust's Restaurant and Café, and Jack huddled Susan inside. The backs of the booth he secured for them were high and protective, and Susan leaned against the dark wood as if she were exhausted.

"That certainly came as a...surprise," she said falteringly.

"A pleasant one, I hope," said Jack. "May I please order you a restorative?" She nodded, and he asked the waiter to bring two glasses of brandy and water.

"It was pleasant," said Susan. "But what if the audience hadn't laughed?"

"But they *did*. In fact, it was the funniest Mixon comedy I've ever seen. And you just watch—every comedy from now on will have a dozen chorus girls straight off the music hall stage."

"'Young Lady in High Society'?" Susan quoted suddenly, remembering the card at the beginning of the picture. "What *did* you tell Mr. Fane about me?"

"I did a little embroidery on Miss Light's identity, that's all," explained Jack. "When I first spoke to him of your scenario he was going to dismiss it. After all, who was I to recommend a writer to him? All I'd done was to fix a gear on one of his cameras. So I begged his pardon, but told him that what I held in my hand had been written by a lady in society who much admired Mr. Mixon and was of a literary turn of mind and wished to try her hand at formulating a scenario for a moving picture. I made you sound very top-of-the-brow."

The waiter brought the drinks. After nodding to Jack over the rim of the glass, Susan sipped at the light-colored liquid. It burned—and it made her feel better almost immediately.

"Did Mr. Fane ask how you came to be acquainted with a young lady of such exalted station? And how you gained her confidence?"

"He did. I said that I had once been engaged as a mathematical tutor to the young lady, and that I still had entree to the house as a tutor to her younger brothers. Twins, I said. And that on my last visit, while waiting for the twins to return from an amateur sporting match, I had fallen into conversation in the conservatory with the young lady, and she had confessed her infatuation with moving pictures and Mr. Mixon. When she discovered that I lived in the same apartment house as Hosmer Collamore, a gentleman actually acquainted with Mr. Mixon, she confided the manuscript to my care."

"I think you're the one with the imagination at this table," said Susan. "Perhaps you and not I should be writing scenarios. Did Mr. Fane believe you?"

"I don't know," said Jack. "But he looked at the scenario, and he bought it."

"And you don't think he would have if he had known it was written by an out-of-work actress living on West Sixtieth Street with a three-legged dog and a broken limb?"

"I think that Mr. Fane saw an opportunity for some publicity in producing a moving-picture written by a society lady who does not wish her name to be known. I don't believe that the writers of these photoplays are usually mentioned at all—and Mr. Fane wrote an entire story up there about the mysterious Miss Light."

Susan grimaced.

"I know what you're thinking, but please don't," said Jack.

"What am I thinking?" said Susan.

"You're thinking that he didn't buy the story on its merits as a story. But I can assure you he did."

"But you just said—"

"Did Mr. Fane change any of it?"

"No," said Susan.

"Did he ask for others?"

"Yes."

"Did he buy your others?"

"Yes."

"And Hosmer tells me they've already gone out to some great rolling farm in New Jersey to shoot the outdoor scenes for the second Mixon play. Mr. Fane might have bought *one* scenario from the society lady for the novelty of the thing—but he would not have bought three."

Susan realized that Jack was right, but she felt that she'd duped the Cosmic Film Company somehow. As if her success were not due wholly to her talent, but due—at least in some part—to Jack Beaumont's smooth story.

"But you think," she said, "that it would not be wise to confide the truth to Mr. Fane?"

Jack pondered the question for a moment, taking a big sip of his brandy and soda and dribbling a fair amount on to his shirtfront in the process. "I think that you should wait till Mr. Fane and the Cosmic Film Company are so dependent on your services that Miss Sarah Light could come forward as the kaiser himself and Mr. Fane would accept her."

Susan leaned across the table and dabbed at Jack's shirt with her napkin.

❧ ❧ ❧

"Mr. Fane wants more," said Jack. "He says you are his steadiest, most reliable writer."

Susan positively beamed with pride, and in all her vocabulary couldn't come up with words to do justice to her happiness. She leaned against the windowsill and tilted her head back and looked up into the cloud-filled early March sky above.

Jack slouched in her armchair, legs stretched out halfway across the room, turning his hat around and around on his lap. He was safe, for Tripod was roaming the streets.

"He thinks I leave the studio and take the bus uptown for a clandestine meeting with the young lady in society. We meet at a restaurant where she wears a black veil, and she hands me the latest scenario in an envelope beneath the table. He says that you should think of making *that* into a picture."

A springlike breeze had unsettled Susan's hair, so she let it down, shook it out, and once more arranged it loosely atop her head. "You sound as if you are at the bottom of a blue funk."

Jack shrugged, and continued to fumble with his hat. It suddenly slipped from his grasp, rolled across the floor, and before he could get to it, neatly upended itself in Tripod's water dish. It was a typical wardrobe accident for Jack—unlikely, and nearly terminal for the article of clothing involved. Jack grimaced, but didn't seem a bit surprised at the fate of his hat. "Your work is going so well—" he said.

"And yours isn't?"

"I can't seem to get my mechanism to work properly," said Jack. "I took it to Mr. Fane today to show him, and the thing fell apart, but not till it mangled the film in the camera. Even Hosmer laughed."

"You don't have the time to work on it," said Susan. "That's all. You're always running about for me, or else you're downstairs fixing some decrepit piece of machinery for someone who doesn't have the money to pay you for it. The reason I've been successful is that I don't have anything to do except write. I have you to do my shopping, you to run the scenarios down to the studio, and you to keep me company and pick up my spirits. That's why *my* work is going well. I know that if you only had time—"

Susan stopped suddenly in mid-speech. She realized with a start of unpleasant astonishment that she was sounding just like the dreadful heroine of *He and She. She* had a splendid career going—going better than her husband's, in fact. But when *he* slid into a depression because of his inferior position, she gave it all up. She wondered now if Jack was feeling jealous. Maybe he was angry with her for doing better than him. She had to find out.

"Jack," she asked without preamble, "does my success upset you?"

He looked up at her, a bewildered look on his face. "No," he replied unhesitatingly. "Have I said something—"

"I'm only asking. You went down to Cosmic today and showed Mr. Fane your machine—and it didn't work."

"That's being very polite," said Jack. "Actually, I felt I was fortunate it didn't explode."

"While at the same time, Mr. Fane bought the scenario you delivered to him."

"After glancing at it for about thirty seconds."

"Some men would feel that..." She trailed off.

"Would feel what?" asked Jack, as if he really didn't understand.

"That it was the man's place to succeed," said Susan.

Jack stared at her. "My invention failed because I hadn't done my work properly. Your scenario sold for the simple reason that you had."

"And that's what you truly believe?"

"Yes." And then, as if this exchange was boring him, Jack said, "Oh, I nearly forgot. Mr. Fane would like you to dash off something for him. He just bought a lot of fancy-dress costumes—English stuff—and he'd like to use it. So if you could come up with something with Queen Elizabeth or Sir Francis Drake, he'd much appreciate it. Also, he'd like a story line in which Ida Conquest gets to be dressed as a boy. All exteriors to be woodland scenes— Central Park, I suppose. By Tuesday."

"He doesn't want much, does he?"

"I told him I thought you could manage. And you can, can't you?"

"Do you think I can?"

"I think you can do anything you set your mind to, Susan."

Susan smiled. So, whatever was going to be between them, Jack Beaumont and Susan Bright, it wasn't going to be a tedious replaying of *He and She*.

❖ ❖ ❖

That evening, Jack brought in Susan's dinner, corned beef and potatoes from a small restaurant around the corner, and shared it with her. She asked him questions about his invention, and learned that one, he was convinced that with enough work, it *would* operate as he envisioned it; two, he only wanted time to perfect it; and three, he hadn't as much time now as he'd like.

"But why are you asking all these questions?"

"Because you know all about my work—you read all of my scenarios—and I know almost nothing about yours."

"My work is sitting at a table in bad light, and filing away at little scraps of metal," said Jack. "I'll admit that it's exactly the kind of thing I like to do and always have. I wouldn't do anything else, even if I had the opportunity. And I *have* had the opportunity. I once made a great deal more money than I do now, but I am much more pleased with this occupation than I would be with any other."

Susan was astonished. Jack Beaumont had never said so much about himself. Certainly what he said—about having once made more money—confirmed her ideas about him. Despite his slightly seedy wardrobe, there was a kind of fumbling grace of manner that someone like Hosmer Collamore, who tried *very* hard, could never achieve. She had suspected that Jack came from much the same background as she. His childhood and adolescence, she was sure, had been spent in surroundings more congenial and comfortable than those they now had. She had never asked Jack about his family, his home, or his education, and she didn't ask now. He had told her a little; perhaps the time would come when she would learn a great deal more.

It was odd. She could imagine themselves in another time and another place, courting under different circumstances. Beneath the stern and watchful eyes of maiden aunts, for instance, in Winter River, Connecticut, or

Elmira, New York. Endlessly chaperoned, learning in a few days all there was to know of one another's histories, antecedents, accomplishments, and prospects. Susan had grown up to think of courtship as a strict ritual, rather like a minuet, in which each move was either right or wrong— and one *knew* which.

But now things were different. There were no rules on West Sixtieth Street, no chaperones—only Mrs. Jadd, who already suspected "the worst." No one told them what they should do, could do, could not do, or ought not be caught doing. Perhaps Susan should allow herself to be seduced by Jack Beaumont, if he made any move in that direction. So far Jack had been the perfect gentleman. He'd kissed her once in the darkened theater, after the showing of Mr. Mixon's second film with Susan's story. A kiss in a darkened theater was not as dangerous or suggestive a thing as a kiss in a sitting room.

When Jack had left, Susan sat down in her chair, and called in Tripod to squeeze in with her. She didn't seem to be able to get anything done without that dog poking his wooden leg into her side until it ached like a laughing stitch. She tried to think of a story that employed Ida Conquest as a boy, Elizabethan costumes, and woodland settings, but all she could think about was Jack Beaumont.

If it had been the kind of courtship she understood— in Elmira or Winter River—Susan would know whether she loved him. But in a city of indecision and wickedness like New York, Susan did not know.

"Do I love him?" she asked Tripod.

The dog growled.

"Yes," said Susan. "I'm quite sure I *do* love him."

With that little question out of the way, Susan began scribbling the scenes for what would turn out to be the Cosmic Film Company's first three-reel production, *Master Manford Hewes*. Ida Conquest would play the title role of a talented young actor who, in reality, was a beautiful young girl, the sweetheart of William Shakespeare.

CHAPTER THIRTEEN

HOSMER COLLAMORE looked distressed as he sat in Susan's sitting room a few days later. For one thing Tripod was standing in his lap and licking his face affectionately, and the dog's pointed wooden leg was embarrassingly situated. It was evident that Hosmer was at a loss to know what to do. He also didn't know why he'd been summoned upstairs by Susan. Perhaps Susan had begun to suspect that he had been comparing her to Ida Conquest, and that Susan had been found wanting, which was true. A young lady with black hair and slim hips and a broken leg, after all, was no match for a splendid creature with extensive curves, bright blond hair, and a style of dress that put one in mind of shop windows at Christmastime. Since he had seen little of her in the past month, perhaps he now sat waiting to be chastised for his neglect.

Susan had no intention of chastising him, but she needed a favor.

"Hosmer," said Susan. "I wonder if you would do something for me?"

"Anything I can," Hosmer murmured unconvincingly.

"Do you know about Mr. Beaumont's new invention?"

Hosmer looked up with astonishment. "What invention?"

"His improvement for moving-picture cameras," explained Susan.

Hosmer laughed derisively, and Susan decided that she really did not care at all for this man. In fact, she began rather to hope that Ida would marry him. A man who laughed at Jack Beaumont's soul-work deserved a woman like Ida Conquest.

"Well," Susan persisted, holding her anger in check, "do you know the invention I'm talking about?"

"I know it exists—at least—in his head," said Hosmer. "I doubt it will ever exist in a camera."

"I've no doubt that Mr. Beaumont will be able to perfect the mechanism, given enough time—and freedom from worry."

"Oh, to be *sure*," said Hosmer, in the unpleasant way that Ida Conquest said those very words. Oh, to be *sure*.

"The problem, I think," Susan said, "is that Jack spends so much of his time in doing small repairs that he—"

"Jack Beaumont does *not* spend his time doing small repairs," interrupted Hosmer. "I took him my alarm clock three weeks ago and asked him to reconnect the bell, and he hasn't found the time to do *that* little piece of tinkering. And I even offered to pay. Now I not only have no alarm to wake me up in the morning, but when I *do* wake up, I don't know what time it is."

Hosmer was the sort, Susan saw for the first time, who harbored small grudges as if they were large ones.

Susan took a deep breath, fighting the urge to say something unpleasant. "I'd like you to help me make it possible for Jack to have the time he needs to complete his camera device—and to repair your alarm clock, of course."

Hosmer looked at her suspiciously, and finally pushed Tripod off on to the floor. He crossed his legs and put his hands into his lap in case the terrier made another leap. "And just how do you propose we help him?"

"By giving him a sum of money that would allow him to work solely on his invention."

"I don't have a nickel to spare," said Hosmer, so quickly that it sounded miserly rather than penurious.

"Well I do," said Susan, "but I don't think Jack would accept the money from me. So I'd like you to offer it to him as a loan, and I will provide the money. I recently came into a small inheritance," she lied unblushingly, to explain the apparently sudden turn in her finances. "Will you help me in this? It is a very innocent stratagem, Hosmer. You can even stipulate that before he does any work on his camera invention, he repair your alarm clock."

Hosmer considered her proposition for a few moments. "If Jack Beaumont wanted money," he said at last, "why doesn't he just ask his rich lady friend?"

"What rich lady friend?" demanded Susan sharply.

"The 'Young Lady in High Society,'" said Hosmer, and Susan instantly colored. Hosmer did a bad job of suppressing an unpleasant little grin; he evidently thought she was jealous. "The one who writes all the stories for Mr. Fane. His lady friend up on Fifth Avenue. Mr. Fane told Miss Conquest that this lady was crazy for Jack, and that she was not only rich in her own right, but that her father owned two gold mines, three railroads, and half a dozen banks in Kansas and Illinois. If Jack Beaumont needs money, he should ask her. That's why he can't get his work done, because he's always traipsing back and forth from Fifth Avenue down to the studio with scenarios."

For some time Susan had wondered how much Hosmer knew about her "alter ego." Gossip at the Cosmic Film Company was obviously rampant. Hosmer's jealousy of Jack's supposed intimacy with the "rich daughter of the industrial magnate" on Fifth Avenue was as pitiful as it was obvious, and probably had been the cause of Hosmer's new antipathy toward Jack. "It's not a simple matter to borrow money of the very rich, Hosmer. And it's certainly not easy for a man to take money from a woman, even though she may have it to spare and he may need it very badly. That shouldn't be so, but it is the way things are. For whatever reason, Jack has *not* borrowed any money from the young lady on Fifth Avenue, and that is why I would like to lend it to him myself."

"How much money?"

"Five hundred dollars."

Hosmer blinked. "Must have been a tidy little inheritance."

"It was. Will you help me?"

❀ ❀ ❀

Susan had already considered the extent of her foolishness in this. Even though, strictly speaking, the five hundred dollars was hers. It would be just her luck to have Mr. Jay Austin appear with the signed receipt demanding a full accounting just as Jack was accepting the money. But she didn't really think that was going to happen.

It was also a foolish thing to give Jack the whole amount, but anything less would have been a half-measure. Even though the gesture was to be anonymous, she wanted the thing done right. What Susan wanted was for Jack Beaumont to feel financially secure. For Jack, Susan suspected, was the sort of man who would never marry till he felt himself in that happy state.

Hosmer arrived again at Susan's apartment about the same time the following evening. He threw himself down in Susan's chair, kept an overly affectionate Tripod at bay with a rolled-up magazine, and said, "I talked to him."

"And?"

"No," said Hosmer, shaking his head. "Most definitely no."

Susan turned away in frustration. Out the window she could see the windows of a dozen other apartments. What sorts of problems did *those* anonymous creatures have? she wondered.

"But he will sell me something for it," said Hosmer.

Susan turned back.

"What? What does Jack have that's worth selling?"

"A half-interest in the patent," said Hosmer. "Which is worth about twenty-two cents, by my estimation."

"Did you say yes?"

"I said I'd think about it."

"Go back and tell him yes."

"*I* don't want half-interest in a piece of worthless machinery."

"Hosmer, stop being such a dunce," said Susan. "He'll assign half the rights to you, and then you'll sign them over to me, and then Jack will get his five hundred dollars."

"Why don't you just stick the money into an envelope and shove it under his door?" asked Hosmer. "Wouldn't that be simpler?"

"No," said Susan. "This way it's not just a loan, and Jack won't feel obligated to you or to anyone." She did not add, *And he may well take a wife on the basis of that five hundred dollars.*

❀ ❀ ❀

The business was concluded the next day. When Jack was out of the building, Susan clomped down the stairs, went around to the bank and closed out her account, rather to the annoyance of the officials of that establishment. In their considered opinion, women were tedious, indecisive creatures, and if they couldn't handle such simple finances as keeping money in the bank, well then it was no wonder they'd never received the vote. And they *wouldn't*, either.

The bank's appraisal of women was not enough to dampen Susan's spirits, however, and she returned home in as good cheer as she had left. She had bought envelopes from a stationery store, and placed nine fifty-dollar bills in one of them. She made up the final fifty dollars with ten of the five-dollar bills she'd earned selling scenarios.

That evening, Hosmer knocked quietly at her door. She opened the door, and Hosmer nodded conspiratorially. He placed a piece of folded paper in her hands, and withdrew with a finger to his lips. As he crept quietly down the stairs, Susan glanced at the paper.

I, Hosmer Collamore, resident of the Fenwick Apartments, West Sixtieth Street, New York City in the state of New York, hereby assign to Susan Bright one-half speculative interest in Mr. J. Beaumont's device for improving the moving-picture camera.

Hosmer T. Collamore
March 9th, 1913

Only a few moments later, Jack raced up the stairs. His tread was quicker and harder than usual, and Susan would have heard him even without Tripod's barking. Jack's excitement seemed to have communicated itself to the dog, for Tripod wouldn't stop throwing himself at the panels, and it was with difficulty that Susan hooked a leash through his collar and dragged him into the bedroom.

Jack was breathless. "No cold meat tonight," he blurted. "No bottled beer. No sliced bread. Tonight I'm taking you to a restaurant. But first we're going to the theater—no nickelodeon, either. And I am paying."

In another moment, and without explanation or a word from Susan, he was gone, leaving her to dress. She went into the bedroom, and looked with despair at her wardrobe. It had not been added to for many months now. At last she chose a long woolen skirt with enormous black and white checks, a simple white silk blouse (her best), and a six-inch wide red lacquered belt. She stood against the hallway door and looked at herself in the reflection of the sitting-room windows—a faulty mirror at best—and then tried to see how she looked when she walked.

Not pitiful any more, just a bit awkward. She wasn't so awkward when she used only one of her crutches, but no woman ever looked *really* fashionable with a broken leg.

Damn Jay Austin.

Then she thought again. No, don't damn him. Because it might just be Mr. Austin's five hundred dollars that would allow the man she loved to have enough self-respect to propose to her.

The play they saw was the second night's performance of Charles Frohman's *The Sunshine Girl*, with Vernon and Irene Castle. Susan was enchanted, not only with the dancing and the music, which were heavenly, but with Irene Castle herself—an almost boyish figure, with her hair cut boyishly short, wearing no jewelry and the slightest of slight pastel frocks. She made every other woman in New York look heavy and overdressed. Once she got her cast off, Susan knew what she was going to do with her wardrobe. By the intermission, she had decided what she was going to do with her hair.

After the theater, Susan expected that Jack would take her to one of the small restaurants in the area, but instead they climbed into a *second* cab and headed south from Forty-second Street. They got out on Sixth Avenue, just below Twenty-eighth Street and Susan was astonished to find that the awning above the door bore the name Mouquin's in flowing script. It was a place she'd only heard about, but she knew it was the oldest and best French restaurant in the city.

Jack had found a suit of clothes that did not look as if they'd been patched to death, but Susan was nervous about his passing muster in such a sophisticated and well heeled a crowd as would most certainly be found in such a place as this. So she was actually glad, as the waiter led them to a table, that those who stared, stared not at Jack's worn suit, but rather at her crutch and the strange bulge the cast made beneath her skirt.

They were certainly not being mistaken for out-of-town Mellons or Huntingtons.

But once they were seated, and the waiter had hidden Susan's crutch behind a potted palm and, incidentally, quite out of her reach, Susan was astonished to find that Jack had no difficulty in deciphering the menu. And to his evident amazement, neither did she—though she had only a few remnants of high school French left at her command.

Susan had consommé printanier, roast teal duck, chicory salad, and crème en mousse. Jack had oysters, pilaf of chicken à la Creole, haricots verts à l'Anglaise, barbe de Capucin salad, and charlotte russe. The bill came to more than eighteen dollars, an amount greater than Susan generally spent on food over the period of three weeks.

It was a wonderful sensation, to be in the midst of such fashion and elegance, and to feel almost as if she and Jack truly belonged there. Even if the money Jack was spending *was* borrowed, even if at the end of the evening they would have to return to cheap lodgings on West Sixtieth Street, even if it might be a very long time before they were able to reproduce the extravagance of these happy hours, when they two, struck with poverty, lived as the rich perpetually lived, Susan was deliriously happy.

Jack had saved his good news for dinner, and Susan pretended to be full of wonder at Hosmer's generosity. She did not think that Jack saw that her surprise was feigned, for she was, after all, an actress. They toasted the camera-man's perspicacity with champagne. They further toasted Hosmer's uncle who had lent Hosmer the money for this obviously wise investment. They toasted Mr. Fane's sound aesthetic and business judgment in purchasing so many scenarios from the Young Lady in High Society. Jack would have ordered another bottle of champagne with full expectation of finding other persons worthy of commemoration, but Susan declined.

They went home in a *third* taxi, and tonight, Jack kissed Susan in her sitting room.

But he did not ask her to marry him.

CHAPTER FOURTEEN

He WAS SHY AND reticent, that was all. He was hiding behind that great brown beard, hiding beneath that old hat the brim of which always shadowed his face, hiding inside the old wardrobe she helped to keep together with a clumsy needle. Maybe there would come a time when it would be enough for a woman simply to write well. Susan wished it were now, for she was little better with a needle than she was with the directions in *Mrs. Farmer's Boston Cooking School Cookbook*.

Within Susan grew the certainty that Jack would not ask her to marry him till he was assured of her affection. That meant she should simply say, "Jack Beaumont, I am hopelessly in love with you."

She couldn't. Something in her upbringing prevented her. She knew that she loved Jack, she was sure that Jack loved her, but she could not force herself to be the first to say those words aloud.

But Susan had a plan.

She stayed up all one night, scribbling and type-writing. She sat bundled, for beside her the window was wide open in the hope that the noise of the machine would be spilled out into the night rather than disturbing Jack below.

At six o'clock the next morning, she knocked excitedly at Jack's door. He came blearily to her summons in a threadbare green silk dressing gown with the initials JAB on the pocket.

"Is something wrong?" he asked. "It's so early."

"Nothing's wrong," said Susan, thrusting a thick, sealed envelope at him. "But I'd like you to take this to Mr. Fane this morning first thing and I wanted to make sure I didn't miss you. It's just another story, but this time I don't want you to read it."

"You've always told me my reading your work brought you good luck."

"You do bring me luck," she replied. "But I don't need luck on this one. This one is special. Now go back to bed, and please knock on my door when you come back from the studio."

❀ ❀ ❀

Hearing Jack's distinctive tread on the stairs a few hours later, Susan threw down the Macy's spring and summer catalogue—in which she'd been dreaming of Bozart rugs, McCray refrigerators and Apollo player pianos—thrust Tripod into the bedroom and firmly shut the door. She moved quickly to the hallway door, pulled it open, and said, "Well, did he buy it?"

"He did."

"Did you read it?"

"I did not, of course. And hello to you too, Miss Bright."

"Hello, Mr. Beaumont," she returned with an apologetic laugh.

"You have no intention of telling me what all this is about, do you?"

"None whatever. Did you see Ida?"

"She sends her love."

"I'm sure," said Susan, with a doubtful glance.

"She pretended not to remember me," Jack admitted.

"Ida doesn't remember anyone below a certain established income," said Susan easing herself into her chair. "I don't know what she sees in Hosmer."

Jack had dropped into a chair himself, and now glanced idly at the bedroom door. It would repeatedly shudder, for with silent hysteria Tripod was throwing himself against it on the other side in an effort to get out and at Jack. "There is a certain type of woman," he said, "who likes to think of herself as an idol. Miss Conquest is one, I believe. Hosmer is a worshipper at her shrine. Isis doesn't kick away her priests."

He reached into his pocket and brought out a small white envelope. He leaned up out of his chair to offer it to Susan, and she leaned over to take it.

She glanced inside.

"There's forty," she said with surprise.

"I bargained for higher wages for the Young Lady. I told Mr. Fane that the price of orchids on Fifth Avenue had just gone up."

"I don't know about the price of orchids," said Susan, "but carbon paper is now fifty cents a box."

❋ ❋ ❋

Susan's cast came off two weeks later.

Jack took Susan back to Bellevue, and waited while the doctor attended her. Distressed by the appearance of her skin, which was white and slack and flaked, she reflected that long skirts would at least hide *that* temporary deformity. She suffered a few moments of panic when she tried to walk again, without the cast, and nearly fell. She was certain that her infirmity was permanent, but the doctor—catching her—assured her that it was only that she was unaccustomed to not carrying the weight of the cast. In time, she'd readjust, and if she exercised properly, there was no reason she would not walk perfectly normally. She would have to use her crutch for a while, but in time she'd be able to do without it.

Susan determined to walk the limp out of her gait, and with the warm weather of spring, this was a pleasurable recuperation. Despite the inconvenience of the four flights of stairs, the crutch, and Tripod's leash, Susan tried to spend an hour every morning in Central Park with Tripod, who threw himself at every other dog he encountered. By experimentation he discovered that his tapered wooden leg could be used as a weapon, and he perfected a sort of sideways offensive lunge that was as effective as it was peculiar-looking.

In the afternoon, she occasionally went out—sometimes with Jack—and did errands. One of her favorite things to do was to look in shop windows to select the things she would buy when she had saved a truly secure amount of money. She'd been in financial straits for so long that she still feared all her good fortune might end, and she would slip down that rough hill again. The hundred dollars of security she now possessed in the bank was going to stay there. No new wardrobe just yet.

And then there was the matter of Jack. Susan couldn't seriously make herself believe that he was inching toward a proposal of marriage. In fact, if anything, he seemed to be inching away.

They still saw each other a lot, that was true, but he now seemed troubled in her presence. He would seem to grow discomfited by some casual remark she'd make in all innocence, particularly if she'd make any mention of money. He took to absenting himself at odd times and with unconvincing explanations. She couldn't determine any real pattern in this new behavior, and she didn't think it was anything as simple as, for instance, *He's afraid of getting married* or *He believes that his camera project will be a failure* or *He's down to his last dollar and thirty-five cents.*

Perhaps someday men and women would sit across from each other, look each other in the eye, and say what was on their minds—whether that something was love, money, religion, politics, or even sexual desire. Susan suspected she wouldn't see it in her lifetime. Jack's trouble was locked up in his breast and brain and the key was hidden under his tongue.

❀ ❀ ❀

On her practical-shopping forays she began stopping in shops that did ladies' hair, asking if anyone knew who Irene Castle was and could cut her hair in the style of the actress's. She had decided that a haircut was a luxury she could afford. Finally, she did find such a person—an old he-gossip with a smooth pink face and lacquered black hair in a tiny blue shop on Broadway between Sixty-first and Sixty-second streets. This gentleman assured her that he had seen Irene Castle many times on the stage, adored her, worshipped her appearance, and said that someday every woman in America would shear off their dreadful long tresses in favor of a style delicious and short. He would be pleased to shape Susan's hair in imitation of Miss Castle's. The crutch was leaned against a wall in one corner of his little shop, Tripod was tied to a chair, and Susan watched in the mirror as her long hair was snipped away.

The feeling of weightlessness she experienced as she emerged from the shop, promising the old he-gossip to return, was exhilarating. She paused on the street and gazed at her reflection in a shop window. It was apparent that she was at the height of *some* sort of fashion—with bobbed hair (which was still rarely seen off the stage), a crutch under one arm, and a three-legged dog on a yellow leather leash.

As she made her way up the stairs to her apartment she noticed that Jack's door was wedged open, a sign that he hoped she'd stop in. This was just one of half a hundred small signals they'd devised, hardly recognizing that they had patterns—lovers' patterns at that.

She pushed open the door, and Tripod very nearly fractured his neck in trying to get at Jack, who was standing at the table by the window.

Before Susan had a chance to say, "Do you like it?"—referring to her hair—she noticed a great change here, too. Gone were the greasy machine parts, the cogs and wheels and valves, that mélange of small industry. There was no longer the smell of oil permeating the atmosphere of the room. That odor had been replaced by the scent of pine soap—evidently even the floors had been scrubbed. The two tables, the divan, and a couple of chairs remained, but otherwise the room was almost bare. In one corner stood three moving-picture cameras, and spread out on one of the tables were the inner workings of a fourth. Indeed, even Jack looked newly scrubbed and neat, in woolen trousers, a clean white shirt, and a tweed jacket that hardly looked patched.

"I'm devoting all my time to my invention," Jack announced succinctly. "And your hair suits you splendidly."

❀ ❀ ❀

Susan's progress now was rapid, and within the apartment building she scorned use of the crutch. Now that Jack's sitting room was presentable, Susan spent as much time there as Jack had previously spent on the floor above. Tripod did not approve of this arrangement, as he was not allowed to visit Mr. Beaumont's apartments.

While Jack tinkered with his cameras, Susan often read magazines. This was not an idle occupation. It was through the dreadful stories published in the ladies' and general circulation magazines that Susan got many of her ideas for scenarios. For instance, a tiny scrap of dialogue in a story called "A Romance of Cash" suggested an entire two-reeler. And once after reading a small paragraph in the *Sun* relating a touching incident in the life of a washerwoman, Susan immediately sat down and penned the scenario for the melodramatic "Cotton Veils," the saga of a washerwoman (played by Ida Conquest) who had once been proposed to by an English duke.

So Susan read and scribbled, and Jack laboriously worked away at his mechanism. But despite all the time that the two spent together, not even a hint of a proposal of marriage fell from Jack Beaumont's lips.

❀ ❀ ❀

One day Jack reported that he had made significant progress on his invention. No thing of beauty, he admitted—an awkward-looking collection of wheels and levers that wouldn't even sit up on a table properly—but when hooked up to a moving-picture camera, it prevented the jiggling and flickering that was so annoying to viewers and gave moving pictures an unrealistic look.

One Sunday afternoon Jack, Susan, Hosmer Collamore, and Tripod made an expedition to the Sheep Meadow in Central Park. With the new device installed in a camera, Hosmer photographed Jack and Susan walking hand in hand; Jack stealing a kiss from Susan; Jack fending off an unleashed Tripod; Jack falling off a bicycle and ripping the knee of his trousers; Susan sitting on the ground with Jack's leg thrown across her lap as she mended the rip; Susan throwing Tripod high into the air and the dog spinning around and around in a way that dogs with four legs are utterly incapable of; and Jack snaring the sleeve of his jacket on a thorny bush while attempting to pick a bouquet of flowers for Susan.

Hosmer planned to have the film developed the following day, but that proved impossible. That Sunday night, Patents Trust hooligans once more broke into the laboratories of the Cosmic Film Company, overturned containers of chemicals, slashed or exposed film, and generally made a wreck of the place. Mr. Fane told Hosmer that he felt certain the ruffians would have set fire to the laboratory if the building had been exclusively the property of the film company. Fortunately, there were unrelated businesses on the first two floors of the building, and the ruffians apparently had *some* honor.

This latest vandalization by the Patents Trust was a real blow for Cosmic. Four two-reel features, three one-reel shorts, and the completed portions of Susan's "Cotton Veils" were completely lost. Everything would have to be reshot, and the studio would have to reoutfit the laboratories completely. This meant that there would be a week and a half in which no new Cosmic Film Company photodrama could appear in the theaters of the country. There would be no income to offset these extraordinary losses.

"I overheard Mr. Fane tell his friend that Cosmic couldn't take another setback like this—the company would go under," Hosmer confided dismally to Jack and Susan.

"I was under the impression that the Patents Trust was on its last legs," said Jack. "I thought they were losing their power—that the independents were just too strong for them."

"That's so," said Hosmer. "That's probably why this last attack was so vicious. They're desperate. It would be just my kind of luck that the last nefarious act of the Patents Trust would be to drive Mr. Fane out of business—and put me out of a job, and send Miss Conquest back to the stage, just when she is about to become a true star in the moving-picture firmament."

Jack and Susan exchanged glances over Hosmer's head. They both realized that if Cosmic went out of business, Susan would lose her source of income as well. Maybe she could sell her work to other studios, but it wouldn't be easy, and only after some time spent scouting around.

How typical of her life to now throw this in her face, Susan thought. All her eggs had gone into the one basket, and that basket was labeled Cosmic Film Company, and now she was going to watch as Thomas Alva Edison and his friends in the Patents Trust hurled that basket against a brick wall. It really was *very* aggravating. The only consolation she could think of was that when poverty came knocking, she'd greet it at the door with a leg that wasn't in a cast and a becoming style of hair.

❀ ❀ ❀

On the first of April, the weather was surprisingly warm. Susan had donned a gray silk sweater over a white shirtwaist, a long gray linen skirt, a pair of gray Burpon hose (without seams), and a pair of brand-new Niagara Maid silk gloves. With unwonted mystery and one of those blushes that turned his face the color of embers in a dying fire, Jack had promised her "something very special" this afternoon.

He appeared at her door wearing light blue flannel trousers and a dark blue jacket. For once his collar was stiff, and he'd shaved his neck right up to his chin. Looking at him dressed like this, she could very nearly imagine him a young broker or businessman—and not merely an impecunious inventor.

"Aren't you going to ask me where I'm taking you?" he asked, once they were on the street.

"I'll let it be a surprise," said Susan. She had decided not to let anything bother her this afternoon. Any troubles she had seemed miles away as she thought what a very handsome couple Jack and she made. She rather hoped that their destination could be reached by walking. She leaned on Jack's arm in such a way that her limp became almost invisible, then turned and waved to Tripod, who was barking ferociously in the fourth-floor window.

"This is an important day for me," said Jack solemnly. "It will determine the course of the rest of my life." With that he hailed a passing taxicab, and Susan climbed in as he opened the door for her.

Jack gave the driver an address through the window, and Susan did not hear it. The sly smile Jack wore when he climbed in beside her told her he had meant to keep it a secret. In the back of the taxicab, Jack took Susan's hand and squeezed it between his, and suddenly it occurred to Susan what the secret was: Today was the day Jack Beaumont was going to ask her to marry him!

Susan decided to feign indifference. She didn't press or ask why this day was to be so important to him. She even pretended not to take too much note of the taxicab's route, as if to indicate to Jack, *I trust you completely.*

The taxi drew up in front of 27 West Twenty-seventh Street—the Cosmic Film studios. Susan felt a slight twinge of disappointment, but still she asked no questions.

As he was paying the driver, the lining of Jack's blue jacket caught on the cab's door handle and a great piece of it ripped out in a long flap as the vehicle took off toward Broadway.

CHAPTER FIFTEEN

Mr. FANE DID NOT remember that he'd once met Susan Bright. He scarcely glanced at her when Jack introduced them again and was brusque with Jack. "I'm quite behind schedule this afternoon, Mr. Beaumont," he said, gesturing sharply to one of the crews who were setting up a scene in one corner of the skylighted studio at the top of the Cosmic building. "I'm afraid you'll have to be patient. Watch anything you like, just stay out of the way, you and Miss—" And with that he hurried off, rubbing the side of his forefinger against his mustache in a gesture that suggested he was too important a character to be burdened with inconsequentialities.

Jack looked chagrined.

The studio was much busier than at the time of Susan's first visit. A fourth "stage" area had been set up, and Junius Fane was now filming four productions at a time, in hope of recovering from the recent set-backs.

To be out of the way of scurrying workmen, Jack gently pulled her back out of the way against a wall. On one side of them were sections of a rustic fence covered with paper morning glories and on the other was a cardboard cannon that stank of shellac.

Susan looked up at Jack and gently squeezed his elbow. "Don't be disappointed." Jack said nothing. "You were going to tell Mr. Fane today that I am the Young Lady in Society, weren't you?" Jack looked down at her in surprise. "You see, I did guess your secret, didn't I?" she said.

Jack beat the brim of his hat against his thigh and looked around the studio. Susan watched a blush creep up his neck, disappear for a few moments beneath his beard, and then mount to his eyes and brow.

"Not exactly," said Jack. "I had an appointment with Fane today to show him the results of my invention."

"Oh."

"The laboratory here is working again, and Hosmer was kind enough to get our experimental reel processed. It's done now, and Mr. Fane has agreed to look at it. I thought you might enjoy seeing yourself on celluloid, Susan. And of course, if Mr. Fane is pleased with the results..."

"I'm certain he will be," said Susan, thinking of something else. After a moment she added, "Then you still don't think it's the right time for Susan Bright to step forward?"

"No...I don't," said Jack slowly.

And then like a light going on, Susan realized that there was something more to this pseudonymous charade than she had realized. There was some piece of deception she suddenly realized, something that was beyond the simple matter of a false name. And Jack was behind it, she knew, and Jack didn't want her to find it out, and Jack also feared that she would.

She stared at him as if she might be able to read the answer to this riddle on the underside of his chin. He was turned away from her, and that was all of his face she could see. But what was he hiding? And how could she find it out? She knew he'd not tell her directly.

Well, if he was going to be devious, so could she be.

"Let's watch some of the filming," Susan suggested. She thought her voice sounded natural. She'd been an actress, after all, though never in a mystery play.

Nearest them was a set built to resemble an apartment kitchen. The camera was set up at one corner of the open end of the three-walled room, and two lines of white tape forming a wide "V" on the floor marked the limits of the camera's angle of view.

"Now stay within those lines, Miss Songar, or else the camera won't catch you," the director warned her.

Miss Songar could not have been more than sixteen, Susan thought, a slip of a thing in a print dress and a light blue apron. On film, Hosmer had explained to Susan once, light blue would show up as pristine white; whereas a truly white apron would have shown up blindingly bright. In order to avoid the harsh shadows that the lights produced, the young actress's face was heavily powdered and her lips emphasized with bright lip paint. Her eyes were lined with green pencil, making them preternaturally large and expressive. Miss Songar's long thick hair was wound up atop her head and she was vigorously applying a broom to the plank floor of the stage. The little crippled girl with the accordion played "Home Sweet Home" off to one side.

"Now sweep, sweep, Miss Songar. Your husband is about to come home, and he's promised to bring you a gift. You've prepared him his favorite supper. God's in His heaven and all's right with the world. Yes, that's it."

The director reached out and slapped the crippled girl on the arm, and she immediately stopped playing the accordion and cried out in a nasal voice, "Waa! Waa!"

"That's your precious baby, Miss Songar!" shouted the director.

Miss Songar thrust out one hand—the one holding the broom—as far as she could and leaned in the other direction, her other hand cupping her ear. An expression of attention overtook her face, and her large eyes widened.

"That's right!" cried the director. "Now concern for your baby. Register, Miss Songar!"

Miss Songar registered concern, then love, and then she hurried off to the side of the stage, crossing the white line.

The director handed her a bundle of blue linen, arranged it in her arms, and then pushed her back across the white line.

"Waa! Waa!" cried the crippled girl, and then began playing a lullaby on the accordion. Miss Songar sang along in an accent that suggested to Susan that she came from Brooklyn.

The director banged a block of wood on the floor three times. "Turn left!" he commanded. Miss Songar turned left. "Love. Expectation. Your husband is at the door. He loves you. You love him. You both love the baby. Here he comes. Hold out your arms, but don't drop the baby."

A young man who had been slouching listlessly near the white line suddenly leapt into the range of the camera with his arms spread wide. He grabbed Miss Songar and embraced her. He looked at the baby, registered love, and looked at his wife again with devotion, pride, and pleasure. The two then looked at the baby and registered hope in the future of the human race. The young man's face was painted white with lips the color of cherries.

"Stop the camera!" cried the director.

Miss Songar's arms drooped, and the blue linen slipped from around the "baby," a block of scrap wood about a foot long with nails pounded into it. The accordion gave a sour, deflating squeal, and the young man took a brush out of his pocket and brushed off some powder that had spilled from Miss Songar's face on to his shoulders.

"How many feet are left?" the director asked the cameraman.

"Two hundred," said the cameraman, peering at a small counter at the side of the camera box.

"That's plenty," said the director, then speaking to the young actor with the white cheeks and the cherry lips, added, "Clear out, Bob, and take that whining block of wood with you. That was very good, Miss Songar, and as long as we have film in the camera, we're going to do another scene. Put on that other apron, please, and disarrange your hair. This will be a little later in the story. Here is the situation: Your husband is in jail, having been framed for the murder of an industrialist. Your younger brother has been abducted by the gang that actually committed the crime. The landlord has sold all of your furniture—Mr. Cox, remove that table—and a deranged neighbor has flung your infant out the window. So when the camera begins to turn, I'd like you to register distress. A fair amount of distress, I think, Miss Songar, would be appropriate."

To get Miss Songar in the mood, the accordion player began a somber rendition of "Just Before the Battle, Mother."

❈ ❈ ❈

"One of yours?" Jack asked quietly as they moved away.

"*Not* one of mine," said Susan, heading for another set. As she looked across the studio she saw Mr. Fane directing Ida Conquest, and was hit by a sudden realization. Wasn't it just her fate—her stupid typical fate—that she and Jack should arrive on a day when Mr. Fane was filming a scene from *that* picture she'd written? She'd better keep Jack away from there, she thought.

But Jack was heading directly toward the set in question—three walls defining a space about the size of Susan's sitting room. Susan followed helplessly, hoping that perhaps they wouldn't do the whole scene, or else that she could get Jack away before the end if they did.

Hosmer turned the camera as Ida Conquest sat alone in the "room," leaning over a desk, scribbling away on a pad of yellow paper. Pushed aside on the table was an old typewriting machine with a sheet of yellow paper stuck awry in the bale.

"Throw down the pen," said Mr. Fane.

Ida threw down the pen.

"Register frustration. Register weariness."

Ida tore at her hair and stretched her neck.

"Get up and go to the window."

Ida went to the window, then leaned out and gazed longingly up at the sky. She wore a blue jacket and a blue skirt, with a wide expanse of shirtwaist, the uniform of the office girl.

"Now you get a terrific idea for a new story," said Mr. Fane. "Register excitement."

Ida pulled her head back inside, then her mouth dropped open and her eyes brightened.

Jack sneaked a questioning look at Susan.

"Go back to the table, now," Mr. Fane said. "You want to get your brilliant idea down on paper. That's right. Now pull over the typewriting machine, and go to it."

"Don't know how," hissed Ida without moving her lips. Hosmer was still turning the camera and Ida couldn't appear to be speaking when no one else was in the room.

"Press down the keys," said Mr. Fane, with no trace of sarcasm in his voice, "one after the other."

Ida tried it, and looked no less efficient than most office girls confronted with a typewriting machine for the first time.

"Faster," said Mr. Fane.

Ida tried faster, but then the keys jammed, and Ida went into a charming flurry to get them unstuck.

"Good business," said Mr. Fane as Ida wiped her fingers delicately on a scrap of paper.

"*Knock, knock, knock,*" cried the director. Then turning to a young boy nearby, he said, "Dog."

The boy opened a basket that he held in his arms. A small spaniel instantly leapt out of it, ran on to the stage, and threw himself against the door of Ida's sitting room.

Jack turned and looked at Susan hard. "I guess they couldn't find a dog with three legs."

Yes, Susan had to admit, it was quite obvious that this was her story.

"Hide your work, quick. He's at the door," Mr. Fane hissed in a stage whisper.

Ida stood up, looked about the room, clapped her hands at the dog, and then dragged a folding screen across the floor and set it up in front of the table. She grabbed the dog, gripped it beneath her arm, glanced at herself in the mirror, straightened her hair—

"Knock, knock, knock."

—and hurried to the door.

She opened it. Outside the door stood a tall man in old trousers and jacket.

"I'm sorry to bother you, Ida," the man said aloud.

"Call her Susan, dammit," said the director. "Audiences read lips. In the play her name is Susan, not Ida."

"Could you sew this on for me?" the actor finished without a pause. The mistake wasn't so great that the camera had to be stopped. Then he held up his arm and showed that the flap of his jacket pocket had been half torn off in some mishap.

Jack cleared his throat and glanced at Susan again. He tugged at the ripped lining of his own jacket. "Is his name Jack?" he asked in a low voice.

"Ah—" Susan began.

"Jack," said Ida/Susan with a gaiety that seemed entirely inappropriate, "you are very clumsy." She took hold of the flap and tugged it playfully. The dog made a lunge at the actor Jack, but Ida pulled the dog back and wagged a warning finger at him, at the same time frowning and shaking her head left and right. Actor Jack threw himself into an easy chair and draped the edge of his coat over the arm.

"Now you be good," said Ida/Susan to the dog, pushing him beyond the white line, where he was grabbed up again by the young boy and thrust back into the basket.

Susan now could see that they were going to do the whole scene, so she tried to pull Jack away.

"No," he said, "let's watch."

What had seemed such a wonderful idea when she'd thought of it was turning into just about the most dreadful idea ever born in Susan's fevered brain. Her plan had been simple. Write a scenario about Jack and Susan—Jack a handsome, impoverished inventor and Susan a would-be writer turning out serials for monthly magazines. Jack lived in a room directly below Susan's. Susan had a dog that disliked Jack. There was a little contretemps when Jack grew jealous of another man who lived in the same building. Just as the contretemps was about to be resolved, Susan discovered an actress in Jack's sitting room, and now *she* was jealous. Everything turned out well in the end. In fact—

Ida/Susan knelt girlishly at the side of the easy chair. With exaggerated flowing arm movements, she pantomimed sewing the pocket flap back on to the jacket.

"I'm the one should be on my knees," said actor Jack.

"Whatever do you mean?"

"I mean to propose to you, Susan."

Ida/Susan registered surprise.

Actor Jack registered sheepish modesty.

Ida/Susan registered love.

Actor Jack registered increasing hope.

"Let us change places," he said.

Ida/Susan registered maidenly modesty.

"Get up from the chair," said the director. "Now, Ida, you sit down in the chair. Kneel, Jack. Now look in your left pocket. No, it's not there. So look in your right pocket. That's it—take out the ring. Show the ring."

"It's so big," squealed Ida/Susan.

"I sold my invention today. I am rich. Will you marry me, Susan?"

"Oh yes, Jack. Yes." Ida/Susan fairly gushed.

"Let him put the ring on your finger, Ida. Embrace, you two. Dog!"

The boy with the basket let the spaniel out again, and it rushed on to the set and began tearing at the tail of actor Jack's coat.

But so great was the happiness of actor Jack and Ida/Susan that the exertions of the dog went entirely unnoticed.

"Stop the camera!" cried the director.

Hosmer ground the camera to a halt.

Ida/Susan and actor Jack got to their feet.

Actor Jack kicked the spaniel away.

It was a pity, thought Susan, that moving-picture studios did not have trapdoors the way stage theaters did. She would have been very pleased at that moment to simply drop out of sight. She dared not look at Jack. How could she have come up with a plan so stupid? Jack, she had thought, had merely been unsure of her feelings toward him. He wouldn't ask her to marry him simply because he didn't understand the nature of her feelings for him. Susan thought she had figured out a way to tell him she loved him without appearing to throw herself at him. Jack was to have seen the photoplay in the theater and been so convinced of Susan's love for him that he'd return to the Fenwick and immediately drop to his knee before her chair, and beg her to marry him.

A witless, charmless idea altogether. It would have failed in any case. What must he be thinking standing there beside her, beneath these bright lights, with workmen hammering in the background, and an accordion playing over across the room, and a dog barking crazily.

She looked up at him.

He was not blushing. In fact, all the blood seemed to have drained from his face.

"Does it have a title?" he asked, looking straight forward.

"I called it *Susan's Serial.*"

CHAPTER SIXTEEN

JACK AND SUSAN *walking hand in hand in Central Park.*
Jack stealing a kiss from Susan.
Jack fending off an unleashed Tripod.
Jack falling off a borrowed bicycle and ripping the knee of
his trousers.

These were the images moving across a stretched
sheet tacked to the wall of a windowless room in the laboratory of the Cosmic Film Company.

Jack sat next to Mr. Fane, and Susan sat farther back
near Hosmer Collamore at the projector. The day's filming
had ended only a quarter-hour before.

It was the first time Susan had seen herself on celluloid, and the experience was unsettling. She looked
thinner than she had imagined herself to be, and her skin
looked pale and her hair intensely black. She cringed to
see the hitch in her right leg, though she knew it had
improved since that day in the park. But most of all,

she was embarrassed to see herself and Jack together, cavorting in playful innocence—an innocence that had now been spoiled by the revelation in that dreadful scenario, *Susan's Serial*, that she loved him. Women simply did not declare their love. Women were like puppies in a shop window. They could frolic in their cages; they could gaze moonily at passersby; they could be adorable and irresistible. But they weren't allowed to choose with whom they'd go home. Like puppies in a shop window, women were chosen.

An altogether disgusting state of affairs. She was also angry that Jack was displeased with her gesture—he'd not even spoken to her. Angry with herself that she had made it. Angry with life, and fate, and damned Hosmer Collamore now running a moving picture that mocked her misery. She and Jack and Tripod would never be as happy as on that innocent Sunday in Central Park.

Mr. Fane rose from his chair and went up close to the sheet on the wall. Susan's laughing face was displayed across the back of his jacket, like some maniacal harpy. He stood aside and peered at the images.

He moved to the back of the room, near Susan, and conferred in a low voice with Hosmer. He peered at the projector and sat down near Susan and watched the rest of the reel.

"Now run it again," he said. The film ran free of the spool and flapped against the metal projector as Hosmer turned it off. "Use a different machine."

In the few minutes it took Hosmer to set up the new machine, Mr. Fane occupied himself with a little notebook and a stub of a pencil. Jack, a few feet in front of Susan, did not turn around. Susan's leg began to itch, and it felt as if she still had the cast on it.

The lights were turned out again, and Hosmer began the film once more. Susan could scarcely bear to watch. She turned halfway in her chair and only glanced at the images out of the corner of her eye.

The door at the back of the room opened softly, and an ample figure rustled in. It was Ida Conquest. In the dim light Susan could see she had not yet removed her powder, and her face had a ghostly glow.

"That's enough," said Mr. Fane, standing up as the reel once again came to an end. Hosmer turned on the overhead light in the room.

Jack turned around at last and looked at Junius Fane.

"Mr. Beaumont," the owner of the company said, "I must say I was dubious about your idea. I didn't expect it to work, and I wasn't even certain that I wanted it to. But you've convinced me. I could see no jiggle. Not when I stood at the back of the room, not when I looked up close. It makes our present pictures look as if they'd been shot out of the back of a moving taxicab. Congratulations."

Jack grinned. Susan saw beads of sweat forming on his forehead at the hairline.

"Hosmer," Mr. Fane asked, "you assure me that you shot these scenes in the normal way?"

"Yes, sir, just as I shoot them here—just as I shoot them for you."

Fane nodded thoughtfully, then sat down and took out a fountain pen and a sheaf of bank checks. "Mr. Beaumont, I'm going to write you a check for five hundred dollars. I'd like you to install your device in every camera owned by the Cosmic Film Company." Jack beamed. "I would also advise you, sir, to patent this device as quickly as possible. If you can retain control of this thing, you will be a very rich man."

Hosmer winked his congratulations, and Ida threw an actress's warm smile. Mr. Fane said no more, but his five-hundred dollar check had spoken eloquently enough.

Having turned down an invitation to dine with Junius Fane and Ida, Susan and Jack were left alone in the small, windowless room. Jack turned backward on his narrow straight-backed chair. A single Edison bulb burned in a lonely socket in the ceiling.

"I'm very happy for you," said Susan in a strained voice. She was, too.

Jack nodded. "*Susan's Serial*—is that what you called it?"

She wanted to turn away from his gaze, but she couldn't.

"You didn't even change the names," he said flatly.

She didn't reply.

"Hosmer has figured out that you're the Young Lady in High Society, you know," said Jack. "I saw it in his eyes. I don't think Mr. Fane knows—yet."

"What about Ida?" Susan asked.

"If she hasn't pieced it together, I'm sure Hosmer will tell her."

"No more secrets," said Susan, with the sour taste of irony in her mouth.

"I have to confess something to you," said Jack.

"Confess?"

"Yes. Remember when you gave me that scenario to bring to Mr. Fane you asked me not to read it?"

"Yes," Susan said a bit uncertainly.

"Well, I read it anyway."

"*What?* You mean...you mean to say you knew...that you've known...that you've been..."

He nodded. "Not only that," he continued, his face blank, his voice a monotone, "I knew that they were shooting the last scene today—the one where Jack asks Susan to marry him."

She threw her purse at him.

He ducked to dodge it, lost his balance, and tumbled off the chair to the floor, breaking a leg of the chair in the process.

"You knew!" Susan screamed, paying no attention to his fall.

"I knew," he admitted, an amused glitter in his eyes.

"You...you deceived me!" Then she felt silly for having said that. It was just the sort of thing young women in magazine serials always said midway through the installment. "But why didn't you—"

"I was just following the scenario," said Jack. "I had to wait till my invention was sold before I could ask you to marry me."

Susan stood rooted to the spot with anger and frustration. Jack was still struggling, not very successfully, to get up from the floor.

"I am so *angry*," said Susan.

"Why? You were the one who wrote the scenario. I was only playing my part." He hadn't gotten all the way up from the floor; he remained on one knee. "I have a splinter," he said, picking at the cloth of his trousers. "So do you know yours?"

"My what?"

"Your part," Jack said. "Let me refresh your memory. I'm on my knee—just as I am now. I ask you to marry me. For a moment you register confusion. Then you register love for me. And then the title card is cut in, and it reads—"

"The title card reads: *Oh yes, Jack, gladly.*"

❁ ❁ ❁

Sitting in the small windowless room with the single harsh Edison bulb in the ceiling they held hands and talked on and on. Jack described the moment when he first dared hope that she cared more for him than she did for Hosmer Collamore. Susan expressed disbelief that Jack would ever have regarded the cameraman as a rival. Misunderstandings were untangled. Small arguments were laid to rest. Happy insights were revived and shared.

"It's late," Jack said at last, as if he were afraid that their happiness would not persist beyond the confines of this narrow chamber.

Susan glanced down at the watch that was pinned upside down to her shirtfront. "Half-past ten."

"They've probably forgotten about us," said Jack. "We didn't come in here till nearly seven, and by then most everyone had already gone."

"Could we be locked in?"

"No," said Jack, "there must be someone about. Hosmer said there's now a watchman."

Jack went to the door of the room and opened it. The laboratory floor of the Cosmic Film Company was completely dark. The windows had been blacked over, and not even light from the street entered the building. Weak yellow light spilled out of the projection room behind Jack and Susan, but this served to illumine not much more than a strip of black wall ahead of them. Worktables and cabinets were nothing more than bulky black outlines arrayed across the wide expanse.

"I feel foolish," said Susan.

"A simple mistake," said Jack. "I don't imagine the night watchman is going to mistake us for Trust hoodlums—if we can find him."

"The elevator's over there somewhere," Susan said, pointing off toward her right. "Should I switch off this light? It's not doing us much good anyway."

Jack nodded, but it was so dark Susan couldn't see the nod, so he said, "Yes, switch it off."

She switched it off and pulled shut the door of the projection room. Then, hand in hand, they groped their way carefully in the direction of the elevator. Jack succeeded in kicking over a wastebasket, knocking a stack of files off a desk, and jamming his thigh against a corner of a table. Susan progressed without mishap until they got nearly to the elevator.

Then Susan tripped over something and pitched headlong to the floor.

"Are you all right?" Jack cried out.

"Yes," said Susan softly, "something broke my fall."

"What?" asked Jack, helping her to her feet.

"A body."

❀ ❀ ❀

"He's breathing," said Jack, having found the man's face and applied his ear close against it.

"Do you think it's the watchman?"

"It must be," said Jack in a low whisper, shaking the man's shoulders. "But he's got a bad lump on the back of his head which means that maybe we're not alone here."

Susan swallowed audibly, then whispered, "Maybe we should try to call the police. I'll see if I can find a phone."

Jack shook the unconscious form again. The man groaned, but he didn't come to.

Susan found a desk, but there was no telephone on it; she fumbled her way over to another. Just then there came a shrieking, grinding, metallic noise. "What is that?" said Susan, no longer whispering.

"The elevator," said Jack. "It's going down."

"What does that mean?"

"I don't know," said Jack. "Maybe someone's leaving the building—or maybe someone's on the ground floor and is on the way up."

Susan wiped her now sweaty hands across the second desk and knocked a telephone to the floor. The operator's tinny voice was distant: "Central. Central." Susan got down on her hands and knees and crawled around the desk till she found the receiver.

"Please connect me with the police," Susan said urgently.

"Thank you," said the operator with odd formality, and on the other end, a telephone rang.

"Headquarters," immediately said a voice on the other end.

Susan sighed with relief. "Yes, I'm at Twenty-seven West Twenty-seventh Street, at the Cosmic Film Company and the watchman here has just been knocked unconscious. Could you please send somebody right away? We—"

"Twenty-seven what?" the policeman asked.

"Twenty-seven West Twenty-seventh Street. We—"

"Who is we?"

"My name is Susan Bright, and—"

"Susan!" called Jack.

"Just a moment," said Susan, putting her hand over the mouthpiece. "What is it?" she called out.

"Do you smell something?"

Susan breathed in deeply and then uncovered the mouthpiece.

"Twenty-seven West Twenty-seventh Street?" the policeman was asking.

"Yes," said Susan, "and send the fire brigade as well."

CHAPTER SEVENTEEN

IT WAS IMPOSSIBLE to tell where the smoke was coming from, but from the growing acridness in the air they presumed that the fire was near.

This became more than a presumption when they saw a dull glow at the far end of the room toward the front of the building.

Then, to their horror, there was an explosion. Evidently a cache of chemicals used in processing film had been ignited.

Flames roared behind the door for a moment and then began pouring out into the room.

Jack and Susan's faces were red and garish in the light of the fire. At least now they could see. Jack rushed over to the elevator and pulled the lever that summoned up the lift. But there was no responding noise of grinding machinery.

He pulled the lever again as Susan tried to rouse the unconscious watchman.

"They must have cut out the elevator machinery as well," said Jack.

"Then we'll have to use the stairs," said Susan.

"A good idea," Jack said, "but it would be a better one if the stairs weren't on the other side of the fire. I've used them several times when I've been here and not wanted to wait for the elevator."

"Maybe we can slide down the elevator cables," said Susan.

"Another good idea," said Jack. "Do you want to throw the watchman over your shoulder, or shall I? Or should we just leave him here to burn?"

The night watchman was a huge man.

"All right," said Susan. Another, larger explosion came, and it sounded like it blew out some windows in the front, which gave the fire new oxygen. "I've come up with two bad ideas, you come up with one good one."

The whole far end of the room was bright and hot now, and giving off a dull roar. The open entrance to the stairs that led down to safety was now brightly and frustratingly illuminated.

Near them was a long narrow table, that held half a dozen film-splicing machines, evenly spaced down its length. Jack ran down the length of the table, hurling the machines to the floor. When it was clear he went over to the watchman, reached under the unconscious man's arms, and dragged him across the floor to the table.

"All right, Susan. Take his feet."

The two tried to lift the dead weight from the floor, but sank down under the watchman's bulk.

They tried again, and this time they succeeded. With loud groans they got him over the lip of the table and onto the scarred surface.

"Now what?" said Susan. "Is he more comfortable up here?" Then she added, in an apologetic tone, "I'm sorry. I'm always sharp when I find myself in mortal physical danger."

"I understand," said Jack gallantly. "Now we push the table." And he began to do just that.

"Where?"

"Into the fire." He pointed toward the open stairway door beyond the wall of orange flame and roiling black smoke.

She looked at him, opened her mouth to say something, didn't say it, closed her mouth, and put her shoulder into it.

They pushed the table straight across the floor, and into the flames.

The long narrow table reached across the barrier of burning chemicals, the forward legs drawing along little flaming channels with them. The fire was so hot that Jack and Susan could already smell the charring wood on the underside of the table.

The watchman lay on the center of the table, flames leaping up on either side.

"Up you go," said Jack, and he lifted Susan up on to the table before she had a chance even to think.

Susan began to limp down the table, but found her way blocked by the watchman, whose girth did not allow her a safe foothold on either side.

"Go on!" shouted Jack above the roar of the flames.

As lightly as she could, Susan pressed her good foot on to the chest of the watchman and sprang forward.

She stumbled sideways, her other leg swinging dangerously close to the flames. She managed to make her way to the end and climbed down on to the floor on the other side.

"I'm all right, Jack!" she shouted.

Jack now stood with his feet planted on either side of the watchman's head, preparing to leap to safety.

"Oh, no," said Susan, for at that moment, the watchman's eyes popped open—and immediately filled with fear and confusion. His hands flew out at his sides into the flames, shot back up again.

At that moment, Jack leaped.

Instinctively, and perhaps thinking that Jack was the person who had attacked him, the watchman grabbed Jack as he hurtled over. Jack's leap was broken, and he fell sideways, tumbling into the flames.

❀ ❀ ❀

All the nurses wore blue-and-white skirts, and Susan remembered two or three of them from her own stay in Bellevue.

"How is your leg?" one of them asked quietly. It was past midnight, and the hospital was as quiet as it ever got. Most of the patients were asleep.

"Mended," said Susan. "I'm here to visit a friend."

"Which one?"

"Mr. Beaumont."

"Oh, yes," said the nurse, who had a figure like Ida Conquest's. "The concussion."

"Is he very bad?"

"Burns on his arms and neck. He comes around now and then. He'll be all right. Speak to the doctor, though. I'm not supposed to know anything." She wandered off down the dark corridor.

The doctor was in the room with Jack, and Susan had been told she could go in just as soon as he was finished.

It was Susan who had dragged Jack out of the flames, flipped him over, pulled him out of his burning jacket, and shoved him down the stairs out of immediate danger. Susan also had gone back into the burning room and led out the bewildered watchman by the hand. She'd gotten them down as far as the second-floor landing before the police and fire brigade showed up and took over for her. Jack had been taken away on a stretcher.

That had been only a few hours ago.

Susan had talked to the police at headquarters on Grand Street, drunk three cups of coffee, devoured a ham sandwich, and taxied up to Bellevue. Standing there now in the hospital corridor, she was suddenly aware that all her clothing stank of oily smoke.

"Miss—" The hand touching her shoulder startled her. She turned to find herself staring into the strained face of Junius Fane.

"Miss Bright," said Susan.

"I'm told I've you to thank that more damage wasn't done and the upper floors were preserved," Mr. Fane said. "Though I'm not certain what you and Mr. Beaumont were doing there at that hour."

"Jack and I lost sight of the time, Mr. Fane." She thought of a convenient lie, and then said: "Jack had come up with an idea for an improvement on the projectors as well, and was—"

"I don't really care *why* you were there, what matters is that you called the fire brigade. And you saved the watchman's life, too, I hear. Is Mr. Beaumont badly injured?"

"Well," said Susan, "he was unconscious, and there are some burns, but—"

"I came to thank him."

"I think we should be able to go inside in a few minutes," said Susan.

There was a moment of silence between them, then Mr. Fane said, "This evening, after we left the projection room, Colley told me something very interesting."

Susan looked up sharply at the owner of the film company.

Junius Fane smiled. "He told me that he suspected that *you* were our fabled Young Lady in High Society." Susan didn't answer. "Does that silence signify yes? Or does it mean no?"

"It signifies yes," admitted Susan with a small smile.

Junius Fane glanced at her, appeared to consider the business for a moment, then laughed, and grasped Susan's hand, shaking it heartily. "The Patents Trust has done a lot to try and put me out of business, but you have done as much—and more—to keep me in business."

"Mr. Fane," Susan protested, "I'm glad my work has been a help to you and your company, but I have to tell you that I did it for the money."

Junius Fane blinked. "Money?"

"Yes. I had broken my leg, Mr. Fane, and had no income. The money you paid me for those scenarios kept me from—well, I suppose I ought to be candid, it kept me from starving."

"Miss Bright, the reason I maintained belief in the existence of the Young Lady in High Society was that she never asked recompense for her work. The Young Lady in High Society had only one desire—and that was to see her stories on film."

"But I received money for those stories!"

"Perhaps you did, but it didn't come from me."

Susan fell back against the wall, her head swimming.

Just then the doctor came out of Jack's room. "He's awake, but I've given him an injection, and in a few minutes he'll be asleep."

The doctor stood aside, holding the door for Susan.

Junius Fane entered the room behind her. It was a long room, with a row of half a dozen beds along each wall separated by white curtains. Susan and Junius Fane walked quietly, for the hour was late and most of the patients were sleeping. Susan got to the end of the room, but still had not found Jack. She looked around, baffled anew.

"Susan." It was Jack, calling weakly. She turned in the direction of his voice. Even when she saw the man who said her name again, a tall man with his head pressed against the headboard and his feet stuck through the bars at the bottom, she didn't recognize him. Jack's beard had been shaved off, and white bandages had been wrapped securely about the upper portion of his chest.

He looked completely changed—and yet strangely familiar. Even his voice sounded different—but disquietingly reminiscent of one she knew. It was as if Jack had been transformed into a man that was part himself and part someone else. She became more convinced that she was going insane.

Junius Fane shook his hand. "Mr. Beaumont, I thank you. Just now I told Miss Bright that I—"

Mr. Fane's speech faded from Susan's consciousness. For as she stared down at Jack Beaumont, she realized with blinding suddenness and utter clarity that he wasn't Jack Beaumont at all.

He was Jay Austin.

Jay Austin who had broken her leg.

Jay Austin who had written her whimpering letters from Chicago.

Jay Austin who had slipped the five hundred dollars into her cape.

Jay Austin who had offered her scenarios to Junius Fane *gratis*.

Jay Austin who had each time brought back an envelope with five-dollar bills in it.

Suddenly she remembered Jack's threadbare dressing gown with the monogram JAB. John A. Beaumont. John Austin Beaumont. J. Austin Beaumont. Jay Austin.

John Austin Beaumont had humiliated her, making her livelihood spurious and her independence a sham. Her love had been given to a man who didn't exist.

"—and also, I should say," said Mr. Fane, half-turning with a smile for Susan, "that your and Miss Bright's little deception has been revealed—"

He broke off in astonishment, for at that moment, Susan lunged forward, grabbed the end of the white iron hospital bed and shook it as hard as she could.

"Jack Beaumont," she shouted at the top of her voice, "may there be a hell! And may you be sent there! And may you roast in it for all eternity!"

She gave one final shove that smashed the bed up against the wall, knocking over the bedside stand and smashing a pitcher of water onto the floor. A nurse came running down the corridor. Susan crashed into her on the way out. Blinded with tears, Susan flailed through the doors into the corridor.

The ward awakened with puzzled incoherencies, but above the noise and confusion she heard that man—whoever the devil he really was—hoarsely calling her name.

"Susan! Susan!"

Part II

JACK

CHAPTER EIGHTEEN

JOHN AUSTIN BEAUMONT lay restless in his bed at Bellevue Hospital. The nurse had offered him a sedative, but he'd refused it. He'd preferred to fret about Susan Bright, and his deception of the past months.

He didn't regret it, of course, because it had come round to the point he had wanted to reach. That point being that he had asked her to marry him, and she had replied, as on a card in a moving picture, *Oh, yes, Jack, gladly*.

"Is there some way that I can send a message?" Jack asked the nurse who came around the next morning, bringing a tray of wretched gruel.

"There's a boy who'll go anywhere for a quarter and carfare," said the nurse. "The son of one of the ambulance drivers."

Jack wasn't surprised to hear it. Ragged platoons of boys had established themselves in every corner of the city to make the course of true love run smooth. The ones on the west side of town generally charged no more than a dime. Bellevue, Jack observed silently, was on the east side, and the price was higher. Jack, laboriously scrawling with his uninjured left hand, penned a note to Susan. He had intended to spell out to her a long explanation of precisely why he had done what he had done, but his penmanship wasn't up to that. He satisfied himself with:

> PLEASE COME
> JACK

She didn't.

He waited all day, through a change of bandages, the examination of two doctors, a humiliating incident with a bedpan, and a noontime meal so wretched he was tempted to ask for his breakfast gruel again. At three o'clock, tea was brought around and Jack managed to spill an entire pot of it across his good left hand, leaving red, stinging burns. The nurse eyed him with an expression that clearly said, *I know your type.*

He once again summoned the ambulance driver's son, gave him a dollar, and handed him another note. This was addressed to Hosmer Collamore, in care of the Cosmic Film Company, 27 West Twenty-seventh Street. It ready simply:

> PLEASE COME
> BELLEVUE HOSP.
> JACK BEAUMONT

The worst thing about a hospital, Jack decided bitterly, was not the pain of the accident or the disease that put you there, not the casual humiliation and embarrassment and general sense of worthlessness that pervaded your paltry soul, but the frustration attendant on any attempt to guide your destiny from the confines of a narrow iron bed and thin white sheets.

Here he lay, bandaged and burning, listening to the damn birds in the damn tree outside the damn window, while Susan Bright sat at home, thinking the worst of him and saying to that damn dog, *You were right about him all along, Tripod.*

Jack was pushing away the supper tray, which made him think that he should have eaten more of his luncheon, just as Hosmer Collamore entered the ward, peering down the line of beds in search of him. Jack waved his better hand.

"You're a hero," said Hosmer, peering into Jack's face to make certain the beardless face was indeed Jack. Satisfied he had the right patient, Hosmer offered his hand to be squeezed by Jack's less burned one.

"I'm an unhappy hero," said Jack. "Have you seen Susan today?"

"No, but Mr. Fane made an announcement about her being the Young Lady in High Society, and he said that the entire company owed their jobs and livelihoods to her and to you for saving the building from burning to the ground last night. And then there's the night watchman. He owes you his life, and he said he's coming to visit you and bringing his wife and five children. They're all going to thank you in person."

"I'd much prefer a sandwich and a cup of coffee. It's a wonder anybody ever gets well in this place. I have to see Susan."

"I assumed she'd be here."

"We had a slight misunderstanding."

"Lovers' quarrel?" Hosmer said with a leer.

"Something like that," returned Jack uncomfortably.

"Want me to give her a message?"

"Yes. Please ask her to come here, no matter what she thinks of me, no matter what she thinks I may have done, and no matter who she thinks I am."

"Interesting quarrel," said Hosmer, suppressing his curiosity.

"Not really a quarrel," said Jack, "only a misunderstanding. A small misunderstanding at that." He opened his mouth to say something more, but then desisted.

Hosmer waited for that something else, and when it didn't come, he asked, "What if she won't come? What if she says no? What if she says, 'I never want to speak to Jack Beaumont again?' I'm not saying she will, mind you, but what if she does?"

Jack blushed up to the roots of his hair. He, of course, had a fear that that was exactly what Susan would say. Then Hosmer would come back with the message of rejection, and Jack would have to tell him the whole story, and plead with him to become an emissary of reconciliation. A delay of at least twenty-four hours in which Susan Bright would brood over the wrongs and humiliations done her.

"Would you consent to be my intermediary?" Jack asked suddenly.

Hosmer cocked his head and didn't reply for a moment. Then he said, a little mysteriously, "I could be afraid of Suss when her mad is up."

"'Her mad is up' only against me, Hosmer. I'm going to explain the whole story to you, so that you can explain it to her. Because the way she probably feels about me right now, I don't think I could get her to sit still for an explanation, even if you could persuade her to come here."

"Here's the ears," said Hosmer, placing his hands on either side of his head. "They're bending and attending."

"To begin with, my name really *is* Jack Beaumont."

"Never doubted it. Should I have?"

"When I first met Susan, I was going by the name Jay Austin."

"I see," said Hosmer, with a knowing wink.

"Hosmer, please let me go on, or we'll never finish with this. My full name is John Austin Beaumont, and I used the pseudonym because"—Jack paused a moment while a truly terrifying blush suffused his face and caused it to burn like his hands burned. He wiped beaded perspiration away from his forehead with a corner of sheet—"because I was not in a position to have it known that I was pursuing a young woman in the theater."

A puzzled expression crept over Hosmer's features, but he said nothing. The story suddenly seemed more interesting than he had previously thought.

"I was at that time—we're speaking of early January of this year—in a position of some prominence downtown. The fact is, I was managing director of a fairly large financial investment company on Wall Street. You've probably never heard of it, but I was ultimately responsible for the investment of tens of millions of dollars a year."

"Are you sure a burning beam didn't fall on your coco last night?" Hosmer wondered.

"I'm telling you the truth," said Jack seriously. "The company is owned by my uncle, and it has been in my family since the early part of the last century. It will be mine someday—if I continue to please my uncle."

"You're just a tinkerer! A damned tinkerer fit to fix my alarm clock, that's what you are!" the cameraman exclaimed, as if offended by the thought that Jack Beaumont might turn out to be something more.

"Tinkering has always been my hobby, that's all. Please let me finish, Hosmer. My uncle was, and is, an old-fashioned sort, and he feels that actresses are—well, you know what people think of actresses, and always have thought of actresses—so when I sent a letter backstage to Susan, I did not use my own name. Just a precaution—the sort of precaution I always take in my work. But that very night, there was an accident—"

"The anarchist?"

"That's right. And I was the unfortunate and unwitting cause of Susan's breaking her leg. She was laid up here in this very hospital, as you know. She wouldn't see me, she wouldn't accept my assistance, she wouldn't answer my letters or notes."

Hosmer shifted in his chair. He was looking at Jack with new eyes. It wasn't that he exactly believed Jack's story about having authority over tens of millions of dollars, but he was considering the possibility that Jack might be more than an impoverished tinkerer living third floor front in a second-rate apartment building on West Sixtieth Street. At any rate, Hosmer was paying close attention.

"But there was a solution to my problem. Susan wasn't refusing to see everyone, she was just refusing to see Jay Austin. She did not even know that Jack Beaumont existed. I grew a beard. I went through my wardrobe and pulled out all my oldest clothes. I rented the room directly below hers, and across the hall from you."

"Fortunate it came available just at that time," said Hosmer skeptically. "Mr. Delamore and his wife—"

"—had no intention of moving out," Jack interrupted, "until I persuaded them that they could afford a much more substantial rent in a much nicer section of the city." Hosmer's eyes widened. "So I moved in. Even though we'd met only once, and though she'd seen me only at night, and at the time I was coming down with the grippe so my voice was hoarse and distorted, I was still afraid Susan would recognize me. So I changed the way I treated her. I was gruff at first, as if I cared nothing for her company, and only gradually changed. I don't think she ever suspected that I was anything but an impoverished inventor. Not until last night, that is, when she saw me without my beard, and heard my croaking voice."

Hosmer thought for a few moments. "Were you going to tell her...?"

"Very soon. And before we were married. Lucky girl—she was going to discover that her impoverished husband was in reality a man who had more than his share of wealth."

"This is the story you want me to take to Suss?"

"She hates it when people call her that, Hosmer."

"She won't believe a word of it. Not sure I do, either."

"Every word is true. No more deceptions."

"I suppose you mean for Suss and me to believe that you have been running a financial empire from that greasy little flat across from mine?"

"Not at all. For the past two months I've been exactly what I appeared to be: an inventor living on the money he makes repairing broken alarm clocks and typewriting machines. An inventor who also hopes to make a good deal of money on the camera patent he's about to take out."

Hosmer shifted uncomfortably in his chair. "You know that five hundred dollars my 'uncle' invested in your patent? That wasn't my uncle. That was Susan's money."

"I know that."

"So, despite the fact that you're rich—at least you say you are—and Suss had nothing, you knowingly took all the money she had in the bank."

"Susan was doing well enough with the scenarios she was writing. She was making more money at that than she would have ever made on the stage."

"What money? Mr. Fane didn't pay—"

"I paid her, Hosmer, and told her it was all from Mr. Fane. I imagine that Susan is a little upset about that too, if Mr. Fane told her."

"I don't know about that."

"Well, if she doesn't know, then I don't think you need to tell her."

Hosmer's eyes darted nervously about. He cracked his knuckles. "What about your uncle? If he doesn't like actresses, what does he think of nephews who wear old clothes and repair alarm clocks and live on the wrong side of town?"

"He wouldn't approve, if he knew. But he doesn't know, and what he doesn't know won't hurt him. He thinks I've taken a trip to Havana for my health. I told him I'd been coming down with too many illnesses this past winter. He's expecting me back next month, full of vigor."

"It's a romance," Hosmer remarked after shaking his head for a few moments.

"But you believe me now?"

"It doesn't matter what I believe, you only have to worry about what Suss believes. If I was Suss, I wouldn't believe much."

"Proof's easy," said Jack, with more confidence in the favorable outcome of this than he actually felt. "So you'll speak to Susan? Will you tell her what I just told you? That I did everything for love of her? That I love her still? That I beg her forgiveness? And that we can be married anywhere and anytime she pleases?"

"Sure," said Hosmer, after a moment of reflection, "and if I can't do anything with her, then I'll speak to Ida. And Ida'll make all things right. Right as a rain-barrel."

Jack hoped that Hosmer would not have to resort to the assistance of Ida Conquest.

Jack waited out another day in the hospital. His bandages were changed again, and a nurse rubbed salve on his burned skin. His throat—feeling charred after the long conversation with Hosmer Collamore—felt better after he drank some thick, syrupy liquid. He began to dream of long life with Susan—in more comfortable surroundings than those they had enjoyed together till now. He envisaged the time when this interlude would be looked back on as a time of high romance for them. He wondered if they'd have children, and to while away the time, he began to think of names for them.

Such thoughts were more pleasant than meditations on subjects that were probably nearer to reality. These included the possibility that Susan would never speak to him again, that the untimely discovery of his deception had spoiled all possibility of their ever uniting, that Hosmer and Ida and President Wilson together couldn't convince Susan that Jack's perfidy hadn't been perfidy at all, but merely an expression of his affection for her.

There was no sign of Susan the next morning, and no Hosmer either.

Nor did anyone come to visit that afternoon.

Each and every one of the other patients in the ward received visitors. There were flowers on all the other bedside tables. Jack fretted and twisted, and sent the ambulance driver's boy with more notes to the Fenwick.

No reply came from either Susan or Hosmer.

Jack continued to fret and fume, despite the nurse's warning that if he kept on like this he was never going to get well.

Five days after the fire in the Cosmic Film Company, Jack was released from the hospital. He was bandaged across his chest beneath his clothing and one side of his face and neck still showed signs of having been burned, but not severely. The doctor had suggested that he allow his beard to grow again to cover a possible healing scar, but Jack had refused, despite the pain that shaving caused him. He didn't want Susan to be confronted with the old, false Jack Beaumont.

When Jack left the hospital, he was wearing an old suit of clothes donated by a church charity. His own clothing had been too badly burned by the fire to be wearable, and there was no one to bring him clothes from the Fenwick. His pockets were empty, for all his money had been spent on sending messages. So, despite his impatience to get back to the Fenwick and find out what was going on with his reconciliation plans, he was forced to walk home. He looked like a drunkard dressed in a suit of mission clothes, searching out a bar that would provide him with drink on credit. He even took the precaution of avoiding policemen, who might have collared him for being in the wrong part of town. So using side streets and a corner of the park, Jack made his way back to the Fenwick.

He discovered that he'd lost the key to his room, but that presented no problem, since the door was standing wide open. Odd, Jack thought, but he'd worry about that later.

Hurriedly he changed clothes, putting on his only decent suit. There was no point now in looking like a beggar when he presented himself to Susan. Hastily he finished getting ready, and then stepped outside into the hallway.

The next two minutes determines my fate, he thought.

He knocked first on Hosmer's door, but there was no answer.

He went up the stairs and knocked on Susan's door. No answer there either. There wasn't even the familiar commotion of Tripod hurling himself against the door.

"Susan! Susan!" he called.

The door behind him in the passageway scraped open. Mrs. Jadd stuck out her head.

"She's gone. And good riddance."

"Gone where?" Jack demanded.

"Wherever that other one has gone."

"What other one?"

"Mr. Collamore. They run off together. Elopements," Mrs. Jadd intoned judgmentally, "are wicked things."

CHAPTER NINETEEN

"WHERE DID THEY go?" cried Jack in an agony of desperation.

"Don't know," said Mrs. Jadd, with evident pleasure. She shushed her twins, who had been whining and peering around her skirts into the hallway, and pushed them back inside the apartment.

"*When* did they go?"

"Let's see," she said thoughtfully, "wasn't today, wasn't yesterday. They left the day before that."

"And you don't have any idea—"

"Always knew there was something going on between those two. A respectable apartment building is no place to carry on a romance, not when there is children around to be infected. It's a wicked city, Mr. Beaumont, and Susan Bright was a shining example of it."

Jack didn't stay to argue Susan's moral posture with Mrs. Jadd. He immediately paid a visit to the landlady, Mrs. McCalken, who lived two blocks away. Mrs. McCalken knew only that both Susan Bright and Hosmer Collamore were paid up in their rent. They'd left no forwarding address, though she'd specifically asked them to do so.

"And it was your impression that the two of them left together?"

"Keeping company, as my ma used to say," said Mrs. McCalken, wagging a square head on a fat neck. "Keeping company, Mr. Beaumont."

Jack wandered dazedly back out into the street. The bandages around his chest felt as if they were about to choke him they were so tight. His great fear those days in the hospital had been that Susan would never forgive him for his deception, though he'd allowed himself to think that with time and perseverance he could eventually convince her. She loved him; she'd even agreed to marry him— under his real name, just let her remember that!—and now she had thrown it all over just because he was rich when he had told her he was poor? It didn't make any sense!

Well, actually he wasn't really *rich*—yet. He had only a comfortable income from his job with the family firm. But he would be decidedly rich when his uncle died and left him not only the business but the substantial private holdings that had been amassed through three generations of Beaumonts in Manhattan and upstate New York. His uncle could have no objection to Susan, for Miss Bright was very much a lady in appearance, manner, dress, and carriage. Also, Jack had done a little investigating, and discovered that her stock was quite good; she was from one of the best families of western Connecticut. There would be little difficulty in suppressing, for a few years at least, information about Susan's brief and inconclusive theatrical career. Jack's uncle need never know about that.

But those, it appeared now, had been the idlest of idle dreams, for Susan had done what Jack had *never* imagined. She'd run off with Hosmer Collamore. *Hosmer!*

Jack and Susan had laughed at Hosmer together, at his attempts, never wholly successful, of purging his accent of its Brooklyn origins. They'd poked fun at his peacock pride, his pomaded mustache, and his maladroit adoration of Ida Conquest. Jack had to admit, however, that he'd proved a good friend, assisting Jack with the promotion of his camera invention, in suggesting an attorney to secure the patent rights, in being occasionally a good companion. Nevertheless, that Susan should run off with this man was well nigh inconceivable to Jack. In fact, the more he thought about it, the more he was convinced there was a piece of the puzzle that was still hidden from him.

He intended to find out what it was.

His first move was to taxi down to 27 West Twenty-seventh Street.

There was no longer any sign on the building indicating the premises of the Cosmic Film Company. Jack looked up at the facade. Windows on the third and fourth floors were broken, the sashes charred and black. He went into the cramped little lobby and tried to call down the elevator. It wasn't working, and he supposed it must have been damaged in the fire the previous week. He climbed the stairs.

A rope blocked the third floor, and Jack breathed through his mouth to avoid the stench of charred wet wood. Peering into the room that had housed the film laboratory, he saw that it was deserted. Tables and other furniture damaged in the fire had been abandoned. No one had cleaned up, no one had made repairs. A cricket chirped in a pile of dense rubble in the corner. Otherwise all was silent.

The fire had burned the stairway above the third floor, and it was impossible for Jack to go higher in the building, but because the elevator was not working, Jack realized that the other two floors of the film company must also be deserted. So where were Junius Fane, Ida Conquest, and the thirty or so other employees of the

Cosmic Film Company? Had they all been given time off while repairs were made to the premises?

But no repairs were being made.

Perhaps they had moved to another location?

Jack went down one flight, and knocked at the door of the dress manufactory on the second floor. A girl in a long blue skirt inched the door open. "Yes please?"

"I'm looking for the Cosmic Film Company."

"They piked it," said the young woman mysteriously.

"The whole company?"

"Every bit."

"Where did they go?"

"Don't know. Don't nobody know. Used to have us make their costumes and didn't pay on time though they was right in the rooms above, and that's cheek if you ask me what I think about it. Always getting broke into, and now this fire, and look—" She pulled open the door another inch or two, and Jack peered inside. At the front of the loft, the ceiling had collapsed in a wet mire of plaster and pipes and burned wood.

"Lost eighteen bolts of silk," the girl continued. "You ever buy silk by the bolt, mister? You got any idea what that costs? It costs dear, is what it costs, and that silk is gone. So's Cosmic, and I ain't a bit sorry."

With that she shut the door with finality.

Jack was not getting very far with his investigation. The burns sustained in the fire, as well as several days of physical inactivity and mental anguish, had debilitated his system. He was exhausted, and took a cab back home. He intended to lie down for an hour or two and think about what to do next.

That small respite was not allowed him, however. As he climbed the stairs toward his apartment, there on the third-floor landing stood a figure. It was late in the day, and the light was never too bright in the hallways of the Fenwick anyway, so Jack did not immediately recognize his visitor.

"Mr. Beaumont?" the man said, and the voice was familiar.

"Mr. Garden!"

Mr. Garden was the junior partner—though he was nearly sixty years old—of the law firm which handled the private affairs of Jack's uncle. Jack made a quick and simple deduction: Nobody in his "real life" was supposed to know that he was anywhere near West Sixtieth Street; they were supposed to think he would be in Havana for a few months. But now here stood Mr. Garden, and if Mr. Garden knew of his whereabouts, then very likely Jack's uncle knew as well.

It was a deduction that did not bode well for Jack, and he suddenly felt even wearier than he had in the taxi coming home. Well, there was nothing to be done but ask the man inside.

Mr. Garden looked about Jack's sitting room with an expressionless curiosity that did nothing to put Jack at ease.

"We understand that you were in hospital," Mr. Garden began after a moment. He was a thin, aristocratic man with a bright red face, and shining white hair. Jack had always thought that Mr. Garden resembled a beet in a snowstorm.

"I'm out now," Jack offered lamely. He always felt like a little boy in the lawyer's presence.

"Yes," said Mr. Garden. "We hope you are recovered."

Mr. Garden frequently used *we* in an ambiguous, somewhat regal sense. In this case, did it include his uncle? Jack thought it better not to ask.

"I have to recuperate for a while."

Mr. Garden didn't reply to this, instead he simply gazed out the window for a few moments, and then he looked at the calendar on the wall. Then, as if the calendar had reminded him of the subject of time in general, he announced: "You have lived here for three months, two weeks and one day."

"Something like that," said Jack uncomfortably. This visit was just the sort of thing to cap an already trying day.

"You still maintain your bachelor apartments on Twenty-third Street, however?"

"Ah, yes," said Jack, with the uneasy feeling that this truthful answer was somehow going to get him into trouble.

"Isn't that—*extravagant*?" asked Mr. Garden.

"The rent is excessive on neither place," said Jack.

"Rent is always excessive if you can't afford it," remarked Mr. Garden.

Jack had a feeling that Mr. Garden was about to get to the heart of the matter. "Mr. Garden, I am in considerable pain," Jack said. "Considerable physical pain, and considerable pain of the heart as well."

"Ah yes, Miss Bright."

Yes, Jack thought, not really surprised, *he knows about Susan as well.* "Mr. Garden, would you please tell me the purpose of your visit this afternoon. Tell me as quickly and as succinctly as possible. If it's bad news, putting off telling me won't make it any better. If it's good news—"

"Oh, it's certainly not *good* news, Mr. Beaumont."

"I thought not."

"Mr. Beaumont, a few weeks ago, an acquaintance of your uncle's happened to be dining in Mouquin's."

Jack looked up sharply. So it had been a mistake to go there after all. He had chosen it because none of his friends liked the place—it was decidedly old-fashioned. But he should have realized that it was likely to be visited by gourmands of his uncle's generation.

"And as you were in the company of a female cripple, your presence hardly went unnoticed."

"Susan is not a cripple. She was only on crutches. In fact, I was the one responsible for breaking her leg."

Mr. Garden smiled a thin little smile that said, *I'm not a bit surprised to hear it.*

"Your appearance was mentioned, *en passant*, to your uncle, who was, as you might imagine, quite surprised to learn that you were in town. For to his knowledge, you were in Havana—for your health"—Mr. Garden spoke the last words with supercilious disapproval. "Naturally, your uncle telephoned your apartments on Twenty-third Street to determine why you had not called on him immediately upon your return, and why you had not resumed your position of responsibility in the firm. No answer was forth-coming, Mr. Beaumont, and your uncle became worried. He instituted inquiries. He questioned his friend as to whether he might not have been mistaken in marking you in the restaurant. The friend said that despite a growth of facial hair that he had not seen before, *you* were most indubitably *you*. Your uncle dispatched telegrams to Havana. He paid a personal visit to New York's commissioner of police."

"Oh, lord," sighed Jack.

"You remained elusive, Mr. Beaumont, until several days ago, when you were reported to be a patient in Bellevue Hospital. It was an easy matter then to discover your address from the hospital authorities, and a series of interviews with the inhabitants of this apartment building provided a substantial account of your tenure here. All of this was reported to your uncle, Mr. Beaumont, and I do not believe that I go too far in interpretation when I say to you that your uncle was very displeased to learn of it."

"I can begin to imagine," said Jack ruefully.

"'Unquenchable ire at an unforgiveable betrayal,' is a phrase that springs to mind," said Mr. Garden.

Jack uncrossed his legs and discovered that one of them had gone to sleep, and now was heavy as lead and tingling with pins and needles. He ignored the discomfort and crossed his leg the other way. "There's more," Jack said. "I feel quite sure there's more."

"Oh, yes," said Mr. Garden. "To put it bluntly, as you requested, you are relieved of your position with Beaumont, Beaumont, and Beaumont."

None of those three Beaumonts was Jack himself, but referred to his uncle, his late father, and his much later grandfather. Jack had always looked forward to the day a fourth Beaumont would be added. That day was suddenly receding into the distance.

"My uncle is going to sack me?" said Jack. He was calm—in the way a ship's captain is calm when a torpedo has blown a hole in the hull, lightning has struck the mainmast, and general mutiny has just been declared among the crew.

"No," said Mr. Garden, ever precise. "He already has. I do not betray a confidence, I think, when I also tell you that he has struck you from his will."

"He's done all this because I didn't go to Havana?"

"Because you didn't go to Havana, because you lied to him, because you have lowered yourself to the position of an impoverished tinkerer, and consorted with actors and"—Mr. Garden's voice lowered dramatically—"moving-picture people. Mr. Beaumont, your uncle considers that you have brought eternal and irreparable shame on the house of Beaumont, Beaumont, and Beaumont."

"Not exactly," Jack pointed out, "if my uncle is the only one who knows about all this."

"He is not, in point of fact. Notice of your brave and daring rescue of the night watchman at the Cosmic Film Company appeared in the *Sun* and the *Times*. It escaped our notice at the time, for we thought naturally that you were in Havana, and the article referred to some other John A. Beaumont, Esq."

"'Brave and daring...'" Jack repeated thoughtfully.

"Bravery and daring have their place," said Mr. Garden sententiously, "on the high seas, on the battlefield, in the jungles of Africa. But bravery and daring have no place in a company devoted to financial investments. In fact, so far as your uncle is concerned, bravery and daring are substantial disqualifications for the position which you so lately occupied."

Jack stretched out in his chair and inadvertently banged his head against the wall; it seemed appropriate. "Mr. Garden, is this all? I really was advised by my doctors to get some rest."

"Not quite all," said Mr. Garden. "I've saved the good news for last."

"There's good news?"

"Yes. No cloud is without its silver lining, after all. No longer attached to the house of Beaumont, Beaumont, and Beaumont, you are now perfectly free to marry Miss Bright. Your uncle hopes you will be very happy together—in some other part of the country."

"Mr. Garden?"

"Yes, Mr. Beaumont?"

"Did anyone ever tell you that you look like a beet in a snowstorm?"

CHAPTER TWENTY

Jack KNEW WHY his uncle was doing this to him—
any excuse for a disinheritance. Jack's uncle had remarried
recently, a lady from the South—that region of the country
that breeds ladies who are the most mercenary creatures
on earth. Especially the widowed variety, with offspring
from the previous marriage. And this particular widow
had three sons, each more dissolute than the last, and
her plan was to siphon off the Beaumont inheritance into
their rapacious hands. Jack, like his father before him,
had never gotten along with his uncle. It had been a great
nuisance that by the terms of the will of Jack's grandfather,
the firm's assets had gone entirely to Jack's uncle. Now it
appeared to Jack that he was to be cut out entirely.

Soon after the wordless departure of Mr. Garden, Jack
lay down on his bed and thought about all this, but soon
fell asleep and dreamed of Susan in Hosmer Collamore's
arms. It was a nightmare.

He awoke in a sweat and was immediately overcome by an obsession: to find out where Susan and Hosmer had gone. The matter of his stolen inheritance could wait for a while. After all, his uncle wasn't dead yet.

His current financial situation, however, was a concern, especially if it proved necessary to go chasing Susan and Hosmer far. He had not received any salary since he'd left Beaumont, Beaumont, and Beaumont on his "trip to Cuba," but had lived off a small supply of cash he'd brought with him from Twenty-third Street, and that supply was almost gone. In fact, he had less than ten dollars. His checking account contained nearly two hundred dollars, but that would be eaten up by the hospital bill.

Therefore, he concluded, all the money he had in the world was the five hundred dollars given to him by Susan Bright (through the agency of Hosmer Collamore) for the rights to the patent on the motion picture camera.

He wondered if it would make a difference to Susan to know that he was now exactly what he had represented himself to be—an impecunious inventor, whose sole resource was the money he'd got from her anonymous generosity. She probably wouldn't believe him if he told her, and, he reflected ruefully, he couldn't blame her for that.

Jack began to pack his belongings, then realized there was no point in maintaining the imposture of a threadbare wardrobe any longer. Though he was in no financial condition to buy anything, he had much better clothing in his apartment on Twenty-third Street. He stopped packing, looked around the room, and his mind again returned to Topic A: How to find Susan?

To find her, he must also find Hosmer, which would probably be easier. The first step would be to find out what happened to the Cosmic Film Company. The company seemed to have vanished from its former burnt-out premises, and the operator at Telephone Central only knew that the phones had been removed, and there was no new number for Cosmic. Still, it seemed unlikely that such a large and prospering enterprise would go out of business overnight and simply disappear without a trace, so he allowed himself some hope that he would be able to find it in a day or so.

He stuffed his ten dollars into his pocket and had his hand on the knob of the door when there came a knock.

Jack opened the door and found himself staring into the faces of two persons he had never seen before—a large man and a not much smaller woman of middle age, dressed in what appeared to be their Sunday best.

With an explosive sigh, the woman dropped to her knees in the doorway, grabbed Jack's hand, and covered it with kisses. Before astonished Jack could protest, the man had grabbed his other hand and began pumping it so vigorously that Jack feared a wellspring would gush from the top of his head.

"Madam, please..."

Ignoring Jack's protest, the woman on her knees rubbed her cheek over the back of Jack's hand and then kissed it some more. Hosmer's old apartment across the hall already had a new tenant, an old man with arthritic shaking hands, who now opened his door and peered out disapprovingly.

"Thank you, sir," said the man who was still heartily shaking Jack's hand. "Thank you. I thank you, my wife here thanks you on her knees, our children at home— there's five of 'em—they'd be here to thank you too except two of 'em has the mumps and the other three was looking peaked, and Mary here thought it best they not come with us, though they was a-achin' to."

"Do you have the right apartment?" asked Jack. "Maybe you want Mrs. Jadd upstairs."

"John Beaumont," said the visitor, still pumping, "John Beaumont, I thank you from the bottom of my heart. I bless the day your mother first laid eyes on your father's brow."

"I blesses the bed that cradled your infant form," said the woman, staring up at Jack with tears in her eyes.

"Who are you?" asked Jack.

"The Cosmic watchman," said the man solemnly.

Suddenly it all made sense.

"Where is the young lady?" cried the wife. "We wants to thank her too."

"Please come in and sit down," said Jack abruptly. "I need your help."

Husband and wife glanced uneasily at one another. To them, help meant money.

"Don't worry," said Jack, who immediately understood those looks, having learned a few things living life as a straitened mechanic, "it has nothing to do with money."

Husband and wife came into the room. Jack asked their names, and found that they were Mr. and Mrs. Kosdercka—but everyone called them Mr. and Mrs. K.

"No more about saving your life, Mr. K., please," said Jack, "because if you can help me, you'll have paid me back more than fully. I just need the answer to one question: Where is the Cosmic Film Company?"

Mr. and Mrs. Kosdercka looked at each other. Mr. K. looked down at the floor and said, "I don't know."

"You do know," said Mrs. K. "Tell the young man. I'd be weeping over your grave right now if it wasn't for this gentleman and his young lady friend."

Mr. Kosdercka still hesitated. "Not supposed to tell. Not even supposed to know."

"It's because of the young lady who helped to save your life that I'm asking. She was abducted," said Jack, not even blushing at the lie, "by a man employed by Cosmic, and I was hoping that, by speaking to Mr. Fane or someone, I could find the villain who made off with her."

Mrs. K.'s eyes widened at the romance and intrigue of the thing.

Mr. K. considered the business. "You know Mr. Fane, do you?"

"We had business dealings," said Jack, truthfully. "And now I need to find him, that's all."

"They all took off."

"That's obvious. But where did they go?"

"Didn't want nobody to know," said Mrs. K.

"The Trust," whispered Mr. K. leaning forward conspiratorially, as if representatives of that organization might be eavesdropping from an adjoining room.

"That's why they decamped? To avoid the Trust?"

Both Mr. and Mrs. K. nodded.

"Where did they go?" asked Jack. "Brooklyn?"

Mr. K. shook his head. "Across the Hudson."

"New Jersey?"

"California," said Mrs. K. and slapped at her husband's hand for his deception.

"California? The whole company?"

"Some place where they grow oranges. Can't recall the name."

"Hollywood," Mrs. K. supplied.

❀ ❀ ❀

Jack could not believe that Susan had run off with Hosmer Collamore with the intention of marrying the man. Logic dictated that Susan Bright had simply gone to ground. Perhaps she had moved to another part of Manhattan; or was residing above some laundry in Brooklyn; or had gone home to Connecticut to nurse her wounds. That's where he should be searching for her—in rooms above laundries, and in small rustic hotels in rural Connecticut.

But there are times when inspiration supersedes logic. This was one of them. Jack knew that he wouldn't find Susan in those places but in a place called Hollywood in California.

The town was so small it didn't even appear in his pocket atlas. So despite logic and deduction and probability to the contrary, Jack withdrew his five hundred dollars from the bank and purchased a train ticket for Los Angeles.

He packed two small valises of his better clothes from the Twenty-third Street apartment. Then he went back up to the Fenwick with a briefcase and dumped all his papers and plans and drawings into it.

Then he discovered that the final drawings he'd executed for the patent application on his camera improvement were missing. Evidently during his tenure in the hospital they'd been stolen from his room. He then understood why the door of the room had been wide open on his return. The thief hadn't even bothered to close it again.

Anyone with those drawings could patent the camera, and reap all the monetary benefits that accrued from any use of the device.

"Damn," cried Jack, plugging his hat on his head and flying out the door. His train left in half an hour.

❀ ❀ ❀

Jack fretted in his seat before the train departed Pennsylvania Station. He steamed in the dark tunnel beneath the Hudson River. He stewed through Newark and Elizabeth. Life, he concluded with bitterness, was one damn thing after another.

He could have stayed in New York and tried to find the thief who'd purloined those drawings, but Susan would be ever farther away. Her distrust of him would deepen with time. Or worse, she'd forget him. He had to find her again as soon as possible. He couldn't afford precious days tracking down a robber, of whose identity he had no idea whatever.

It probably was another of the Trust thugs. Thomas Alva Edison, that revered white-haired old man, had somehow heard of Jack's invention—spies in the Cosmic studios, perhaps—and had hired some graduate of Blackwell's Island to get into Jack's apartment. The inventor of the light bulb now sat in a comfortable chair in Fort Lee, studying Jack's drawings, and chuckling to himself—as frantic, distracted Jack rode in a cheap compartment on the train headed for Washington, D.C.

Jack questioned the conductor as to whether any film company troupe had recently ridden the train, but the man said no. Of course, the Cosmic Film Company could have taken any number of different trains, or even a different line, for that matter—or had made no impression as a group of travelers. When the train stopped at Trenton, Jack got off and put the same question to several station employees, and again received a negative reply. But in turning away from the ticket seller's cage, Jack caught sight of a familiar face, in a tinted postcard tacked to a board. It was Ida Conquest, in her costume as the Aeroplane Girl, and the card was *signed*.

"That postcard," Jack demanded of the ticket agent. "That girl—"

"Oh yes, she *did* come through here. Could tell that one was an actress, all right. A fine figure of a young woman. Selling the cards out of her pocketbook, and only charged a dime—including the autograph."

"When did she come through?"

"Today's Wednesday. Not Tuesday. Not Sunday, 'cause I wasn't on. Must have been Monday."

That was all the ticket seller could tell Jack but he knew that he was on the right track. He imagined them all traveling together—Ida Conquest and Junius Fane, Manfred Mixon and Miss Songar, the cameramen and the chemists, Hosmer and Susan. All on their way to that town in California, too small and insignificant to have its name on the map.

He was two days behind them, but if he managed to catch every possible connection, and maybe if the company decided to rest a day somewhere, then he might very well catch up with them before they reached California. But even if they stayed the same distance ahead of him, he could not imagine that he would have any difficulty in finding them once they'd reached their destination.

Train journeys were usually boring, but Jack, even in the midst of his anxiety, felt that he was on an adventure. On that night back in January, when he'd so innocently sat in the third row of the orchestra of the New Columbia Theatre, he was just John Austin Beaumont, managing director of the prestigious and long-established firm of Beaumont, Beaumont, and Beaumont. He had admired a young actress, as many rich young men admired pretty young actresses, and as such young men do, he'd sent a note around to her dressing room. After that, not a thing in the world had gone as he could have predicted.

And now only a few short months later, Jack was without a job, without an income, was engaged to a woman who had skipped out in the company of another man, and he was sitting in a railway car at the beginning of a journey that was going to take him all the way across the American continent.

The train arrived at Union Station in Washington, D.C., and Jack got off. He was now forced to make an important decision. He could take the northern route to California, that is, by way of Chicago. Or else he could take the more southern route, from Washington to St. Louis, and from there across the prairie and the desert. This was supposed to be a tedious and dreary ride, though it was cheaper.

Jack, having known Junius Fane and being acquainted with his methods of doing business, judged that he was a man to choose tedious, dreary, and cheap above anything else, so Jack purchased a ticket for an express train to St.

Louis. Perhaps, if the Cosmic Film Company had been forced by circumstance to take a train that made frequent stops, Jack would gain a day on Susan.

The train was scheduled to leave in another hour, at eight o'clock in the evening. It would arrive in St. Louis fifteen hours later—a prodigious speed—stopping only in Louisville, Kentucky. He went into the railway station saloon and downed a brandy and soda in honor of Susan Bright. He downed another to the eternal damnation of Hosmer Collamore.

Jack devoured a ham sandwich, drank another brandy and soda, and made his way to platform 12, where his train waited, steam hissing from under it on to the platform. The train originated here at Union Station, so he was able to climb on without delay. His reserved seat was in a quiet, out-of-the-way spot next to a window. He looked for a few minutes at the Tauchnitz Edition he'd picked up in a bookstall in the station, but it couldn't hold his interest. The brandy made him sleepy, and he watched his fellow passengers saying their good-byes to relatives and friends and then boarding the train. Jack couldn't keep his eyelids open, and he nodded off for a few minutes, under the genial effects of the brandy. He was jolted awake by the simultaneous blast of the train whistle and the shrill laughter of a child.

Jack opened his eyes.

In the seat just opposite him was a little boy, about seven years old Jack guessed, wearing a velvet suit with pearl buttons, in imitation of the child hero of some dreadful touring company production of *Little Lord Fauntleroy*. The boy was standing on the seat, pointing out the window and giggling in a near hysterical fashion. The boy's mother, seated across the aisle, and evidently believing her maternal responsibility ended with the velvet suit, made no attempt to quiet the child.

Jack turned and looked out to see what had so excited the child. Another train was situated on the other side of the platform, and it too was filling with passengers, as could plainly be seen through the lighted windows.

One of those passengers was a great fat man, who was now struggling with two enormous suitcases—trying to get both himself and the suitcases down the narrow aisle. He was bumping heads and knocking hats askew, and one of the cases had just spilled open, scattering clothing everywhere.

Jack laughed too, and was still laughing as his train gave another whistle, then a lurch and began slowly moving on its way to St. Louis.

Then suddenly the laugh froze on Jack's face, for he realized that the fat man causing all the trouble in the other train was Manfred Mixon, the Fabulous Funny Fellow of Cosmic Features.

The entire Cosmic group probably was in that train not twenty feet away on the other side of the platform.

Jack stared frantically out at the lighted windows as the express for St. Louis picked up speed. Then, there in a car toward the front, Jack saw Susan. She sat with her chin on her hand, staring at Hosmer Collamore, who was leaning toward her, holding up something small and sparkling.

Was it a ring?

Jack jumped up from his seat, pushed Little Ford Fauntleroy out of the way, and clawed at the window.

"Susan! Susan!" he shouted.

She couldn't have heard him, of course, over the clattering of the train, and through the barriers of windows, but Tripod was there. Tripod heard Jack's anguished cry, or caught sight of Jack's anguished face, or intuited Jack's anguished presence. Tripod leapt up onto the seat beside Susan, and began barking furiously out the window.

Susan turned, and at the last possible moment, she caught sight of Jack.

The image remained frozen in Jack's mind; Susan's eyes wide in surprise and disbelief, her black hair glistening beneath the yellow light of the train compartment, her mouth open in astonishment.

The St. Louis Express pulled out of Union Station and hurtled Jack Beaumont through the Maryland countryside and on across America.

CHAPTER TWENTY-ONE

ALL THROUGH THAT dark night, Jack stared at Little Lord Fauntleroy—who snored in a way Jack couldn't remember that seven-year-old children snored—and thought of Susan Bright.

Susan Bright in the railway carriage, sitting across from Hosmer Collamore, and Hosmer holding up something small and bright and shiny—doubtless an engagement ring.

The train that bore Susan and Hosmer, Jack had learned from the conductor, was also headed for St. Louis, but by a different, slower route. Susan's train would meander along to the north, halting at every milk-stop hamlet across Ohio, Indiana, and Illinois. The Cosmic Film Company would arrive approximately six hours after Jack. Not only had Jack caught up with Mr. Junius Fane and company, he had leapt over them!

During the half-hour stop in Louisville, Jack stayed on the train and munched hot corn brought through by a boy in a jacket that was too short in the arms and trousers that were too long in the legs. He leaned out of the window and guzzled down a tin of coffee that scalded his throat. Whenever he'd traveled by train before, he'd gone first-class, and he'd dined on linen and silverware in the dining car. His West Sixtieth Street playacting quickly had become real indeed, and this "being without" was not a pleasant sensation. Once every couple of minutes he surreptitiously touched the wad of bills in his pocket—all his money in the world—to make certain it was still there.

Not long after the train left Louisville, it began to get light outside, and as he stared out the window at alternating patches of forest and field, and the occasional small town, Jack laid plots.

Susan had seen him.

Susan had recognized him.

Susan would be expecting him in St. Louis.

She might even find a way to keep him off the train to Los Angeles.

She might herself linger behind and take a different train out. There were all kinds of possibilities.

If Jack could somehow get on the same train as Susan he knew that in the two and a half days that the journey to California required he could convince her that she still loved him and that she ought still to marry him—despite former deceptions, despite Hosmer Collamore's protestations, despite Tripod's innate distrust of him. Jack had somehow to forestall Susan's efforts—efforts she was sure to make—in avoiding him.

By the time the train pulled into St. Louis, Jack thought he had found a workable plan, but he had only six hours to implement it.

When the train arrived in St. Louis, Jack hurried off, checked his luggage, asked a few directions, and then went out into the city. Fortunately, the station was centrally located, and in less than four hours he had visited a used-clothing store, a pharmacist's, a barber's, a store catering to the wants of the theatrical profession, and a veterinarian's office.

He returned to the station, found a quiet bench in the corner, and prepared to wait for the train that was carrying the Cosmic Film Company—and, he hoped, Susan—toward St. Louis.

His own mother would not have known him. He wore a three-piece checked suit—large, square checks in blue and green, in fact—a dented plug hat, discolored spats over muddy shoes, and thick round eyeglasses that magnified and distorted the contours of his face. Above his upper lip he had pasted a heavy yellow mustache that matched the color of his hair as the barber had dyed it. He smoked a long, thick, cheap cigar, and was now a personification of that well-known American figure, the drummer. He was disguised as a traveling salesman.

The train from Washington arrived, and Jack had the electrifying satisfaction of seeing Ida Conquest—on the arm of Junius Fane—emerge through the doors from the platforms.

Then came the less exalted members of the company, other passengers, and—finally—Susan Bright and Hosmer Collamore. They were the last, Jack reckoned, by certain needs of Tripod, who trotted along—*pad pad pad tap*—at Susan's heel.

Jack sank back against the bench and peered at the couple over the top of his spectacles.

Neither of them noticed him, but Tripod stopped dead in his tracks in the middle of the marble flooring of the station, sniffed the air, growled, and turned his canine head slowly in Jack's direction.

Susan turned and called, "Tripod, come."

Tripod would not. He continued to growl.

Susan put down her bags and reached down to scoop up the dog in her arms. Tripod evaded her grasp and headed straight for Jack.

Jack was prepared. "Here, boy," he cried in a loud, fluting voice that was nothing like his own—and which he had practiced in the streets of St. Louis for several hours, to the astonishment of the natives.

Ready in his hand was a soggy biscuit, and he tossed it toward the dog.

Pad pad pad tap. Pad pad—

Tripod sniffed at the biscuit. Tripod looked up at Jack. Tripod looked down at the biscuit again, and gobbled it up. Then he lunged at Jack.

Just then Hosmer arrived on the scene and grabbed up the dog, muttering a brief apology, just as Tripod's jaws opened with malicious intent focused on Jack's checkered trousers. He carried Tripod back across the waiting room to Susan.

Susan took the dog, and glanced across to Jack. Jack grinned a wide grin at her beneath his thick mustache. He'd blacked out two of his teeth.

Susan smiled tentatively back. She obviously hadn't recognized him.

Tripod was already looking a bit drowsy in her arms, and after what Jack had put in the biscuit, he'd sleep for almost ten hours.

Susan stared at the suddenly oddly laconic dog in her arms, and then she and Hosmer joined the others lined up in a corner of the station to receive tickets from Mr. Fane's assistant.

A few minutes later, Jack went to the ticket window, and said quite straightforwardly, "Give me a ticket on the same train as that group over there, please."

"Slowest train on the continent," the ticket seller warned. "Stops for every cow and tick between here and the Pacific Ocean."

"Exactly what I wanted," said Jack.

"Track seven, leaving eight o'clock tonight."

❁ ❁ ❁

Four trains a day left St. Louis headed for California, two to San Francisco and two to Los Angeles. Most people traveling to Los Angeles took the morning train. This late night train had nothing to recommend it but cheapness. It had a great number of baggage cars, mail cars, and transport cars of other sorts besides the two small, rather dilapidated sleepers. The Cosmic Film Company had taken over nearly all of one of these sleepers, the last car of the train. In lieu of a caboose, the conductor had a small compartment at the back of this car.

Jack was given a seat in the forward car, where his fellow passengers were an assortment of types: real drummers with their battered sample cases, East Coast bankrupts headed for West Coast opportunities, sad-looking widows with orphaned children who were going toward who-knew-what, and a couple of frowsy young women who looked as if they knew their way around.

The berths were already made up when the passengers got on board the train. It was frustrating for Jack to know that Susan was right there in the next coach, a sleeping dog draped across her feet like a lumpy hot-water bottle, and Hosmer Collamore who knows how close by. Nevertheless, he knew there was no way to approach her tonight and that he'd have two whole days and more in which to work his way back into her heart—and he'd do it, despite Hosmer Collamore, despite Tripod, despite Susan herself.

The train lulled him to sleep with its rhythmic clickety-clack—and woke him up again every half hour or so with lurchings and squealings of brakes, as it made yet another milk-run stop.

Next morning the train was in Kansas somewhere, and slowly the passengers roused themselves. A porter turned the berths back into seats, and another porter came through selling coffee and rolls. The railroad had spared every expense on this particular train, including that of a dining car; perhaps they reckoned that the train made more than enough stops to satisfy the passengers' gustatory demands.

Jack stared out the window at the passing prairie, newly green and yellow in the spring sunshine, and wondered when he should make his move. It would be best if he could get Susan out of the other coach and into this one, but that might not prove easy or even possible. His ingenuity wasn't up to it. Probably he was just going to have to walk in, drop to his knees, tear off his false mustache, announce culpability and plead forgiveness, and apologize for having administered a sleeping potion to Tripod.

Of course, that would mean that the entire Cosmic Film Company would be witness to the scene, but Jack hadn't come halfway across country to back out now on account of possible embarrassment.

Maybe it would be better to throw off the costume beforehand. There was something melodramatic and improbable about false mustaches to begin with, and besides, it was partly deceit that had got him into this trouble with Susan in the first place, so perhaps it would be best to appear before her in his true identity.

The door at the back of the coach opened just then and Jack saw the conductor there, in conference with Junius Fane. Jack did not want to take the chance of being recognized by the owner of the film company, so he took down one of his bags and carried it with him into the gentlemen's lavatory at the front end of the car. There he proceeded to reconstruct Jack Beaumont.

He removed the checked suit, and stood in his garters and shirtsleeves. He gingerly stripped away the fake yellow mustache, the spirit gum—and a decent-sized patch of skin. He put away the eyeglasses, and ruined one of the railroad's towels in attempting to rub some of the yellow dye from his hair.

He threw away the spats and shined the shoes. He put on a good—though not his best—suit of clothes, even going so far as to attach a watch and chain to his vest. He tied, untied, and retied a four-in-hand foulard, then peered at his face in the mirror and applied a dab of alcohol to his upper lip.

Outside the window, the prairie continued to roll by endlessly. At a town called Kiowa, the train stopped, for no apparent reason, since there was no one at the station that Jack could see, no one got off, and the train took off again almost immediately. For a few moments, Jack thought he heard Mr. Fane's voice in the passenger section of the coach, which was curious, but Jack had other things on his mind, and certainly did not want to be seen by Junius Fane.

After the train was on its way again, making the slight incline into the Smoky Hills in the western part of the state, Jack emerged from the gentlemen's lavatory with his suitcase. The two blowsy young women saw him, leaned their heads together, whispered, giggled, and then turned in their seats to stare at him as he moved down the aisle to his seat.

Others in the car stared also. The traveling salesman who had gone into the men's lavatory half an hour before had emerged as a Wall Street broker.

The time had come. He blushed, but did not hesitate.

He placed his bag in the small compartment above his seat next to his other valise, grasped the points of his vest, and pulled them down—modern man's gesture of readiness to do battle—and strode the rest of the way down the aisle toward the rear door of the coach.

He reached for the door handle.

At that moment, with a grinding of brakes and shrill protests from the wheels, the train ground to a sudden stop.

Jack fell backward and sideways into a nearby seat, bumping up against a man who was holding a burning cigar. The stogie singed a hole through Jack's trousers, causing considerable discomfort against the flesh of Jack's thigh.

"Oh, God!" cried Jack, dancing away in pain.

Ladies were startled, a couple of children had been thrown from their seats and were now crying, but apart from the little round burn of flesh on Jack's thigh and the hole in his trousers, little damage had been caused by the clumsy application of the brakes.

"Where are we?" asked Jack, peering out of the window, but seeing nothing but the same endless vista. "We stopped only ten minutes ago."

The other occupants in the car looked at one another, a little tensely Jack thought, and the gentleman with the cigar laughed suddenly and said, "Well, maybe it's a desperate gang of train thieves, come on board to rob us all—"

Then everybody in the car laughed as well, except for Jack, who wondered if he ought now to change his trousers before presenting himself to Susan.

He decided against this, and once more reached for the handle of the door. But the door opened of its own accord. There, blocking his way, stood a short man, wearing blue jeans and a checked shirt. A red bandanna masked the lower portion of the man's face, and he carried a revolver, pointed directly at Jack's belly.

"Lively now," he said briskly. "Tumble out, everybody, and keep your hands above your head! 'Cause I'll drill you if you don't!"

CHAPTER TWENTY-TWO

BECAUSE HE WAS standing in the aisle, Jack was the first of the passengers to be hustled off the next to the last car of the train. Susan was the first passenger herded off the last car.

They met at the bottom of the steps, and for a moment stood staring at each other.

"You?" Susan said, in a tone that expressed no particular emotion.

But before Jack could say anything, they were both prodded forward with gun barrels. In another few minutes, everyone on the train had been arranged in a ragged circle in the short grass by the side of the track.

The short man in jeans and another accomplice, also with a bandanna over his mouth, covered the passengers with revolvers—unnecessarily large weapons, Jack considered. A third member of the gang held the reins of five horses at the rear of the train, while a fourth guarded the engineer and the fireman at the head of the train. The locomotive blew off a great deal of frustrated steam; the sun was bright and hot above, and Jack had never realized that so large a stretch of land could be treeless.

Susan stood next to him, but she resolutely refused to notice his presence. They held their hands above their heads, in approved victim fashion, and Jack tried to grasp Susan's in his own. She jerked away.

"Stop it," she hissed. "Whatever you have to say to me—whoever you are, and whatever your name is today—now is *not* the time to say it."

Jack thought that Susan might be right.

The thieves began to work from the outside in, searching the gentlemen of the party for valuables. To Jack's surprise, there seemed to be no panic in the crowd of perhaps thirty passengers, not even among the widowed mothers. The children seemed to think the whole thing was some kind of adventuresome lark, and leered grinning at the thieves from behind their mothers' skirts. Jack was relieved. In well-conducted robberies, innocent people didn't get shot and die. If everything continued as easily as this, Jack might have the chance to speak to Susan without the worry of an inconvenient bullet hole in his body or hers.

"As Ma couldn't come along today to act as matron," said the gunman who had appeared in Jack's car, and who was evidently the leader of the gang, "we're going to trust the ladies to search theirselves. Diamonds and jewels and money in the hat as we pass it along."

Immediately to Susan's left, there was a sudden commotion. "No!" screamed Ida Conquest, "I'm not going to give up my diamonds! You'll have to shoot me first!"

With that dreadful resolve, the actress broke ranks and fled toward the train. The decorum of the robbery had been instantly—and dangerously—destroyed, thought Jack. It was unclear to Jack what advantage Ida thought she would gain by reboarding the train, since there were few places to hide in a passenger car at rest in the middle of the most desolate part of the desolation that was the state of Kansas. The train would never move forward till the thieves released the engineer and the fireman. Nevertheless, Ida ran; and the leader of the bandits turned his gun in her direction and shouted, "Stop!"

Unthinkingly, Jack raced toward the desperado and flung himself against his back. There was a dreadful blast in the morning stillness as the gun went off, but the bullet went wild, and Ida turned with a look of astonishment on her face.

"Run, Ida!" Jack shouted.

The thief regained his balance, and his eyes were wide with surprise for a moment as he stared at Jack.

Jack kicked the revolver out of the bandit's hand. Cringing, he expected every moment to feel the sharp sting of a bullet in his breast from the revolver of the second robber, who was standing just behind the first gunman, but no bullet stung, so Jack pushed the leader into his henchman, and they tumbled to the ground. Then he cracked each in the jaw with his fist, as hard as he could, which was hard enough to bruise his own knuckles, and hard enough to send the bandits roiling in pain. The bandit at the back of the train abandoned his horses and rushed to the assistance of his comrades. From the front of the train, the fourth man abandoned the engineer and the fireman, and ran to investigate. Quickly Jack grabbed up the two revolvers that had fallen to the ground and backed up against the train, one revolver pointed to the right, the other to the left.

"I'm sure nobody wants to die, so put down your guns," Jack said.

The third and fourth bandits did not. Jack wasn't certain what to do. He glanced at the circle of passengers, who stood stock-still in astonishment.

"Put down your guns or I'll shoot," Jack cried. He stood alone, an armed bandit on either side, holding a revolver trained on each, trying to remember the last time he had fired a gun.

"*Put down your guns,*" he repeated, in a tone of voice which he hoped suggested that he would do something if they didn't.

Junius Fane gave a nod, though why he should be nodding to Jack, Jack had no idea, unless it was to give silent approval to Jack's bravery. In any case, the bandits—to Jack's amazement—dropped their weapons.

Jack breathed a sigh of relief, but at that moment, two strong arms were thrown about his neck. The arms of Ida Conquest.

"My hero!" she screamed, right in his ear. "You saved my life, my virtue—and my diamonds!"

The diamonds—if indeed they were diamonds—that she wore were sharply faceted, and dug little holes into Jack's neck and cheeks as she kissed him on the mouth.

"Ida," said Jack, trying to push her away without using one of the revolvers to do it. It was still necessary to hold the two thieves at bay. Their weapons lay nearby them on the ground.

Finally, someone else did something. Manfred Mixon, who had stood throughout the ordeal with comically quaking knees, grabbed up one of the guns, and pointed it at the head of one of the bandits. One of the children picked up the other surrendered weapon, and swung it round and round in a circle, and all the passengers began to laugh.

"Wonderful! But I guess that's enough," Junius Fane shouted, waving at someone inside the train. "Stop the cameras."

❀ ❀ ❀

"How was I to know?" Jack asked Susan. He'd *begged* five minutes' conversation with her. She'd assented with a dour nod.

"Mr. Fane made an announcement that there was to be a mock holdup."

"That must have been when I was changing my clothes. And it looked real. The bandits looked real. Their horses were real. Their guns were real."

"But, thank heaven, loaded with blanks," said Susan. "As it was, those blows you landed were real. Didn't you recognize Mr. Perks and Mr. Westermeade? You'd seen them often enough at the studio."

"They were wearing masks, remember?" Jack protested. "I was sure that the holdup was real. And I was certain that the bandit leader was going to shoot Ida in the back."

"You must have thought you were saving her life," said Susan thoughtfully. "You were very stupid, but very brave." She didn't speak in a tone of voice that Jack could construe as admiration.

The passengers had returned to the train, laughing and excited by the staged robbery and by Jack's unplanned part in the moving picture adventure. The two actors, with bruised jaws and loosened teeth, were being tended to in the conductor's little cabin at the rear of the train. Jack and Susan sat at the back of the second to last car and talked in whispers, uncomfortably aware that everyone else in the car was making no secret of their interest in their exchange.

After a few moments' pause, Jack tried to think of a way to bring the conversation around to the subject of their engagement. He admitted to himself that Susan probably didn't consider it still on. The same subject was evidently on Susan's mind, because she also didn't seem to know how to begin.

"Hosmer told me about your most recent pack of lies," she began.

"Every word was true," Jack protested.

"I'm to believe that you are, in reality, a Wall Street broker, and that you gave up your family, your home, your position, and your friends, in order to impersonate a penniless inventor so that you could be near me? This is what I'm to believe? And find endearing? And to look upon as proof of your affection for me? You ask me to think of months of daily deception, high-handedness, and prevarication as a sign of your regard and respect? I'm to thank you for allowing me to believe that Mr. Fane was paying me thirty-five dollars for every script I wrote, when in reality, it was *you* who was placing five-dollar bills in those envelopes? I'm to think it was merely a beau's clever stratagem to advance me five hundred dollars so that I would have the opportunity of lending it to you again?"

Jack was silent under this barrage. She wasn't firing blanks. Jack's only comfort was that this speech was obviously rehearsed, which meant that she'd been thinking about him. Not with any generosity, it was true, but at least he'd been on her mind.

"The only things I have to thank you for, Jack Beaumont, or whatever your name is—"

"My name really is Jack Beaumont, I promise."

She ignored the interruption. "—the only things I have to thank you for are severe humiliation, a broken leg, and the loss of my career on the stage."

"Are you going to marry Hosmer?" Jack asked suddenly.

Susan stared at him. "Weren't you listening to me?"

"Of course. But are you going to marry Hosmer? I saw him showing you a ring."

Susan spoke very deliberately. Outside, the sun spilled across fields of spring wheat. "Whether I marry, when I marry, and whom I marry are none of your business."

"But it is my business," Jack protested, "because you said you'd marry me."

Susan shook her head in apparent disbelief. "I agreed to come in here to talk to you for the sole reason that I intend for this to be the last time that I ever speak to you in this life. If there is a heaven, if there is a hell, if there is something in between, and we, by chance, meet in any of those places, you're welcome to renew your suit. But not here, in New York, or Kansas, and particularly not in California. Let me try to put this simply, Mr. Beaumont—I never want to speak to you again. I would also like never to see you again, hear of you again or see your name in print except perhaps with a black border around it. Also, since you're evidently such a rich financier, I'd like my five hundred dollars back."

"It's not your five hundred dollars," said Jack. "*I* gave it to you in the first place."

"Jay Austin gave it to me," returned Susan coldly. "And as Jay Austin doesn't exist and apparently never did exist, the money is very much mine. So I want it back."

❋ ❋ ❋

Susan didn't believe Jack when he told her that he'd been fired and disinherited, and that what remained of that five hundred dollars was his only means in the world. Why should she believe anything he said? When he claimed that his plans for the camera improvement had been stolen, she wanted to know if the lies would *ever* stop. She went back into the rear car, and warned him that if he tried to talk to her again, she'd throw Tripod in his direction.

The train twisted through the mountains of Colorado, where the night was as black as the occasional tunnel. Jack stared morosely out of the window at nothing and was positively rude to the two forward young women who came to the rear of the car to praise with giggles his useless bravery against the moving-picture thieves.

What was he to do now? Here he was, on a train headed for Los Angeles, a place where he knew no one, a place where he had no hope of finding a job, a place he knew nothing whatever about except that oranges grew there and the sun set rather than rose over the ocean. Susan Bright, whom he loved, was no more than twenty feet away from him, but he had no more hope of obtaining her hand than he had of stepping outside, picking up the train, and turning it around heading back east.

"Pretty bleak," he said aloud to himself.

"I beg your pardon?" said a voice at his side.

He turned, and saw Hosmer Collamore smiling down at him. "May I sit?" the cameraman asked.

Jack nodded. Already, at the other end of the car, the porter was making up berths. It was past nine o'clock. Jack hadn't eaten anything all day.

"I meant to visit you earlier," said Hosmer, "but what with one thing and another…"

"Sorry I spoiled your scenes," Jack apologized. "When I didn't see you in the crowd outside, I should have put two and two together and figured that you were inside filming the whole thing."

"Mr. Fane thought we might as well use the trip for profit, and get some footage on the way out. No particular story yet, but there's always room for a train robbery somewhere. And I've been hopping out at every stop, filming the little towns and some of the countryside. Come in handy and save us some time, expense, and travel someday. Anyway, I don't think you spoiled it. We can always write you in as a character, and then you get killed in the next scene—we'll try to find somebody as tall as you to act as double—and Ida can weep bitter tears. Ida has it in her contract that she gets to weep in every picture."

"How are Mr. Perks and Mr. Westermeade?" Jack asked, a little uncomfortably.

"Bearing up. But I wouldn't advise you to visit 'em just now. Wait till the swelling goes down, then buy 'em a box of cigars. Then it'll be right as roses again. Except it doesn't really matter, since we won't ever be seeing you again once we get to California."

Jack looked at Hosmer sharply. "Who's 'we'? What are you saying?"

"Why are you on this train?" Hosmer returned, as quickly.

"I came after Susan."

"Suss don't want you coming after her."

"She can speak for herself."

"Yes, she can," agreed Hosmer. "But so can her husband."

CHAPTER TWENTY-THREE

"HER HUSBAND!"

"We're engaged," said Hosmer complacently. "And when I am her husband, I will have every right to speak for Suss. And right now, as the man to whom she has given her consent, I think I can say I don't like it very much that you came all the way across the country in pursuit of her when it is pretty clear that she doesn't want to be pursued by you. We don't need you running about, making trouble for us. And if you still don't believe it, ask Suss."

"I like that idea," said Jack, getting up instantly, and stretching one long leg over Hosmer's in order to get to the aisle.

"Oh, no," said Hosmer, "ask her tomorrow, when we get into Los Angeles."

"I'll ask her now."

"Porter's already made up the berths, and Suss is lying there in a cotton nightdress and sweet repose, dreaming of me and our wedding night. Ask her tomorrow at the station, and then you may take leave of her and me forever. I was pleased and proud to be your friend on West Sixtieth Street, Jack Beaumont, but it's time for you to move along, and you know it as well as I know it, 'cause one and two make three, three's a crowd, and two can live as cheap as one. So if I were you, I'd dig in my pocket at the station tomorrow, and pull out the money needed for a ticket, and I'd hop on the next train back to New York, 'cause there's nothing for you in California but an aching heart and a burning head."

With that advice, Hosmer Collamore got up and returned to the other car, leaving Jack Beaumont sitting all alone, his head throbbing.

❁ ❁ ❁

The train reached Los Angeles near the end of the following day. The trip across the country had taken three nights and three days. Bedraggled, weary from too little sleep, soot-begrimed and dusty, frayed and short-tempered, the two dozen members of Mr. Fane's organization who had elected to make the move from one side of the continent to the other, staggered off the stuffy railway car into the warm California sunshine.

"It smells the way heaven is gonna smell," said Miss Songar, who had spent the tedious hours reading a testament handed to her in St. Louis by a member of the Salvation Army. The scent of orange blossoms overcame even the machinery stench of a railway station. Massive mounds of red and yellow flowers boiled out of tubs at the doors of the station.

"Makes me feel even grubbier than I did," complained Ida Conquest. "Just look at my feathers."

Jack slipped out with the passengers in the other car, and rushed forward in hope of helping Susan with her bags. Susan had prepared for this contingency and taken Tripod off his leash. The dog leapt at Jack. Jack had also come prepared, and had in his hand another biscuit soaked in the sleeping draught he'd obtained from the St. Louis veterinarian. Too smart to be tricked more than once, Tripod jumped past the biscuit, worked his wagging head up under the cuff of Jack's right trouser leg, and sank his teeth into Jack's ankle.

Jack yelled in pain. Susan slowly came forward, and disengaged her pet. "Tripod speaks for me, Mr. Beaumont," Susan said in a wintry voice. "California, I'm told, has many felicities—its climate, its natural scenery, its healthful air—but it will always be dear to me as the place where I managed to rid myself of you."

Jack bent down and ruefully examined the bloody marks of Tripod's teeth. "Are you really engaged to Hosmer?"

Susan smiled a grim smile. "I am," she said. "I most definitely am."

❀ ❀ ❀

The Cosmic Film Company was booked for the night in a hotel on South Orange Street near the train station. In the morning, they would travel out to the quiet suburb of Hollywood. Jack discovered this from speaking quietly to Miss Nethersole, who had conceived a *tendre* for Jack, and now thought she might have a chance with him if Susan Bright was out of the way.

In a separate taxi Jack followed the company to the hotel and hovered about the entrance till everyone from Cosmic had been inside for a quarter of an hour. Then he went in, approached the desk, glanced at the register, and saw that Susan was in room 506.

"Do you have something on the fifth floor?" Jack asked. The desk clerk looked at Jack suspiciously and shook his head no.

"The fourth floor then?"

Again the clerk shook his head.

"Is room 606 available?" asked Jack, with a sudden thought.

The clerk hesitated. Jack pushed a dollar bill across the desk.

"Yes sir," said the clerk.

Jack could see no tactical advantage in being in the room directly over Susan's, but he had a sentimental memory of West Sixtieth Street, where Susan's bedroom had been directly over his. Perhaps, he thought with the illogic of a desperate man, she would discover that he had asked particularly for this room, would make that connection herself, would be overcome by her old love for Jack, renounce Hosmer forever, and throw her arms around Jack in the hotel elevator. Jack realized his hope was improbable, but not as improbable as the scenarios Susan wrote for Junius Fane.

Also improbably, Jack was not wholly convinced that Susan was engaged to Hosmer. His only evidence was Hosmer's assertion, Susan's confirmation, and the ring that Susan was now wearing on the fourth finger of her left hand. To Jack, these things did not constitute *total* proof.

At eight o'clock, Jack stood at his window and was astonished by the sunset. He leaned out of the window to gaze over the flatness of Los Angeles, and discovered that a dozen or so other hotel guests were also leaning out of their windows—including, directly below him, Susan Bright. He looked straight down at the top of her head. Apparently sensing his gaze, she craned her head upward. Jack smiled down at her.

"Just as it was in New York," he called down the few feet separating them. "Except that now I'm on top of you."

Susan grimaced, and wordlessly pulled her head inside. A moment later, her window slammed shut in its sash.

At dinner that evening, the Cosmic Film Company took over a private room off the main hotel dining room. For another dollar's bribe, Jack secured a table just beside the curtain that separated the two dining rooms. By moving his table a few feet, sitting sideways in his chair, and holding back the edge of the curtain with his foot, Jack was able to hear all and see a little of what was going on inside.

After dessert had been served, Junius Fane stood and made a speech to the company.

"Ladies and gentlemen, tomorrow we will take another train to our new home in Hollywood. A very small, very quiet town, that will not be small and quiet for long. Four years ago, our friendly competitor, the Centaur Company of New Jersey, moved out here to escape the ravages of the Motion Picture Patents Company—that unscrupulous combine that has repeatedly attempted to strangle our livelihoods in total contempt of the Constitution of the United States and the beliefs which we all hold dear, that American men and women were born to compete fairly, and get rich off the sweat of their own brows, and not the brows of others." Fane, who tended to get hot when he talked of the Patents Trust, paused a moment to recover himself and regain the track of his remarks. "Since the arrival of the Centaur Company, others have followed, and I predict that before long, Hollywood will be a more glamorous name than Fort Lee. We will be happy here. Here we, and our children, and our children's children shall be blessed, and we shall prosper. When God made the earth, he finished his good work, and then tilted the planet a little, so that all the greatest of his splendors spilled down into California. In New York a millionaire's ransom would not pay for the flowers that grow in ditches here. J. P. Morgan has not such a breakfast table as we may have here simply by walking on to the street and plucking oranges off the trees and lemons from the vines. I'm told that every house comes with an avocado patch, so that there will be no danger of starving or freezing to death."

The members of the company glanced at one another. *Any* talk of freezing or starving was not an encouraging augury of their future success.

Fane went on: "We will be able to shoot entirely out of doors, three hundred days of the year. Clouds, I'm told, are allowed only on the weekend, for the better promotion of the moving-picture industry. For exteriors, there are city parks in abundance, and bucolia in the form of farms. We have beaches and the sea, we have mountains and snow, we have desert and torrential rivers. And, on top of all this, the Mexican border is only a few hours away, in case the Patents Trust send out any of their hooligans. Ladies and gentlemen," the director concluded expansively, "we have fallen into a soft crib."

Jack paid little attention to Fane's speech. He was much more interested in the activities of Susan and Hosmer, who were seated at a table in the corner of the room with Miss Nethersole and Mr. Perks—one of the gentlemen whose teeth Jack had loosened by the side of the railroad track. Several times Susan had inclined her head in Hosmer's direction, and had spoken directly into his ear. Jack's blood boiled up into his face.

As the company party broke up, Jack hurried away to the smoking room and sent an anonymous message to Hosmer that a gentleman wished to speak to him on a matter of some urgency. As he waited for the cameraman's appearance, Jack watched a game of billiards in progress, imagining a Méliès transformation of every billiard ball into Hosmer Collamore's head.

❀ ❀ ❀

"Just as I thought," Hosmer said, with a smug smile. "I knew it was going to be you—I don't know anybody else in Los Angeles. I thought you were going to turn right around and go back to New York. But here you are, still bothering me and Suss."

"I have to ask you a question," said Jack.

"It's not polite to invite a gentleman into a gentlemen's smoking room without also inviting him to partake of spirits and tobacco," said Hosmer. "And as you are the politest fellow I know—when you aren't knocking bandits on the chin—I'll have a glass of brandy and a thirty-five-cent Havana."

Jack went to the bar and brought back two glasses of brandy and a twenty-five-cent cigar for Hosmer.

"I have just one question for you," Jack repeated.

"'Fire when ready,' as the conspirator said to the executioner, who turned out to be his brother."

"Are you really engaged to Susan?"

Hosmer grinned. "Suss is beside herself, contemplating our conjugal felicity. As am I."

Jack swallowed off his brandy, got up, went to the bar to get another, bought the bottle while he was at it, came back, sat down, poured a glassful, drank it, poured another glassful, refilled Hosmer's glass, and said, "I think you're just saying this because Susan asked you to because she knew it would upset me. Hosmer, you can now tell me the truth."

"I have told you the truth, and so has Suss. Who will you believe? Will you believe the preacher who marries us? Will you believe the clerk at the honeymoon hotel who watches me sign in as Mr. and Mrs. Hosmer T. Collamore? Will you believe five hundred angels blowing on trumpets and singing, 'Love, love, love'? Jealousy has blinded your eyes and closed your ears and put a torch to your mind— that's what jealousy has done to you, my friend. I would suggest that you go east again, forget Suss, and marry some real young lady in high society—one who doesn't really care what you tell her your name is."

Jack filled his glass again. Hosmer held his out, but Jack ignored the gesture. He put the bottle down on the opposite side of the chair.

"I'll tell you what," said Hosmer. "You can go with me to city hall tomorrow and watch me apply for a license to be married. It's Suss who is pressing for this wedding, by the way," he added with a leer that made Jack want to smash some heavy object against his yellow teeth. "In fact, she can't wait, and I'm not sure that we will wait."

"What does *that* mean?" Jack demanded.

"Means she's asked me to her room. Means she wants to plan the honeymoon. You know what I mean, don't you? Plan it out. Set the details. *Rehearse.*"

"Get out," said Jack quietly, "before I push that empty glass down your throat."

Smiling, Hosmer rose and sauntered out of the gentlemen's smoking room, leaving Jack alone with his bottle of brandy and the gentlemen playing billiards.

❀ ❀ ❀

Jack returned to his room with the bottle. He sat down at the window with his glass and stared out at the multitudinous stars of the sky and the lights of Los Angeles, which were few and far between. The air of the sprawling city was fragrant and sweet; Jack's heart was hard and black. He thought of throwing himself out the window just for the satisfaction of knowing that Susan and Hosmer would see him on his way to his death. *That* would spoil their little tryst. He would even leave a note, blaming Susan for everything. *Then* she'd regret terminating the engagement. But what if, as he'd suggested to Hosmer, the whole thing *were* a lie just invented by the two of them to irritate him? The engagement to be married, the illicit meeting in Susan's room? Then suicide was probably not a good idea.

Jack wished he could see through the floor with Roentgen rays, but no machine was at hand to produce them. The thought, however, gave him another idea—simpler and not very scientific, perhaps, but...

He taped his shaving mirror to the handle of his umbrella. He had wondered why he had bothered to bring an umbrella all the way across the continent, since he had been told it never rained in California. Now it seemed like a most provident object to have picked. He leaned out of his window and lowered the umbrella, holding on to its tip so that he might catch a reflected glimpse of the interior of room 506. This operation took a while, for Jack had finished off a bottle and a half of brandy, the mirror was small, and it was difficult to maneuver an umbrella just by its metal tip. Fortunately Susan's curtains had not been drawn and there was a light on in the room. Still, the only thing Jack could see was that the pattern of her carpet was the same as his.

Jack pushed aside the empty bottle of brandy and climbed halfway out the window, straddling the sill and holding on to the frame with the calves of his legs. This allowed him to position the umbrella at a different angle, and he could see more clearly into the room.

He wished he hadn't. For what he saw was two piles of clothing on the floor—a man's and a woman's.

Desperately, he leaned even farther out, to see if he could improve the angle of the shaving mirror. The tiny reflecting surface suddenly swung into a different position, and Jack could see the bed. And in that bed, locked together in an embrace between the covers, were a man and a woman.

Just then the metal umbrella tip slipped between Jack's sweating fingers and plummeted downward toward the sidewalk below. Jack made an instinctive, ineffectual lunge for it—and lost his grip on the ledge.

Jack thought he was going to die, smashed on the sidewalk into more pieces than his shaving mirror. In his fall he wouldn't even have the comfort of knowing he had left a note blaming Susan for everything. A pointless death, that did nobody any good.

But he didn't die. He didn't even fall.

Two strong hands had reached through the window, grabbed him, and pulled him inside.

"Thank you," Jack began, trying to shake his rescuer's hand even before he knew his identity. His rescuer, however, wanted no thanks. It was a policeman.

"You're under arrest for Peeping Tomism."

CHAPTER TWENTY-FOUR

THICK VINES OF climbing roses intertwined all over the somber red-stone facade of the Los Angeles city jail. This peculiar resemblance to a bower, however, didn't make it any pleasanter for Jack to be dragged there on his first night in California, facing a charge of Peeping Tomism. He was booked by a weary sergeant who stated merely that he had seen Jack's type before and would doubtless see Jack's type again. He was thrown into a large cell with half a dozen men drunker than he.

The next morning he discovered that charges against him had been dropped. Who had spoken in his behalf he could not discover. He was free to go, and the sergeant suggested that he get out of the place before someone else came forward with a complaint against him.

Jack walked out of the police station with the intention of taking a taxi back to the hotel. He had hailed a cab, but before getting in, Jack reached into his pocket and to his horror discovered that the bills that had been in his pocket the night before—all his money in the world, except for seventy-eight cents in change—was gone. He waved the taxi on and frantically tore at his pockets, turning them inside out. He took off his jacket and searched it minutely. He patted his body to see if he could find the thick wad of bills that he already knew he was not going to find.

Obviously, he'd been robbed the night before. A cell mate, taking advantage of his boozy sleep, had quietly rifled his pockets and taken away every dollar, leaving him only some change.

He went back into the police station and politely explained to the sergeant that he'd been robbed of over three hundred and seventy-five dollars. The sergeant told him pointedly that there were statutes against lying to officers of the law, and that he had best take heed of them.

"There were thieves in that cell last night."

"And Peeping Toms, too," said the sergeant. "But the thieves is going to jail, and the Peeping Tom has had the good luck to go free."

Jack walked back to the hotel, hesitated a moment at the entrance, and then entered with as much dignity as he could muster. The desk clerk eyed him balefully, with a glance that seemed to say, *Now I know why you were so particular as to your room location.*

Jack approached the clerk and asked, "Has the Cosmic Film Company checked out yet?"

"*You* should take a bath," said the clerk, sniffing the air. "That's what *you* should do instead of asking questions about things that don't concern you." Jack was surprised at the clerk's rudeness. "The management would like to ask you to vacate your room as quickly as possible," the clerk continued. "I don't believe I need to tell you why."

How he was going to pay for the room he had no idea, but he put that thought out of his mind. "I'll take the bath first," said Jack.

It was not easy to wash away the stink of the alcohol and the jail and his misery, but Jack scrubbed. And when he was finished scrubbing, he applied to his hair a packet of yellow dye he had purchased from the barber in St. Louis.

He went back to his room and put on his best suit of clothes. Over that he put on the checked suit of the traveling salesman and stuffed his pockets with underwear and socks. Walking out of the room, he abandoned everything he could not carry out on his person.

He went down in the elevator with the plug hat over his head, smoking a cheap cigar. Hidden behind a fake mustache, and swathed in a halo of foul blue smoke, Jack Beaumont sauntered out of the hotel without paying his bill. On the street he asked the first indigent-looking man he saw for the address and direction of the nearest pawnshop. It was a half a mile away. There he pawned the checked suit, the plug hat, and three pairs of gold cuff links. He came away with eight dollars and seventy-five cents. A Chinese prostitute, who had ignored Jack on his entering the shop, pulled on his arm as he left it. "Two bittee lookee, four bittee feelie, six bittee, doee," she whispered. Her hair was as black and as lustrous as Susan's, but Jack said, "I've a train to catch," and pressed on.

❀ ❀ ❀

The train ride from Los Angeles west to the sleepy community of Hollywood was quite different from the trip from New York to Los Angeles. The car was more like a trolley than a real train—and the landscape was totally different from anything he'd seen before. The train passed through hundreds of acres of fruit groves—oranges and lemons, mostly—and across flat barren fields where tall oil derricks pumped petroleum out of the earth with stately motions. The locomotive and half a dozen cars passed small ranches with cattle and goats, and—to Jack's astonishment—one farm devoted entirely to the raising of ostriches. For the feathers, he thought, remembering Ida Conquest's wardrobe.

Jack leaned far out of the window, with the wind (and the locomotive ashes) in his face, in hopes of recovering from the effects of the alcohol he'd consumed the night before. He bought three bottles of Moxie from a little boy who marched up and down the aisle of the car.

Half an hour later, the train arrived in Hollywood, a quiet town with street after street of small comfortable homes and brown empty hills. If it hadn't been for the strange and rampant vegetation, Jack would have thought he was in some bedroom suburb of New York. It wasn't easy to believe Junius Fane's declaration that this town would rival and surpass Fort Lee as the center of the moving-picture industry in America. Hollywood, California didn't look as if it was prepared to take on much more than a busload of Elks on holiday. But then, considering the notice that Jack saw in the train station with the information on it that alcoholic beverages were not for sale anywhere within the city limits, Jack thought that the Elks might just as well stay away—and the moving-picture industry, too.

❀ ❀ ❀

Leaving the station, he walked a few blocks north till he came to a wide, divided, dusty, hot thoroughfare. It was called Santa Monica Boulevard, and he picked out a bench that was slightly away from the traffic. He sat down and tried to figure out what to do next. What had happened to him and to his life, he wondered? A stupidly normal childhood in stupid Elmira. A pointless education at Yale where he'd sung in a club and learned to drink and figured out how to pass examinations with a minimum of preparation and had memorized scurrilous lyrics to every song Stephen Foster ever wrote. A dull apprenticeship in the offices of Beaumont, Beaumont, and Beaumont, where almost despite himself he'd learned what he needed to know to carry out the family business when the time came for him to take it over. An essentially dull life, mapped out in the old-fashioned Beaumont way from Beaumont cradle to Beaumont grave. But down the line, in his twenty-seventh year, something had very definitely changed, and the catalyst for that change was a fledgling actress named Susan Bright. As soon as he saw her, things began to happen to him of a sort that had never happened to him before. He ran into bomb-hurling anarchists on the street, he took up false identities, he saved night watchmen from being burned alive, he interfered in armed train robberies, he was arrested for Peeping Tomism—and now here he was, sitting on a green bench in the hot California sun, stuporously staring at a noisy traffic of automobiles and trucks and taxis and trolleys, with no place to lay his head this night.

Behind him, the barren hills north of Hollywood rose forlornly against the pale blue sky. The air was so clear here it was impossible to tell how distant they were. This was a great change from the smoky, soot-filled air of New York. He walked up toward those hills with seven dollars and some change in his pocket. Maybe he could take lodging in a cheap hotel for three or four nights, or perhaps find a cheap rooming house for a week. Out of sight of Santa Monica Boulevard, the streets were completely residential in character. He marched up to the first house he saw and paused a moment before knocking.

A sign beside the door read:

ROOMS FOR RENT
NO JEWS
NO ACTORS
AND
NO DOGS

Being none of these things, he knocked. A thin, sour-faced old woman came to the door. She looked as if she never spent a moment of her life in the California sun. Her face was like library paste.

"Have you a room to rent?"

"Are you a movie?" she demanded suspiciously.

"I beg your pardon?"

"You know what I mean. Do you work in the moving pictures?"

"No," Jack answered truthfully.

"Don't believe you," snapped the old woman. "You have the face of a liar. Bet you drink, too."

"When I can get it," said Jack.

"Won't find lodging around here, then. Don't want movies in decent people's homes, don't want drinkers, don't want people that drive auto-cars twenty miles an hour up and down the streets running down the sober and religious, that's what we don't want, and that's what you are—I can read it in your face like it was written there in your suffering mother's blood—and you won't live *here*."

With that, she slammed the door in Jack's face.

It wasn't the only such greeting he got. At a dozen other doors he was turned away with a curt, "We don't rent," or with a more direct, "We don't rent to the likes of you." The splendor of the sky and the beauty of the flowers were a mockery. Jack had never felt as stranded as he felt this first afternoon in his new home of Hollywood. The westering sun was hot, his head buzzed and throbbed, the Moxie that he'd guzzled on the train was building up uncomfortably in the lower portion of his body, he was stared at by everyone he passed, he was close to penniless, and on top of everything Susan Bright was engaged to Hosmer Collamore and he had seen the two of them locked under the covers of the bed in room 506. The latter made Jack feel worst of all.

He had been steadily working his way up a steep hill, stopping at every house that had a sign advertising rooms for rent, and asking at the others at well. It would have done no good to tell potential landlords that he had nothing to do with the moving-picture industry, but was, in fact, a Wall Street broker. No one would have believed him. The fact that he was not even carrying a satchel was suspicious as well. Eventually he made a final fifty feet up a steep incline and found himself in a state of near total exhaustion, leaning against a post that bore a bell and a sign reading Sunset Boulevard.

It was a wide avenue, unpaved, full of dust, with automobiles parked here and there on either side, like black beetles sleeping in the gathering dusk. He remembered that the building Mr. Fane had found to be the new home of the Cosmic Film Company was on Sunset Boulevard, and he had even written down the number—8400—that Miss Nethersole had provided him. He turned left and walked toward that address.

The street was level, and that was a relief. Houses were sprinkled against the hill that rose immediately upward from the boulevard. The breeze from the ocean was at his back. There was no particular reason to go to the studio, for he had no hope of a pleasant reception there. But there would at least be familiar faces, and a familiar unfriendly face was preferable to a face that was hostile and strange.

The new Cosmic Film Company building looked like a livery stable—in fact, it had been one until two weeks before. It not only had the outward aspect of a home for horses, but it smelled as if a few animals might still be in residence. The wide doors had been built to accommodate a double carriage. They were open and Jack stepped inside.

Little had been done in the way of conversion for use by a film company. Jack saw a great number of doors, none of them labeled, along both sides of a long whitewashed corridor. He opened several of these cautiously, but the rooms were empty. He discovered that this line of what was apparently the Cosmic Film Company offices were no more than the former horse stalls, cleaned out and white-washed with doors set in where before there had been gates and windows. The place smelled of newly-sawed wood, varnish—and horses.

At the end of the corridor, Jack heard movement and muffled voices behind a door larger than the others. He decided not to investigate.

Instead, he opened one of the other doors, crept into the room, now occupied by a swivel chair, a desk, a filing cabinet, and a wastepaper basket made of twisted wire. He took off his jacket, removed his vest and folded it for a pillow. Then he put his jacket back on, lay down on the floor, and immediately fell asleep.

❀ ❀ ❀

He was awakened by the barking of a dog. Tripod. Then after that came Susan's voice. "Oh, my lord," she said, "what mischief are you doing here?"

"Sleeping," said Jack groggily. He sat up, or rather, tried to sit up. It is not a pleasant or easy thing to sleep on a hard floor all night. "I was in jail, and all my money was stolen—"

"Jail! I'm glad to hear it," said Susan. "Be quiet, Tripod. I'll let you loose in a minute."

"I couldn't afford a hotel, and nobody in this town will rent to the movies—"

"This is my office," Susan interrupted tartly. "And when I chose it, I wasn't told that it would also be used as a dormitory for ex-convicts." She threw herself into the swivel chair so hard that it rolled across the floor and very nearly took off Jack's right ear.

He jerked his head out of the way just in time.

Despite the discomfort of the floor, Jack felt a little better than he had the morning before. This was to be expected since he'd managed to sleep for fifteen hours, and he'd recovered from his overindulgence in brandy. He'd had nothing to eat, however, and his stomach growled warningly. "You don't happen to have a sandwich, do you?" asked Jack. "And please keep that dog away. I don't want another bloody ankle."

Junius Fane stuck his head in at the door. "Susan, I'd like you—" The director suddenly noticed Jack sitting on the floor, with his head against the wall and his feet beneath the desk. "Oh. You have me to thank for getting you out of jail," Mr. Fane said, apparently not thinking it odd that Jack Beaumont was sitting on the floor of Susan Bright's brand-new office at eight-thirty in the morning. "I persuaded the management not to press charges—I owed you a favor for what you did for me in New York. Susan, could you come with me, please? Oh, and you too, I suppose, Mr. Beaumont, as long as you're here. There's something you might like to see down at the end of the hallway."

After tying Tripod's leash to one of the handles of the filing cabinet, Susan followed Junius Fane out the door and down the corridor. She did not speak another word to Jack.

Staying out of range of Tripod's leash, Jack dragged himself upright with the assistance of Susan's desk and wandered out into the empty hallway in search of a bathroom. Finding one, he washed his face, shook out his shirt and trousers, and wiped off his dusty shoes. Then he went to find Junius Fane.

He found Fane, Susan, and several of the actors—including Ida Conquest and Miss Songar—in a darkened room at the end of the building. A projector had been set up and sun-drenched images were being shown on a canvas screen. The footage was of Jack, bravely interfering with a holdup.

In the darkness, he blushed, seeing himself so very tall and stern. He remembered what he had been thinking when these pictures were made—he had been contemplating putting bullets into the hearts of Mr. Perks and Mr. Westermeade, imagining them real bandits. How could he have been so foolish? Then on the screen Ida Conquest threw her arms around Jack, thanking him for saving her life, her virtue, and her diamonds. She even turned—just so—and the camera took full advantage of the grateful kiss she planted on Jack's mouth. Hosmer, filming from inside the train, had caught everything: Jack's stalwart behavior in the face of danger, his concern for the safety of the other passengers, his confusion at Ida's kiss, and finally, his unmistakable astonishment at discovering that the entire business had been only a setup.

The film then rolled on, showing shots of small towns and mountains and forests and deserts, taken from the windows of the train.

Junius Fane was not interested in this stock material. "Is Beaumont in here yet?" he called out, rising from his chair into the light from the projector.

"I'm here," said Jack.

"Splendid stuff," said Fane.

"Oh, yes," murmured others in the room, "perfectly splendid." Susan murmured other words.

"Have you ever acted before?" Fane asked. The projector whirred on. A snowcapped mountain peaked against Fane's neck.

"No," replied Jack, "never."

"Well, it doesn't matter," said Fane easily. "Because you are a natural actor. I just wish that I had known this in New York. A true, natural hero—perfect to play opposite Miss Conquest here. Ida, didn't you think that you and Mr. Beaumont looked splendid together? Didn't he show you off to advantage?"

"Sure as sugar," replied Ida.

"I'm going to hire you right now," said Fane, "on the spot. Somebody fetch our standard contract. Doesn't matter what it says, as long as there's a place for him and me to sign. We'll worry about the details later, but I want him on the Cosmic payroll before some other studio gets to him."

Jack stood speechless. Cactus whirred across Junius Fane's chest.

"Hosmer, stop the projector and run it back so that we can watch Beaumont's scene again. Susan, you pay particular attention, because I want you to concoct a script around this footage. Introduce Jack's character as the hero. He's in love with Ida, but too shy to tell her so. He follows her out west. He makes an advance. He is rebuffed in the dining car. Bandits attack the train. Ida's life is threatened. Her virtue is in danger. Jack saves her life and her virtue—"

"And her diamonds—" Ida prompted.

"And then let him save her life again. No, wait, change that. She should save *his* life. That's it. She has to make a choice between her virtue and her diamonds or Jack's life."

"I know which I'd choose," Susan muttered darkly. "In a minute."

"She chooses to save Jack's life, of course," said Fane. "And that proves she loves him. Let's have a scene at the beach, too. Maybe she chooses between her diamonds and saving Jack from being eaten by sharks. I'm sure you can come up with the details. And keep the titles down, Susan. With Jack and Ida up on the screen, we're not going to need words to tell the audience what is happening between them."

"Does Mr. Beaumont die at the end?" Susan asked.

"Certainly not. This is a moving picture. We will leave unhappy endings to the stage, Miss Bright. And to bad novels, which is where they belong."

CHAPTER TWENTY-FIVE

SOMEONE FOUND A blank contract, and Junius Fane pushed Jack into the nearest office to have him sign. "Have you a pen?" Fane asked.

"No," replied Jack.

"Susan, please get Mr. Beaumont something to sign his name with."

Susan wouldn't do it. "Junius," she protested, "I am sure you know the story of how this man tricked me."

Jack, who had been reading the contract, glanced up and smiled a little smile of apology at Susan Bright.

"Oh, of course. Everyone in the company knows," returned Fane easily, insensitive to whatever additional pain this might afford Susan. He rummaged in a box of supplies and came up with a fountain pen for Jack.

"Well, then, do you really want to hire a man who is an inveterate liar? A man who makes up wild tales about anything? And everything?"

Jack blushed, but he did not look up from the contract.

"All actors are liars, Susan," replied Junius Fane easily. "And the better the liar, the better the actor. Jack—may I call you Jack?" Jack nodded with a polite smile of acquiescence, then returned to the contract. Mr. Fane went on: "Jack showed a natural talent before the camera, and I am convinced that he will—with his disregard for danger and his own physical well-being— be a distinct asset to our little acting company. I was at a bit of a loss what to do when Mr. Fitcher decided to remain in New York with his parents. I had no one of the proper height to play against Ida. Ida looks best against someone who is quite tall, and as you see, Mr. Beaumont is exactly the right height. Besides, I'm not hiring Mr. Beaumont simply because of his splendid performance before the camera and his height. I'm also hiring him because of his mechanical abilities. It's not as easy to get things done in California, I'm told, as it is in New York. I'll feel safer having Mr. Beaumont around if things go wrong with the cameras or any other mechanical equipment."

"But he's a stockbroker! He's not a professional mechanic, and he never was! He lied about that too!"

"That's as it may be, Susan, but then all I can say is that Mr. Beaumont is the best damned amateur mechanic I've ever come across." Then turning to Jack, he said, "It's time to sign the contract."

"I've inked in a few changes," said Jack, handing the contract to Fane, who took it and looked it over.

"I should argue about these alterations," the director said, "but I know that you are a man of independent means, and I suppose that if I do not agree to your stipulations, you will simply walk out the door. I don't want to lose you, so I will sign. Mr. Beaumont, you're an extortioner."

With a nod to Jack, Fane signed the contract and blotted the signatures, then folded the document and put it into his pocket. Then, just before leaving, he said, "Susan, look for a place for Jack to live, would you?"

When he was gone, Jack smiled at Susan. Susan stared back at him with enraged astonishment and blurted, "Tripod is exploring the hillside, but I wish he were here to tell you what I think of you. I refuse to have anything to do with you."

"You don't have to," Jack said smugly. "You're a writer. I'm an actor. You can sit inside this dark office all day and write, and I'll be outside under the splendid sun, smelling the splendid air, standing in front of the camera being taller than Ida."

"I won't work with this company while you're in it," Susan went on.

"I'm given to understand there are other moving-picture companies in Hollywood. Perhaps, after a while, you could find employment in one of them."

"That's what *you* should do," said Susan. "I had this job first. You don't need the money anyway. The only reason you're doing this is in order to annoy me."

"In the first place," said Jack, "I do need the work, if I'm to sleep with a roof over my head, fill my stomach with food, and pay back the five hundred dollars you demanded of me, though it was, of course, mine to begin with. In the second place, you should remember that it was I who obtained this work for you. And, in the third place, I know my presence is an annoyance to you, so I will endeavor to stay out of your way. I wish you all joy in your married life. Hosmer will make a wonderful husband and father. Your children are sure to win prizes for beauty and intelligence."

❊ ❊ ❊

Junius Fane had been apprised of the difficulty of obtaining lodging for "movies" in Hollywood, for the town had not yet become reconciled to having a sinful industry take root within its boundaries. So, employing a sympathetic agent, Fane had rented a row of new, cheaply constructed two-bedroom furnished bungalows on the southern edge of Hollywood in which to house his little company. The tiny yards in back of these houses were fenced, and beyond the fences were massive flat fields with stately pumping oil wells and trolleys moving back and forth on their way to and from town. Bleaker dwellings could not be imagined; they were all of the same design and bore only rudimentary, machine-made ornamentation. The yards were dirt, and the sun shone blisteringly on the tile roofs. Nothing grew, nothing attracted the eye.

But there were no signs against Jews, actors, and dogs. The rent was, as Mr. Fane had predicted, less than they would have paid in New York. Fane himself took the last bungalow at the eastern end of the muddy street, and Susan shared the one next door with Ida Conquest. The third bungalow from the end had been taken by Hosmer Collamore and into this tiny house Jack was also billeted.

Hosmer welcomed Jack with a surprisingly cordial little speech: "I hope we're going to be friends again. I've got nothing against you—never had, never did, and never will—and if you're a man you'll say the same to me, Jack Beaumont."

Jack's first instinct was to pummel Hosmer Collamore into the middle of next week, but then it occurred to him that Hosmer and Susan were not married yet, and that perhaps he would be wise to bide his time in this matter. So, blushing at his duplicity, Jack shook Hosmer's hand, and said, "When's the wedding?"

"We're going to get settled first," said Hosmer, and then added with a wink, "but it doesn't matter so much to me anyway, for just look out that window there. There's no fence between the houses, and the nights are dark out here—if you get my meaning."

Jack got Hosmer's meaning, all right, and it made him want to hammer Hosmer straight through the calendar, not pausing even for holidays. But he judiciously did and said nothing.

Jack took the bedroom at the back of the house. For him, the job of unpacking was quickly accomplished; having abandoned his luggage at the hotel in Los Angeles, he had only to empty his pockets. The room's furnishings consisted of a bed, a dresser, a mirror on the wall above the dresser, and an ugly carpet on the floor. A window with a rickety sash looked out on to the oil fields, and another window with an equally rickety sash looked out at Susan and Ida's bungalow. Jack moved his bed—too short for him by at least six inches—so that he would be able to spy on the house next door.

He lay down to see what he could see from the bed's new position. It would be easier to see into Susan's windows at night when the lights were on. Tripod was in the yard, accustoming himself to the new difficulties of running about in dirt. This was proving to be much more difficult than moving on sidewalks; wooden legs sink in dirt.

Jack's luck was improving, he thought, if Tripod had been slowed down. As if sensing Jack's thought, the dog trotted across the yard, and growled beneath the window, where Jack sprawled on the mattress.

Jack lay back and thought about Susan. It was wounding that she had gone to bed with Hosmer Collamore. Perhaps she would have gone to bed with Jack if he had asked. Jack hadn't asked because he hadn't wanted to seem forward— and he hadn't wanted her to do something that might have been against her principles or inclination. Now he wished he had at least broached the subject.

Jack knew that other men, in his position, would have lost all respect for the woman, upon learning that she had gone to bed with another man—or even if she had gone to bed with themselves, for that matter. Most men wanted to marry virgins. Just as an experiment, Jack tried to lessen his regard for Susan. It didn't work. He still felt the same about her, even knowing that she had invited Hosmer to her room in the hotel. He knew that he would love her even if every night Hosmer walked across the yard, scraped his shoes on the doormat, and knocked discreetly at her back door, and she let him in. Jack wasn't sure why this didn't matter to him, but it didn't. All he wanted was Susan.

He wanted her here with him on this naked mattress. He wanted her head and her thick black hair pressing against his chest. He wanted to see her legs, and make sure that her injury was healed. He wanted to kiss her legs and apologize once more for having caused her so much pain and suffering. He tried to imagine her body and what it looked like beneath her clothes; he found he had no difficulty in doing so. He recalled the shape and the taste of her mouth. He—

He got up and pulled down the shades, and then he thought about Susan a while longer.

❊ ❊ ❊

A few hours later, after Jack had brushed off his suit and washed out his shirt and underwear, Susan Bright herself—in the flesh, and not just in Jack's febrile imagination—knocked at the door.

"Hosmer's not here," said Jack.

"I came to see you," said Susan.

"Please wipe your feet before you come inside. I wish there were some grass growing around here."

"Me too. I brought you something to read." She handed him a dozen typewritten pages.

"What is this?"

"It's the script for the picture you're to start shooting tomorrow. I just finished it. It's called *Plunder*, and the holdup is, of course, the climax. But I thought you might like to see what else happens to you."

In the sparsely furnished living room there was a low uncomfortable settee and two low uncomfortable chairs. Susan sat on the settee and Jack sat across from her and read through the scenario.

A few minutes later, he looked up. "This seems quite…thrilling," he said uncertainly.

"Mr. Fane is very pleased with it," said Susan complacently.

"In the first scene," said Jack, flipping the manuscript to the front, "I'm run down in the street by a motorcyclist."

"Mr. Westermeade, minus two teeth," said Susan. "I don't think he'll have much objection to that. Mr. Fane says that it can be filmed on Sunset Boulevard."

Jack turned a few pages of the script. "Here I'm nearly hit by a speedboat, and then I'm bound and gagged and thrown into a trunk, and the trunk is buried on the beach at low tide."

"Mr. Fane wanted a scene at the shore," said Susan with a hypocritical smile.

"Then here, at the end, after I've rescued Ida, the bandits capture me again, tie me up in cornstalks and leave me to be pecked to death by ostriches."

"Did you see the ostrich ranch the train from Los Angeles passed by?"

"Yes I did," said Jack, with annoyance. "I'm not so certain that I'm going to relish making this picture."

"Well, it does end happily with you married to Ida—if you consider that a happy ending. Of course, that part will be shot first, just in case something goes wrong in any of the thrilling scenes."

"I'm very much relieved to hear it. Did you enjoy yourself, thinking up this torture for me?"

"Immensely," said Susan. "And I have an idea for another script that I'm going to begin on tonight."

"Perhaps you should wait to see if I survive this one."

"In the next," said Susan, "I'm going to have you thrown off a cliff. You know, Junius pays extra for falls—ten cents a foot. I want you to earn as much money as possible, so that you can begin to pay me back the money you owe me."

"You realize, of course, that I don't actually owe you that money," said Jack stiffly. Susan was being unpleasant. He liked it better when she was running from him, and he was chasing after her. He didn't like it when she stopped, turned around, looked him in the eye, and began hurling darts. In the next day or so he was to stand in the middle of Sunset Boulevard and be run down by a motorcycle in order to appease Susan Bright's bloodthirsty temper. "For that five hundred dollars you got a full interest in my patent."

"What?" said Susan, with surprise.

Jack repeated himself. "I said, you got a full interest in my patent. You see, when Hosmer came to me with an offer to buy the rights to my invention for five hundred dollars, I knew that the offer was really coming from you."

"How? How did you know?"

"Because Hosmer wasn't the type to do me favors of any sort—and you were. I also knew that you had five hundred dollars in the bank. So I accepted the money and signed over the rights to Hosmer, knowing that he would, in turn, sign them over to you. And if I can ever find who stole the plans, I'll patent the thing, and in a few years you will probably find yourself very, very rich."

Susan blinked hard. "Someone stole those plans?"

"I've told you that several times, but you never believed me."

"Why didn't you tell me?" she exclaimed. "Let me understand this—for those five hundred dollars I gave to Hosmer to give to you, you turned over the entire income from that invention to Hosmer."

"Yes. And Hosmer turned it over to you."

Susan hesitated a moment, then went on, "And now someone has stolen the plans—have I got it right?"

"Yes."

She thought for a moment, then said decisively, "Then we have to get them back."

"*I* don't," said Jack. "Because even if I got them back, and went through the trouble and expense of having them patented, and then went to the expense of marketing the device—*you'd* get all the money. Which was a fine idea as long as you and I were getting married, but I have no inclination to go to such lengths in order to improve the financial condition of Mr. and Mrs. Hosmer T. Collamore."

Susan was still for a moment. Then she said suddenly, "Do you have any brandy in the house?"

"No," replied Jack. "Hollywood is a dry town. And I don't have any money to buy brandy with anyway."

Susan sat back and thought for a few minutes.

She's sharpening her darts, Jack thought.

"You signed over all of the proceeds of that camera invention to Hosmer, on my behalf..." said Susan.

"For the third or fourth time—yes."

"Hosmer signed over only half of them to me," said Susan. "He kept the other half for himself."

Jack's eyes went wide. "I'm not surprised to hear it. I also wouldn't be surprised to discover that he had stolen the plans himself. After all, he knew they existed, he knew where they were, *and* he knew that they could bring in a great deal of money."

"Could he just patent it in his own name like that?" asked Susan.

"Yes," said Jack. "All he'd have to do is erase my name from the drawings. And if he did patent it under his own name, then he would have stolen *all* of the profits, instead of just half of them. I intended for you to have all that money—however much it turned out to be."

"Thank you," said Susan simply. "That was very kind."

"I had money then. I could afford to be generous. Now I have nothing. If I were doing it now, I'd keep half of it for myself."

Susan got up and went to the window and looked out at the dusty vista. "I really do wish we had some brandy."

"This comes as a surprise to you?" asked Jack. Susan nodded. "You didn't suspect Hosmer of perfidy, as they say in the magazine serials?" Susan shook her head. "Are you still going to marry him?"

"Marry him?" repeated Susan, turning. "What on earth gave you the idea that I was going to marry Hosmer?"

"Well," said Jack, "for one thing, you told me you were. For another, Hosmer told me you were. And for a third thing, despite the fact that I was arrested for Peeping Tomism for my efforts, I did see you two in bed together."

Susan stared. "You think you saw me in bed with Hosmer Collamore?"

"Yes," said Jack, "and I don't mind telling you that I was pretty distressed by it, too. Even if you had called off our engagement. If you'd go to bed with Hosmer Collamore, why wouldn't you go to bed with *me*?"

"Well, for one thing, you never asked," said Susan. "But I would *never* go to bed with Hosmer Collamore."

"I *saw* you," Jack said, "with Hosmer Collamore, in bed, in room 506 of a hotel in downtown Los Angeles, California."

"You didn't see *me*," said Susan. "It must have been Ida. That was her room. I was across the hall in 505. Room 506 was mine originally, but Ida wanted to be able to see the sunset. Now that I think of it, what she really wanted was the connecting door to Junius's room. It wasn't Hosmer and me you saw, it must have been Junius and Ida."

"I just assumed—" Jack sat back in the uncomfortable chair. "But why did you tell me that you were going to marry Hosmer?" he asked after a moment. "If it wasn't true."

"You'd lied to me enough. I thought I'd give you a taste of your own medicine. Actually, I was surprised you believed it. I had every intention of forgiving you for your deception—once I'd gotten over my anger."

"Is that why you decided to come to California, to get over your anger?" he asked dryly.

Susan hesitated. "Yes, and also because Junius offered me a job. Remember, I didn't have any other way to support myself in New York. Also, I was using it for a test—if you came after me, then I'd know that your love was real."

"What if my injuries had prevented me?"

"Well...they didn't."

"Then why didn't you forgive me on the train?"

"Because you started making up more lies. First, that ridiculous disguise in St. Louis—I knew that was you the moment I walked in the door of the station." Jack blushed, and Susan confirmed, "It was *very* obvious. Then, when Tripod fell asleep in my arms, I realized that you had put some sort of sleeping potion in that biscuit you gave him. And then, when I finally sat down with you on the train, you began making up stories about all your money being gone."

"That wasn't a lie," Jack protested.

"It certainly sounded like one. I thought you were never going to tell me the truth. So I couldn't forgive you—not then."

"Do you forgive me now?"

She didn't reply. Outside the sun was setting. It was another spectacular display, though this time it was mostly purple and pink. The light shone becomingly on Susan's face.

"That ring Hosmer was showing you—" Jack began.

"He wanted to ask Ida to marry him," said Susan. "I told him it wasn't a very good idea, that Ida had her sights set on Junius." She held up a hand with Hosmer's ring on it. "So he lent it to me, to help deceive you."

"How much do you suppose it cost?" Jack asked. He got up and moved to the window. The tiles on the roof of her bungalow next door glimmered with the reflection of the sunset.

"I don't know. What difference does it make?"

"Because I'd like to buy it from Hosmer."

"Hosmer stole half your patent, and he probably stole the drawings, too." She took the ring off her finger and gave it to Jack. "He owes you at least this much, I should think."

"You're right," said Jack. He took the ring, took Susan's hand, and slipped it right back on.

He held Susan's hand. "Are you going to take it off?"

"No. Not this time."

CHAPTER TWENTY-SIX

THE MOON LIGHTED the oil fields. It shone and was reflected off the roofs of the little row of houses. Tripod, anxious and growling low, patrolled the yards and occasionally barked beneath Jack's window.

Jack and Susan lay together on the bare mattress. For a long time they were silent, and then they talked for a while, and then they were silent again.

When they did talk, they went over every moment they'd been apart. Jack's misery, Jack's desperation, Jack's fever to find Susan again, Jack's despair. Susan's anger, Susan's disappointment, Susan's fear that Jack would not come after her to California, Susan's doubts as to his trustworthiness.

She rubbed her head against his chest. "I never knew you had hair here," she said. "And so much of it, too. Tell me who you are, tell me where you came from, what you did before you knew me, tell me the lies you told me, and tell me what the truth really was."

"All right. I'll start at the beginning. I was born in Elmira, New York…"

He didn't get much further in his story. Half an hour later, he resumed, and Susan learned Jack's whole, true story.

"But why didn't you tell me all that from the beginning?"

"Because if I had, you would have thought I was just another rich young Wall Street broker, seeking a dalliance with a compliant actress. You wouldn't have had anything to do with me, would you?"

"No," Susan admitted, "I wouldn't have. That's exactly what I thought about Jay Austin."

"So I had to pretend to be an impecunious tinkerer. And in fact, that's what I became."

"And now you're an impecunious actor," said Susan. "You don't even have sheets for your bed."

"Well, we could—"

The noise of a door closing in another part of the bungalow startled Jack into silence. "Hosmer," he said. He reached to the floor for his watch and checked the time. "It's past eleven." Jack started to get out of the bed. "No time like the present. Let's confront him about the invention."

"Shhh," said Susan. "No. Not yet. He'd only deny it. I've got an idea. You and I pretend that nothing's changed. That we dislike and mistrust each other. I suspect that the reason Hosmer volunteered to share this bungalow with you is so that he can keep an eye on you. He was very particular to take this bungalow, next to mine, because I think he wanted to keep an eye on *me* as well. Well, let's let him keep an eye on us—and we'll keep an eye on him."

"I don't know if I can keep up a deception like that."

"If you could fool me for months, you can fool Hosmer Collamore for a few weeks. We'll find out what he's hiding and whether or not he stole your plans."

"But—"

"I don't mind your lying," said Susan, "as long as you're not lying to *me*."

Susan put on her clothes and Jack carefully lowered her out the rear window, taking care not to disturb or alert Hosmer, whom they heard moving about in his own room.

"Don't bark, Tripod. I'm all right," she cautioned in a low voice.

Jack leaned out the window. Susan stood on the dry earth, and they kissed.

"Get some sheets," she said, and then crept toward home.

❊ ❊ ❊

The next morning, Jack watched Susan and Ida climb into the back of Junius Fane's automobile for the trip to the northern side of Hollywood and the Cosmic Film Studio, as it was now officially called.

"Wish we could afford an automobile," said Hosmer, suddenly appearing beside Jack, and tucking his shirttail into his trousers. "I've got my eye on a Saxon 'Four'."

"Someday we will be able to afford one," said Jack, "if money falls down the chimney."

"Money doesn't fall down the chimney. Not in California—where there are no chimneys," Hosmer laughed.

"Perhaps I'd have money," said Jack, "if I hadn't signed away my interest in that invention. I hope Susan makes a fortune on it," he said blandly. He mentioned nothing of the plans having been stolen from his room; indeed, he tried to make it seem as if he had not noticed anything at all was amiss.

Hosmer cleared his throat. "Is it already being manufactured? Your invention, that is?"

"I don't know," returned Jack easily, as if it were a matter that no longer concerned him. "Susan has the plans. I suppose it's up to her to have the thing patented, produced, and sold. But if I were she, I'd do it as quickly as possible, because it's the sort of idea that any clever person with a little mechanical aptitude could come up with."

"Then you haven't asked Susan about it," said Hosmer carefully. "About her plans for the device."

"Susan won't speak to me," said Jack. "Not on that or any other subject. It's out of my hands. I'll tell you the truth, Hosmer: West Sixtieth Street is a bad dream to me, and I'd just as soon not be reminded of anything having to do with that place or with my time there. For better or worse, I'm no longer a broker *or* an inventor. I'm apparently an actor. And, speaking of that, it's time for you and me to get on up to the studio. After all, Mr. Westermeade has to run me down with his motorcycle this morning."

❀ ❀ ❀

Besides the offices of the staff, inside the Cosmic Film Studio were two enormous rooms for the use of the carpenters and mechanics, as well as the laboratories where the film was developed, cut, spliced together again, and reproduced as a print. As in New York, much of this work could have been done outside, but Fane still thought he saved money and maintained control by keeping everything under his own eye. On the hillside behind the studio the carpenters had already built half a dozen wooden platforms. Sheets of muslin had been spread over the top of these to filter the strong sunlight. The Cosmic Film Studio was about to swing into action once again.

Ida wore a wedding dress, and Jack was in tails. He was made up with white powder and lip rouge, and he felt exceptionally foolish, standing on a threadbare rug, on a wooden stage, with canvas walls meant to represent someone's front parlor in Connecticut. The California sun burned high overhead, and when he looked above and beyond the painted canvas he saw row on row of suburban homes, oil wells, groves of orange and lemon trees, and in the distance, the glistening Pacific Ocean.

He had only to mouth the words spoken to him by the preacher, and he had to kiss Ida. Susan watched from her station behind Fane's chair. The kiss was filmed three times, for Fane didn't think that Jack put enough feeling into it on the first two attempts. Jack closed his eyes and thought of the night before, and Susan. Then he was able to kiss Ida with enough fire.

Two more scenes were shot on the hillside stages that morning: a wedding dance in which Jack's height and innate clumsiness were exploited and a scene in a dry goods store with Jack purchasing the ingredients for a wedding cake. Manfred Mixon provided a few moments of characteristic comedy.

"You are doing splendidly," said Junius Fane to Jack as the company broke for lunch.

"The kiss was very fine," added Ida. "The third one, I mean."

"Yes it was very fine," said Fane. "I shall look forward to seeing it on celluloid. Colley," he said, turning to the cameraman, "see if we can't have this footage sometime this afternoon. Jack, don't eat too much now, we're going to have you dodging motorcycles, and you're going to want to be moving fairly quickly."

Susan had suggested to Jack that maybe Fane would let her tone down some of the wilder action that she had devised for Jack in the *Plunder* scenario, but Jack said that he thought it would be best to keep up the appearance of warfare between the two of them. Jack knew that every precaution was taken to ensure the safety of the actors in the moving pictures. "Not every precaution," Susan warned him. "Be very careful. I'd be extremely distressed to find myself a widow before we were even married."

So Jack didn't eat anything for lunch. At one o'clock, the company and the cameras moved to the other side of the studio and out on to Sunset Boulevard. One side of the street was blocked off and the automobile traffic, accustomed to such unannounced inconveniences, squeezed along the other side of the boulevard for an hour or so.

"It's simple," Fane told Jack. "Mr. Westermeade, the villain, is on a motorcycle. You've just been drugged with opium and you're trying to get to the doctor for an antidote. The doctor's office is across the street, but Mr. Westermeade is trying to make certain that you don't get there by running you down. And remember, as a result of the opium, you're reeling."

"Yes," said Jack, "I think I understand."

The cameras were loaded, Mr. Westermeade was set up on his motorcycle at the end of the blocked-off half of the street, and Jack was given the signal to begin the action.

Jack reeled out of the door of the studio—supposedly the livery stable where he'd been held hostage for twenty-four hours—and lurched into the street. Westermeade took off on his cycle and headed for Jack. Jack looked down the street, registered shock and dismay, and then stumbled to the other side before the motorcycle got anywhere near him.

"Not quite what we needed," said Fane. "Props! Put a splint on Jack's right leg. Underneath his trousers."

As props was occupied in this operation, Fane explained, "You've just been drugged *and* they've shot you in the leg. It's not a serious injury, and it will get better quickly, but for now it's going to make it more difficult for you to get across the street. Also, I'd like you to drink a couple of glasses of brandy. It will lend verisimilitude to your reeling."

The scene was shot again.

Jack once more reeled out of the livery stable/studio and into the street. He tried to reel as he would have if he had drunk six glasses of brandy instead of just two. The splint on his leg helped, for he tended to spin on it a little. Westermeade came very close to running him over this time. Jack jumped out of the way just in time, fell, got up, and raced forward to the other side of the street.

"Almost," judged the director. "That was almost it. Props! Two more glasses of brandy for Jack. And do we have a bucket for that cycle?"

Props looked around for the sidecar and attached it to the motorcycle.

"Good," said Fane. "Now, Mr. Perks will sit in the bucket—and give him a big stick. And we need a doll, have we got a doll somewhere?"

In another few minutes a stick, a doll, and Mr. Perks had been gathered together, and Fane came over to Jack and said, "We're changing it a little. You've had a double dose of drugs—and you might as well take another glass of brandy before we begin. Also, you've come across an abandoned child with the croup that you have to get to the doctor. Mr. Westermeade is going to come at you with the motorcycle, and Mr. Perks in the bucket has a large stick that he's going to try to knock you in the head with. We don't want to make this crossing the street to look too easy. How's that splint? Still in place?"

"Yes," murmured Jack, as he was handed the doll wrapped in a blanket. He exchanged a glance with Susan, who was standing beside the director.

"Right," Fane said to Susan, "remember that we have to account for that baby somewhere along the way."

"I'll make it one of Ida's cousins. She's supposed to be taking care of it," said Susan. "We can show it again in the kitchen scene that's to be shot tomorrow."

"Westermeade!" called Fane. "Are you ready?"

Westermeade had been driving the motorcycle up and down, practicing his maneuvers. This actor's disappointment at not yet having been able to run Jack down was manifest. Mr. Perks—the other gentleman whose teeth Jack had loosened—was vigorously practicing standing in the sidecar and swinging the yard-long piece of hard pine provided him by props.

Jack stood just inside the door of the studio, swilling down his sixth glass of brandy. They had all been generous glasses, and he now felt their effect on his head and on his balance. His left leg was stiff with the newly tightened splint, so that he now had an idea of what Susan had suffered with her broken leg. He was dirty and dusty from his two previous trips across the road. He stared down into the face of the doll he was holding in the blanket, and was distressed to see its waxen face melting in the heat.

"Are you all right?" asked Susan, coming in the door and leaning close to him and whispering. She'd already checked to make certain no one saw her.

He gave her a quick kiss. "Just remember, if anything happens to me, it's entirely your fault."

"Ready?" the director called from outside. Jack heard Westermeade's motorcycle revving impatiently farther up the street.

"Camera!" shouted Fane, and after counting to three, Jack pushed open the door, and hurtled once again out on to Sunset Boulevard.

The supernumeraries in the scene drew back in alarm, and pointed at him. Jack reeled into the street with the waxen infant, stared with horror at the oncoming motorcycle—stared in real horror, for it was almost upon him, and Perks was swinging mightily with his club.

Jack jumped forward, lost his balance, and spun crazily as the motorcycle whizzed by.

Jack stumbled, clutching the infant against his chest and dragging his splinted leg. He was halfway across the street.

The motorcycle screeched to a circling halt at the other end of the blocked-off passage and then headed back for him.

A truck and two automobiles passing on the open side of the boulevard slowed down to watch the progress of the filming. Jack pitched and weaved in the middle of the street. The curb and safety seemed far away.

The motorcycle bore down behind him again, and Perks again wildly swung the club. Jack jumped to avoid it, but not far enough and he caught the end of the club in the middle of his back.

It propelled him forward against the side of one of the passing automobiles. His foot hit the running board, and the waxen infant flew out of his arms into the lap of the lady passenger, who threw up her arms and screamed. The man behind the wheel, alarmed, dragged suddenly on the brakes.

Jack was thrown off the car, back into the street.

"Wonderful!" screamed Fane. "Keep going!"

The driver then took off as quickly as his machine would let him, and the woman stared stuporously at the melting baby in her arms.

Jack was sprawled in the dust as the motorcycle came at him again. He tried to get up and run, but the splint on his leg prevented his doing more than rolling out of the way. As he rolled in the direction of a second automobile, he lurched forward, grabbing hold of the bumper.

He was pulled out of the way of Westermeade's tires just in time. Perks, in trying to swipe at Jack once more with the stick, lost his balance and tumbled out of the sidecar headfirst on to the pavement. Westermeade, off balance with the sudden loss of weight, and looking behind him to see what happened, plunged into a knot of the supers, who scattered with screams that would never be heard in the completed print of the silent *Plunder*.

Jack let go the bumper of the car when he was past the blockade a hundred feet or so farther down the street. Releasing his grip, he rolled out of the way, gasping for his breath, and thinking that he had just made up for any terrible thing he had ever done to Susan Bright.

Junius Fane himself went over to help Jack up.

"That was it," said Fane. "That was it without a doubt. We're not going to have to do it again."

"Good," said Jack, looking down at his body. There was no blood that he could see, but his clothes were in tatters.

"Take the rest of the day off," said Fane. "And rest up. Tomorrow we'll be driving out to Santa Monica beach. You'll get knocked on the head and then tossed off the pier in the path of a speedboat. After that you'll be tied up, thrown in a trunk, and buried in the sand at low tide. And Friday morning we'll go out to the ostrich ranch. I know there's been some trouble between you and Susan, but you'll have to admit—that girl has one splendid imagination."

CHAPTER TWENTY-SEVEN

JACK NEARLY DROWNED in the water off the Santa Monica pier, while dozens of spectators from the adjacent roller-skating ballroom watched breathlessly for him to rise again after the speedboat flew over his head. He nearly suffocated in the trunk buried briefly in the sand a few hundred yards down the beach. Susan tried to show her indifference as to whether Jack lived or died by taking a few shots in a shooting gallery on the pier. The next day, he was nearly pecked to death by a flock of ostriches, while Susan and Ida nonchalantly shopped for plumes in the small shop attached to the ranch.

When *Plunder* was finished on Saturday, Fane examined all the footage of the fledgling actor and pronounced it very fine. Susan and Jack watched the reels, too—from opposite sides of the room. Susan made more than one disparaging comment on Jack's inability to register the proper range of emotions.

"But it's what I *want*," Fane argued. "I want a man stalwart in the face of every danger. A man who quails before no difficulty, a man for whom mortal danger is as common and as little a thing as...as breakfast."

Jack gingerly prodded the bruises on his torso, his extremities, and the back of his head. "Miss Bright evidently believes that a man should be like a woman, and reveal everything in a gush of emotion," said Jack in a bitter tone. "Miss Bright ought to learn that a man cannot always give himself away in that manner."

"Exactly," said Fane. "Susan, didn't you see how tender he was with Ida? How he kissed her at the wedding, and caressed her neck at the wedding dance? He registered his love for Ida in a perfectly manly way. Hosmer, thank you!"

A few minutes later, giving an arm to each, Fane took Jack and Susan down the hall to Susan's office. Tripod was standing on Susan's desk, and as if he had only been waiting for the chance, he took a flying leap at Jack's neck the minute the three of them stepped through the door. But dogs with three legs are not balanced, and Tripod's aim was off. He flew into Junius Fane's arms. "Write a part for a three-legged dog that leaps," Fane commanded Susan. Then he went on, "Next week we'll be shooting that Mixon farce you and he devised on the train out. It's a little thin, so what I'd like you to do is write in a little romance—"

"Mr. Beaumont and Ida?" Susan questioned. "Ida won't work with Manfred. Says it's beneath her dignity to appear in the same frame with a fat man."

"Not with Ida," Fane said thoughtfully, "with Miss Songar. Miss Songar is very short, and Jack is very tall. Miss Songar is Manfred's niece and heir to a fabulous fortune. She is very short and has a three-legged dog that leaps. This dog leaps upon command, does he not?"

"He'll leap at Mr. Beaumont with or without a command," said Susan.

"Good enough," said Fane. Turning to Jack, he explained, "This will give you some range as an actor.

We've tried you out in melodramatic danger, and now we'll stick you into a comedy and see if you come up breathing."

"I have no doubt," said Susan, "that Mr. Beaumont will prove himself to be as ridiculous as you may please."

"Yes," returned Fane blandly, "I have every confidence in my new discovery. So, Susan, today is Saturday, and I'm going into Los Angeles for a couple of days—business," he explained vaguely. "I'd like you to write the new scenes for the picture next week, and I'd like to see an outline for a three-reeler to be shot the following week."

"It's been written, Mr. Fane, for Miss Songar and Mr. Perks. *The Cameo.*"

"No," said Fane, "I'm giving that to an assistant. I want you to write something for Jack and Ida. More thrills." He thought for a moment. "Set it in a forest. We could go up into the mountains for a couple of days. Half the scenes interior—a prospector's cabin, a general store, the timber baron's palatial home, you know the sort of thing I mean— and the other half of the scenes exterior, mountain forests. Ida is the Timber Queen—not a bad title, either—who's had all her land stolen from her by the evil Timber Baron. She's only got five acres left, and they burn down. Write a forest fire, Miss Bright. I don't believe I've ever seen a forest fire in a moving picture. Jack here is a prospector, down on his luck, who discovers diamonds and gold on her five acres once the forest fire has cleared away the trees. They're set upon by a bandit when they go into town to sell the diamonds and gold. They're tied up and left to die. A group of wild Indians—there're a band of Indians here in Hollywood who rent out for ten dollars a day, fifteen of 'em—come up and start using Jack and Ida for target practice. Jack gets loose, somehow or other, kills all the Indians, and unmasks the bandit—who turns out to be the Timber Baron, and he's really Jack's father. Or uncle. Or something. The title will be *The Timber Queen.* There, Susan, I've practically done your work for you, so you might as well have the thing on my desk Monday morning."

"Yes, Junius."

"And if I leave you two alone together now, you won't claw one another, will you?"

"I have Tripod to protect me," said Susan, taking the dog from Fane.

"If that dog works out next week, write him into *The Timber Queen* as well. I like animals in moving pictures."

❧ ❧ ❧

That afternoon Jack and Susan returned to their neighboring bungalows by different routes, at different times. True to his word, Junius Fane drove off toward Los Angeles. A few minutes later, Jack, looking out of his window and hoping for a glimpse of Susan, saw Ida Conquest slip quietly out of the house, and tiptoe with ostentatious stealth across the yard and disappear around the corner.

Jack had little doubt that Junius Fane's snappy Speedking Sixty was waiting for her, out of sight of the Cosmic bungalows.

A few moments later, there was a knock on the door of Jack's room. "Jack?" Hosmer called, "are you in there?"

Jack opened the door. There stood Hosmer, hat and satchel in hand. "I've got a cousin in Pasadena. Pretty thing. Thought I'd visit her. Be back tomorrow night. Can you get along?"

"I think so," Jack said with a grin.

Jack listened for the front door to close. Then he went to the living room and peered out the window and watched until Hosmer was out of sight. Jack waited five minutes to make sure neither he nor Ida returned, then he crept out of the house, and whipped across the yard to Susan's back door.

Tripod's infuriated barking announced Jack's presence.

Susan immediately opened the door and pulled him into the kitchen. She threw Tripod into the dining room and put a chair against the door. "Ida's gone. Till tomorrow night," she said.

"So's Hosmer. I think Ida went off with Fane."

"I'm sure she did," said Susan. "And I think Hosmer probably went off to do something about the stolen patent."

"He said he was going to visit a cousin in Pasadena, but I'll bet you're right," said Jack. "And in that case, I probably ought to follow him."

"Probably," said Susan hesitantly.

"On the other hand, he may really have a cousin in Pasadena."

"It's probably too late to go after him anyway, now," said Susan.

"Yes," Jack agreed readily, then added with a crimson blush, "I bought three sets of sheets this week."

"I don't think we should risk Hosmer's coming back unexpectedly," said Susan.

Jack's face fell.

"So let's stay here," said Susan. "Tripod!" she called through the closed doorway. "If you see Ida coming back, bark!"

❀ ❀ ❀

Jack and Susan did not stir from Susan's bungalow the rest of Saturday and all day Sunday. Tripod's growling grew hoarse at Susan's bedroom door. Toward evening, Jack staggered home. Ida Conquest returned half an hour later, and Junius Fane drove up the street five minutes after that.

Hosmer Collamore, it turned out, did not return on Sunday night at all. When Jack discovered this on Monday morning, he was annoyed on two counts. First, Susan might have spent the night with him without fear of discovery. Second, Jack and Susan's suspicion that Hosmer's absence had to do more with the stolen patent than with a pretty cousin in Pasadena was strengthened.

When Hosmer didn't show up for work at the studio, Fane ranted for a few minutes, fired Hosmer *in absentia*, and stuck Hosmer's apprentice in his place.

So, even without Hosmer, Manfred Mixon's new farcical epic proceeded apace. Susan sat in her office in the morning and quickly typed out the new scenes for Jack, Miss Songar, and Tripod. Fane read them while eating his sandwich at lunch, approved them, sent them over to props for the procurement of the necessary furnishings for the three scenes that were to be filmed that afternoon.

Manfred Mixon's "front parlor" was actually three canvas walls, a threadbare rug, and three or four pieces of old-fashioned velvet-upholstered furniture, perched on a stage on a Hollywood hillside. Jack was very tall and moony, Miss Songar was very short and coy, and Tripod threw himself at Jack at every opportunity—tearing at his trouser cuffs, clamping his teeth down on his watch, and worrying his shoe as if it were a sewer rat.

When his work was finished, Jack crept down the hill toward the back of the studio. Slipping into the thick shrubbery behind the old livery stable, he sidled along the wall until he came to the window of Susan's office. He tapped at the glass.

Susan got up from her desk, shut the door, and went over to the window.

"How did you do?" she asked.

"Well, Fane says that he's going to ask you for a couple of scenes for me to play with Mixon, so I suppose I did well enough. So did Tripod. Every time Fane told him to attack, he attacked."

"I spoke to the men in the laboratory this afternoon. They said that Hosmer came here to the studio yesterday."

"Then he wasn't in Pasadena."

"He stayed for about an hour, and then left. They don't know what he was doing. Do you think we ought to warn Mr. Fane?"

Jack shook his head. "Not yet. Maybe Hosmer was just clearing out. Despite what we think of him, he's a good cameraman. Maybe he just got an offer somewhere. The studios out here make a practice of stealing from one another. I suppose they have to have a little excitement now that they're so far away from the Patents Trust."

"Oh, no!" said Susan.

"What?"

"You don't suppose that's who Hosmer is working for, do you? And has been all along? And that your patent went to them?"

"I don't know," said Jack. "But if he was working for the Trust, then I don't think we've heard the last of him."

CHAPTER TWENTY-EIGHT

WHEN JACK GOT back to his bungalow that day, he found no sign of Hosmer himself. But there was evidence that he'd been there: He'd returned for his clothes—and for good measure he had taken a few of Jack's personal items and all the food in the cupboards.

Nothing more was heard of Hosmer that week. *Plunder* was edited and spliced together. Positives were made, and every title card added the Cosmic Film Studio's new California address at the bottom. Publicity distributed with the prints extolled the lengths to which Cosmic had gone in order to establish a new plateau of moving-picture realism. The breathtaking holdup had been filmed on a genuine Kansas prairie, and the thrilling scene in which Jack Beaumont, the new Cosmic Hero, was dragged down Sunset Boulevard was true and real in every respect, and the couple in the car were genuine, unsuspecting citizens of Hollywood, California, the new home of the Cosmic Film Studio.

A second page of publicity concerned the romance between Jack Beaumont and Ida Conquest, "The Lovers of the Decade." Jack was touted as having been born to a patrician American family, having been educated at Yale, and having been a broker on Wall Street for some years before turning to moving-picture acting as his true profession. Ida Conquest had been born of parents well-known on the classical stages of London and Paris, had worked as a child with the immortal actors of the English stage, and had turned down offers of marriage from titled Europeans.

Jack's biography was gospel. Ida's contained not one iota of truth.

Photoplay magazine had recently begun running photographs of moving-picture stars and wanted a photograph of Jack Beaumont and Ida Conquest. It was thought wonderfully romantic by the editor that Jack and Ida lived in adjoining bungalows in Hollywood. The problem was that the barren yards were not particularly attractive as a backdrop. At Cosmic's expense, therefore, Junius Fane hired a team of gardeners to landscape the two adjoining bungalows. One day when Jack and Susan returned from the studio, they found that they were now living in rose-bowered cottages. Grass had been planted in the front yard. Exotic evergreens shaded the windows. Climbing roses spilled over the doorways. Colorful flowers hedged the new stone walks to the street. A gleaming white picket fence had been erected on the property line between the two houses. (The surroundings of the other bungalows on the street, of course, remained nothing but dust.) Jack stood on his walk, and Susan and Tripod—on a short leash—stood on theirs, and looked at one another in astonishment.

"Just like the illustrations in the weekly serials," said Susan.

"Marry me and we'll live in a vine-covered cottage," said Jack.

Tripod howled in vigorous protest.

"Shhh!" cried Susan, and she hurried inside.

The next morning, Jack and Ida were photographed at the doorways of their respective bungalows, waving and smiling at each other. Then the two "Lovers of the Decade" met and modestly kissed across the gleaming picket fence chastely separating the houses.

Plunder and *The Timber Queen* proved to be the greatest successes yet for the Cosmic Film Studio, and to Manfred Mixon's indignation and fury, the Fabulous Fat Funny Fellow was eclipsed in box office earnings by the Lovers of the Decade. Jack's salary was trebled, to $135 a week, and Junius Fane allowed Jack to keep the bungalow solely to himself. Susan's salary, in recognition of her writing these masterpieces of the genre, was doubled to $110 a week, and Fane hired an assistant for her. (Her assistant was a cross-eyed fifteen-year-old girl with typing ability.) It was not known what recompense Ida Conquest received, but Susan soon noticed new diamond earrings and an entirely new wardrobe in the latest fashion.

Nothing was heard from Hosmer Collamore. Susan telephoned every film company in the area, asking if the man were employed there, but she had no luck in finding what had become of him. Jack visited a lawyer who agreed to investigate whether the camera improvement had yet been patented, and if so, in whose name. But despite this uncertainty regarding the stolen invention, Jack and Susan could hardly help being happy. At night, after Ida had crept next door to Fane's bungalow, Susan crept next door to Jack's. Tripod was left alone in the house, wandering disconsolately all night long—*pad pad pad tap*—through the darkened bungalow.

❀ ❀ ❀

The nights in California were hot and windy in the last week in June. It might have been too hot for Jack and Susan to lie together in the same narrow bed, had Jack not bought a new electrical contraption—an oscillating fan—and set it on a chair next to them. Crickets had taken up residence in the climbing roses outside the windows, and when it was otherwise still, they could hear the rhythmic pumping of the oil wells nearby.

"Are you jealous?" Jack asked.

"Jealous of what?" Susan asked in surprise.

"Of Ida. Those *Photoplay* pictures, Fane's puffery to the distributors and exhibitors. The fact that Ida and I shoot half a dozen love scenes a week now, and every time you take a stroll out to the stages, what you see is me kissing Ida."

"Oh, yes," said Susan, "I'm frantically jealous of Ida. What do you think?"

"I think we should get married."

"Why?" asked Susan.

"Because we sleep together every night."

"Before you came along, I slept with Tripod every night. *He* didn't run out after a license."

"What if we had children?"

"They would be good-looking and intelligent," said Susan.

"But we'd want them legitimate."

"That's why you want to get married, for the sake of children we don't have?"

"No, of course not. The reason I want to get married is that I love you."

"Ah," said Susan into his ear. "That's the same reason I want to marry you."

❈ ❈ ❈

The next evening, Susan asked Ida if she wouldn't bring Junius Fane over for a few minutes after dinner.

"Me?" exclaimed Ida. "What on earth do I have to do with Mr. Fane? Just because he lives next door to us doesn't mean I have any influence with him!"

Jack, who was sitting in the living room of Susan's bungalow in his shirtsleeves, a glass of iced tea in his hand, laughed and said, "Ida, Susan and I know what's going on. We'd be blind if we didn't."

"What?" screeched Ida. "Nothing is going on! Mr. Fane is a married man and my employer!"

Jack glanced at Susan, then spoke: "Come on, Ida, you and I are the Lovers of the Decade. Shouldn't that inspire a little confidence between us?"

Ida Conquest looked at Jack, and then she looked at Susan, and slowly a small idea dawned in her brain. "There is something going on here, too, isn't there?"

"There most certainly is," said Susan.

"I should have known it," crowed Ida. "I should have known there was a reason that damned dog was barking so much!"

So that night, about ten o'clock, four persons gathered in the living room: the president, owner and principal director of Cosmic Films; the Lovers of the Decade; and the head of the story department. Susan said, "I have an announcement. Jack and I are getting married."

Fane said, "But you hate each other."

"Nevertheless," said Susan, "Jack has asked me to marry him and I have agreed."

Fane thought about this for a few minutes, evidently considering what effect it would have on the business. "It's not going to look good for the Lovers of the Decade if one of them is married to someone else," he pointed out.

"They could keep it a secret," Ida suggested. "Or at the wedding Suss could dye her hair, and wear a long veil and we could take pictures and pretend it was me."

Fane considered this suggestion with evident seriousness.

"No," said Jack. "I don't think that's a wonderful idea."

"Could we keep it a secret?" asked Fane. "For the time being, I mean. Till the Lovers of the Decade are played out."

"How much of a secret?" asked Jack.

"Just quiet."

"How quiet?" asked Susan.

"Get rid of that dog," Ida suggested. "That would make it a lot quieter."

For once, Junius Fane seemed careful in his speech. "Ah, if you two would consent to...ah, carry on as you've been carrying on for a while longer, I'll double your salaries."

"You knew!" cried Ida. "How did you know? I *lived* with Suss and I didn't know!"

Jack and Susan exchanged glances, conferring silently over Fane's offer.

"Treble our salaries," said Jack.

Fane hesitated only a moment. "Done."

"Done," agreed Susan. Jack would be making nine times, and she six times what they'd started out with at Cosmic.

❀ ❀ ❀

The wedding was delayed for one reason and another—one reason and another always being one moving picture that Susan had to write, or that Jack had to act in. Finally, Jack said to Fane, "I know you don't want us to do it, but Susan and I are getting married next week. We're taking a week off and going down to San Diego for our honeymoon."

"Why are you two so desperate?" Fane demanded. "Is Susan...?"

"No, she's not," returned Jack. "In fact, we're not so desperate to get married as we are to have a week of rest. Having a honeymoon is just about the only way we can see of getting it."

"I'll let you go on two conditions."

"No," said Jack. "If we want to get married, we'll get married next week. Whether you like it or not."

"All right," said Fane, "then I'll just ask you to do me two little favors before you go off, leaving me and the company and everybody who works for the company high and dry."

"What are they?" Jack asked.

"I'd just ask that Susan write a couple of small scripts for us to shoot while you're away. Something for Ida, in which she doesn't have a love interest. If you're not going to be here, I don't want her playing against anybody else. Maybe she's a nun. Or maybe we can do a historical play— although I hate historical plays. Perhaps Susan should write something about Molly Pitcher. I remember the name from school, and there was nothing about a husband that I can recall. Tell Susan to look up Molly Pitcher in a history book and write a script about her. If Pitcher is married, then have her husband away in the war. If there's not a war, have him away at sea, or looking for the Northwest Passage or something. Ida's been pestering me to play in a costume drama, and we might as well do it while you're out of town."

"I don't think Susan will have any problem coming up with that. What was the other thing you wanted?"

"I want you to do two pictures next week," said Fane.

"I do one a week already!" Jack protested. "It's running me into the ground. Considering how bruised my body is underneath these clothes, it's a wonder that Susan—never mind. I can't do two pictures next week."

"You have to," said Fane. "We can't let the public forget who you are."

"They're not going to forget in a week."

"You don't know the public, Jack. They're fickle. They'll flock to someone else's pictures if they're disappointed in you. And they'll be disappointed in you if they don't get a picture a week. The American public has a hard heart, Jack. I know the American public. My mother was part of it."

Jack considered for a few moments.

"No," he said.

"It'll be easy," said Fane. "We'll just get Susan to write two little scripts, and she'll fix it so you're not in either one of them very much. You'll do one with Ida and you'll spend most of the picture tied up somewhere, and Ida has to rescue you. So all your scenes can be shot in a day or two. And then we'll put you in with Manfred and Miss Songar again. Manfred will be a traveling salesman, I think, going from house to house, and you and Miss Songar are a newlywed couple trying to set up your household. You'll only have to play in a few scenes. You can accuse Miss Songar of carrying on a dalliance with Manfred and storm out of the house. We can even shoot it in your own bungalow, and you can be packing all the while. Two pictures like that—it won't even seem like one."

Jack hesitated. "All right," he said, "but you've got to pay me—and Susan—double for the week."

"Done."

"After all, what could happen between now and next Saturday?"

CHAPTER TWENTY-NINE

"THERE'S A TRAIN for San Diego on Friday night," Susan said to Jack, as she pored over the timetable. "If we're married by then, we can have an extra day at the hotel." They were going to honeymoon at the Hotel del Coronado, on an island off San Diego. Their stay there was Fane's wedding gift to them.

"Are you certain you don't need a—a big ceremony?" Jack asked. "Church, flowers, attendants, wedding breakfasts, and the like? Because we could…"

"You have no family here. I have no family here. We started work on the day we arrived in California, and we haven't paused for breath since. Even Tripod is exhausted when we get back from the studio, and Junius now wants me to write a series of two-reelers featuring Perks and his little girl Millie."

"Let me guess," said Jack. "Millie's an orphan, and an unscrupulous uncle—probably played by her father—has stolen her fortune, and thrown her out into the world with only a three-legged dog to protect her."

"Something like that," said Susan. "Anyway, I'm too tired for a church wedding, and attendants, and wedding breakfasts. Something nice and quiet will do nicely, thank you."

The decision was a wise one. By the end of the week, the two were more exhausted than usual, with Jack acting in two different pictures at once, which required not only the shooting of additional scenes, but two sets of costumes and two different makeups. One was the Manfred Mixon comedy, in which Jack fell off a roof, was nearly drowned in a water tank, and finally was crushed beneath the Fabulous Fat Funny Fellow himself. The other was another in the series of Jack Beaumont-Ida Conquest adventures that had proved so popular. It was called *The Crimson Stain Mystery*. In it Jack played an inventor in love with Ida Conquest, a young, beautiful, and innocent variety performer. Jack's invention, a device that could see through walls and floors and would be of invaluable aid to the police, was stolen by Ida's Old Suitor, and turned over to Rank Villains. The Rank Villains, led by the Old Suitor, captured Jack and Ida in different parts of town and left them to die in improbable ways.

On Friday morning—Jack and Susan's wedding day—Jack stayed home and packed for the two of them. Mixon's comedy had finished filming the day before, leaving him a few hours of respite. When he was finished, he set the bags by the door, left the house, then walked up to Melrose Avenue where he caught a taxi to take him to the studio. He went around back to the stages, and watched the filming of the scenes of Ida's captivity by the Rank Villains and the Old Suitor.

In a tiny bare room, somewhere in the wilds of New Jersey, Ida plays a hand of solitaire, unsuspecting that the cards have been impregnated with a poison that is ingested through the skin. Every game may be her last. She feels faint. She mops her brow. She rolls her eyes, falls back in the chair, recovers herself a little, and gathers the cards together for another round. Moments later, the intrepid Tripod, sensing danger in the deck, leaps up on to the table (in itself no easy task for a short dog with three legs), and snatches away the pack of cards with his teeth. Ida runs after the dog to retrieve the cards, her only means of passing the time. Tripod falls over in a doggy swoon. Ida draws back in horror, realizing that the cards have been poisoned. She snatches them out of Tripod's mouth and flings them out a window. She gathers the brave, self-sacrificing pet to her bosom, strokes his wooden leg, and sheds a quiet tear.

"Exactly what I wanted!" cried Fane.

Jack and Susan, standing apart, politely applauded Ida's performance. Tripod, coming suddenly to life again, stood on the edge of the stage, trying to decide whether to jump into Susan's arms for a cuddle or to hurl himself at Jack.

"Good dog, Tripod," said Fane, giving the dog a biscuit. Tripod wagged his tail, and tapped his wooden leg against the stage in acknowledgment of the director's praise. Fane then announced to the crew, "We'll stop for lunch now! There's only a little to do in the afternoon."

❁ ❁ ❁

Jack's lunch—on this day of his wedding—was a ham sandwich and a glass of sugary lemon soda. He ate it as he was fitted for his costume for the afternoon's shooting. Fane came to him in the wardrobe room.

"What is this padding for?" Jack asked curiously. A kind of thin mattress was being wound around his body and tacked into place.

"That's for the barbed wire," said Fane.

Over the padding Jack was dressed in a cowboy outfit: jeans, a red checked shirt, suspenders, and a wide-brimmed hat.

"I don't remember reading anything in the scenario about barbed wire," said Jack.

"Well," said Fane, "this is the scene in the script where you're hanging from a tree branch, but I thought it would be more exciting if you were hanging upside down from the roof of a barn—we'll use the old barn that's attached to the studio—but first I thought we'd have Mr. Perks wrap you in barbed wire, and then hoist you up, tickle you with a feather and then slash your back open with a whip."

"Did Susan think this up?" Jack asked, adjusting his hat in a mirror.

"It's my own invention," said Fane proudly. Then, drawing Jack aside, he said in a low, conspiratorial voice, "It's all set. Susan went home to dress, and she'll be back up here in a couple of hours. Then I'm going to drive you over to a justice of the peace in Culver City, and Ida and I will act as your witnesses. You'll be on the train to San Diego by seven o'clock."

"If I survive this afternoon," said Jack ruefully.

A decrepit barn was attached to one end of the former livery stable, but it had been in such disrepair when Cosmic took over the place that it had not been part of the conversion. Now it was used to house props, bits of furniture, and rolls of painted canvas. For this scene, the center area had been cleared, a hole had been knocked in the roof to admit sunlight, and a pulley attached to the roof beam. It was on this pulley that Jack was to be hoisted up on his barbed-wire covered rope.

The leader of the pack of Rank Villains who have imprisoned and attempted to poison the Heroine corners the Hero in a barn belonging to the head of the traveling troupe that employs the Heroine. On

> *the walls of the barn are hung the painted cloths representing a European town, mountain scenery, the stormy sea. The Hero is just about to overcome the Rank Villain in hand-to-hand combat when he is struck over the head with the dull end of an ax wielded by the seven-year-old daughter of the Rank Villain. As the Hero lies unconscious on the floor of the barn, the Rank Villain lashes his feet and hands with rope, and then slaps him into consciousness again. The Rank Villain's daughter holds a gun on the Hero as the Rank Villain unrolls a bale of barbed wire round and round his body.*

Jack's look of apprehension as Mr. Perks wrapped him in barbed wire was real enough. He was dubious about the efficacy of the mattress in protecting him against steel barbs.

When this portion of the scene was finished, Fane stopped the cameras, and checked Jack to make sure that he was all right. Jack stood in the middle of the barn, bound and wrapped and gagged. The sweat on his brow glistened in the hot sunlight pouring through the hole in the roof.

"Just nod if you're all right," said Fane.

Jack shook his head vehemently no.

"Well then," said Fane, "we'll make it quick."

Fane backed out of the way. A stout rope, twisted round with barbed wire, had been raised to the roof, placed into the groove of the pulley, and dropped down to another wheel on the barn floor. (There would be no explanation in the picture as to what other use such an absurd device might be put, but Mr. Fane had never been one to be as concerned with plausibility as with drama.)

With a sinister grin, Mr. Perks and his daughter Millie—the seven-year-old was making her debut in *The Crimson Stain Mystery*—turned the wheel.

The rope and barbed wire—attached to Jack's ankles—suddenly pulled taut. Jack lost his balance and tumbled to the floor of the barn. In order not to fall in such a way as to plunge the wire into his body, Jack arched, and landed as much as he could on his shoulders and the toes of his feet.

He eased down against the floor, but had only a moment's respite before his ankles were jerked up into the air.

Mr. Perks and Millie toiled mightily with the wheel. Slowly Jack was hoisted aloft—gagged, sheathed tightly in barbed wire, upside down, sweating in the sunlight.

"All right, Millie," said Fane coaxingly, "bring over that little chair and put it underneath Mr. Beaumont. That's right, make sure the seat is turned out toward the camera. Now stand on the chair and take out your feather. Have you got it? Good. Now tickle his nose! That's right. No, don't look at me, just listen to what I say, and do what I tell you, and you'll be fine. Mr. Beaumont won't hurt you, he's all tied up. Good, now stick the feather in his ear. Do you have two feathers? Wonderful! Take out the other one and stick it in his other ear. Very good, Millie! Very, very good. Now get down off the chair and take it away, because here comes your father with the bullwhip..."

Oftentimes Jack had longed for his quiet, neat desk on Wall Street, with the noise of New York City outside. And this was one of those times. Wall Street had its sharks, that was true, but on Wall Street he'd never been gagged, bound with barbed wire, suspended upside down, and tickled with feathers.

The sweat poured down Jack's neck, welled in the hollow beneath his chin, overflowed that pool and streamed down his cheeks to spill into his eyes. He tried to blink away the stinging water, but it was no use. Jack was blinded.

"Mr. Perks!" he heard Fane call out. "Mr. Perks, where are you? Rest easy for a few moments, Jack, we seem to have lost Mr. Perks. Will somebody go and—"

But Fane's command ended in a strangled cry. And a—

CRACK!

—that was the obvious report of a firearm. An almost simultaneous—

PING!

—on the other side of Jack demonstrated amply that the firearm wasn't firing blank cartridges, but real bullets.

Jack jerked himself from side to side, slinging the perspiration from his eyes. He blinked rapidly, and widened them.

What he saw was even less to be desired than the sight of Perks advancing with his bullwhip.

Three men with masks stood inside the doors of the studio barn. Each held two guns.

Fane lay on the ground.

The two cameramen and Fane's assistant cowered behind a sofa used in parlor scenes.

Millie Perks was hiding behind an urn, visible to Jack but not to the masked men.

CRACK. CRACK. CRACK.

The guns fired again and smashed the cameras.

A fourth masked man, shorter than the others, entered. He halted when he saw Jack and pulled a pistol from his pocket. Raising it in his right hand, he took aim.

With his other hand, he drew down the mask from his face.

Even upside down, Jack had no difficulty recognizing Hosmer Collamore.

CHAPTER THIRTY

"N O!" SHOUTED one of the masked men. "No killing!"
Hosmer paused. Slowly he lowered his arm.

"Get them out of here," Hosmer said, pointing at the three cowering cameramen. "Him, too," he added, indicating Fane, who slowly regained consciousness, but rolled and groaned on the floor.

"What about that one?" asked another of the masked men, pointing at Jack.

"You make sure the fires are set in the offices," said Hosmer. "I'll take care of him."

Soon the barn was cleared of everyone except Hosmer and Jack. The former Cosmic cameraman slowly approached where Jack hung upside down, his head six feet from the floor.

Hosmer stood beneath him, looked up and smiled.

Sweat dripped off Jack's face into Hosmer's eyes, and Hosmer wiped the liquid away.

Hosmer reached up, and pressed the barrel of his revolver against Jack's temple.

"I've always hated you," Hosmer hissed. "I have often dreamed of finding you in just such a position as this."

Jack, having a gag in his mouth, could only respond with a muffled, throaty sound.

"You are tall, and I am not. You are good-looking, and I am not. I wore clothes that were new and expensive, and did not look as good in them as you looked in patched trousers and threadbare jackets. Susan Bright only laughed at me even though I wanted desperately for her to like me. She fell in love with you even when she didn't wish to. I worked a camera for seven years, day in and day out, and you looked at the camera once and found out a way to improve it, and that improvement—if you had managed to hold on to the patent—would have made you a rich man. On top of everything, I discovered that you were born to a rich family, and you threw it all away. I was born poor, and have struggled all my life to get what little I do have. It seems to me that those are very good reasons for being glad to see you in this position now."

Perspiration now poured into Jack's nose, and then was caught in his windpipe. He jerked and coughed with such vehemence that the cloth gag exploded from his mouth.

"Hosmer," said Jack, "I smell smoke."

"That's the studio," said Hosmer. "It's on fire. Soon this building will be on fire as well. Buildings burn even quicker and easier in California than they do in New York."

"*You* set the Cosmic fire in New York," said Jack.

"Yes," said Hosmer.

"You were a spy for the Patents Trust," said Jack.

"Yes," said Hosmer, smiling and spinning the revolver's bullet chamber. The chamber was filled.

"You stole my drawings and turned them over to the Trust, and they patented my invention."

"Yes," said Hosmer.

"Now I suppose you're going to shoot me."

"No," said Hosmer. "I'm going to let you burn to death."

❀ ❀ ❀

With small comfort, Jack thought that he would probably suffocate from the smoke before he actually felt the tongues of flame on his body. The walls of a building burn before the floor. This was of little consolation to him, nor did it matter that the gag was now gone.

"Help! *Help!*" he shouted, but no one came.

The smell of smoke grew stronger.

"I'm leaving now," said Hosmer, who still stood just beneath Jack. "Sweet dreams. Or whatever it is people say before you're about to go to sleep forever. It's a pity you and Susan couldn't make it up before now. I'll make sure I offer her my condolences tomorrow."

"Susan and I were to be married today," said Jack.

"I'll bring flowers then," said Hosmer, with an unpleasant, upside-down grin.

Behind Hosmer, Jack could see smoke seeping in through the wall of the barn where it was attached to the other building.

Jack shook the perspiration from his eyes once more. When they had cleared, he caught sight of Millie Perks, who was now hiding beneath an ornately carved table pushed over to one side. "Millie!" he shouted. "Run."

The child, obedient to a fault, had been waiting for just such a command to seek safety and she hurtled out of her hiding place toward the open door.

Hosmer saw the sudden movement out of the corner of his eye, and he turned instinctively with his revolver, cocking it as he did so. Raising it to the hurrying, tiny figure of the little girl who had witnessed all and heard all, Hosmer started to squeeze the trigger.

Gathering all the force of his will, his strength, and his balance, Jack folded up his body and jerked on his rope, swinging violently to the side. He opened his mouth wide, and then clamped his jaws shut.

Jack's teeth closed on the skin of Hosmer's ear.

The revolver went off, but the shot flew wild.

Millie Perks screamed and dashed out through the door.

Hosmer tried to pull himself away from Jack, but Jack only gripped harder with his jaws on Hosmer's ear. If Hosmer pulled any harder, then the ear would be torn away.

Shouting in agony, Hosmer swung his arm around and slapped his revolver into the side of Jack's head.

Jack's head reeled to one side, but he did not open his jaws. He could taste the cameraman's thick, salty blood in his mouth.

"Let go!" Hosmer screamed. "Let go or I'll shoot you!"

"Jack!" shouted another voice—a female voice—from the door of the barn.

Through the haze of perspiration that blinded his eyes, Jack made out Susan's figure in the doorway. He heard her coughing from the smoke. He could see that she was carrying something, and whatever it was, she dropped it down to the floor.

It was Tripod.

Growling furiously, the dog flew to the center of the barn.

Susan commanded the dog, "Hosmer! Attack Hosmer! Not Jack."

Tripod had no intention of obeying that command, but Jack was suspended six feet from the ground. To get to him, the terrier had to climb up Hosmer Collamore, whose ear was still caught in Jack's mouth.

Dogs are not known for their climbing skills, and it must only be supposed that dogs with fewer than four legs have a harder time scaling heights than dogs possessing the full complement of limbs. So great was Tripod's dislike of Jack Beaumont that he fairly flew up Hosmer Collamore, dragging paws and nails into the fabric of the cameraman's trousers and shirt, in order to get to Jack's neck, so invitingly and vulnerably displayed.

With his ear caught between Jack's jaws, and his flesh being rent in a dozen places by the sharp claws and wooden leg of the terrier, Hosmer Collamore was mad with pain. He cried out and raised the revolver at the dog and fired.

The bullet plowed right through Tripod's leg—

Tripod's *wooden* leg—

—snapping it in half.

Sensing the aggression in this action, Tripod stopped in his ascent and sunk his teeth into Hosmer's wrist, shaking it till the revolver dropped from his grasp.

Susan ran forward and snatched the weapon up from the floor. She cocked it again, and trained it on Hosmer's heart.

"All right," she said. "Tripod, get down. Jack, let go of Hosmer's ear. Hosmer, if you make one move toward me, you're going to be whistling out of your neck."

Tripod slid down Hosmer's body, using his claws as a drag this time. On the ground, he listed seriously toward the back on his shattered artificial leg.

Jack gratefully released Hosmer's ear, then spat out Hosmer's blood on to the floor.

Hosmer dropped to the floor, cupping his injury with his hand and moaning.

"Can you get me down?" asked Jack plaintively.

"Tell me how," said Susan.

An unrolled canvas depicting a mountain range, which had been hung against the wall nearest the studio, burst suddenly into flame. Behind it, Jack saw that the entire back wall of the barn was burning. Acrid, suffocating smoke rolled toward them, and Jack very nearly lost sight of Susan.

"That wheel over there has a lock on it," said Jack, motioning toward the wheel that Perks had turned to raise Jack to his present position. "Unfasten the lock, and turn the wheel slowly."

Susan backed over to the wheel, keeping the revolver still trained on Hosmer, who was now examining the wounds Tripod had inflicted beneath his trousers and vest.

"Don't move, Hosmer," said Susan. But the lock mechanism on the pulley system was intricate, and Susan had to put down the revolver in order to manage it.

The wounded cameraman saw his opportunity to flee the burning building. He got to his feet, and stumbled toward the barn door, now a menacing rectangle of fire.

Susan, keeping her priorities straight, struggled with the lock on the wheel, and finally got it unfastened. Slowly she started to lower Jack to the floor. Tripod stood directly below Jack, leaping up on his three legs and snapping his jaws menacingly.

"Tripod!" Susan shouted. "Stop that! Hosmer's the one you want. Go after Hosmer!"

Ignoring this, the dog continued to snap at Jack's descending head.

"Tripod," shouted Susan hysterically, "if you don't go after Hosmer and leave Jack alone, I will never forgive you, and when Jack and I go off on our honeymoon, I'm going to leave you with Ida!"

The terrier, as if he understood every word, cast one more glance of regret and angry frustration at Jack's head, and then bounded across the barn toward Hosmer—as quickly as he could on three-and-a-half legs.

Having stopped with fright at the burning doorway, Hosmer was about to plunge through when Tripod leaped and snagged the seat of his trousers. The cameraman went down in a billow of smoke.

Jack's head plunked against the barn floor, and then the rest of him settled on the rough wooden planks. The floor was hot.

Susan rushed over and tried to release Jack from his bonds, but the complicated knots in the barbed wire made this an impossible task. "Spread your legs," Susan commanded.

"I can't. They're tied together!" Jack cried.

"Try," said Susan. She took the revolver, pressed the barrel between Jack's ankles, and fired at the knotted ropes.

Jack saw powder singe holes in his stockings and felt it burn his ankles.

His feet were free, though his legs, torso, and arms remained bound with the rope and barbed wire, and he was still lying on the smoking floor of a barn that was burning beyond redemption.

"I'm going to try to lift you up," said Susan, hurrying around and grabbing him by the shoulders. Using all her strength, and with as much help as he could provide under the circumstances, they managed to get Jack up off the floor and on to his knees.

"I can't get up," he said, choking with the smoke that now filled the barn. They were lost in its whiteness, illuminated from above. "I can't even see the door."

"Tripod!" called Susan. "Bark!"

Tripod barked from outside the doorway.

"That way!" cried Susan.

"But I can't move!" protested Jack. "I'm still tied up."

"Try not to breathe," whispered Susan, and she pushed him down to the floor again.

Jack gulped in some smokeless air that remained in a layer a couple of inches from the floor.

Then he felt a jerk, as his legs were suddenly pulled around, and his cheek and neck were scraped against the rough, uneven floor of the barn. He raised his head to prevent further abrasions.

Grabbing the ends of the rope that were still tied tightly around him, Susan began to drag Jack across the barn. He weighed nearly seventy pounds more than she.

It was nearly impossible for her to breathe, and the spurs of the barbed wire caught in dozens of places along the rough-hewn boards of the floor. Still Susan pulled.

Coughing, snagged every foot or so, short of breath, torn and stretched, nearly smothered by the mattress wrapped around his body, with clothing that was already smoking, Jack was pulled to the burning door of the barn and safety. Tripod, barking continuously, guided Susan out of the building.

When Jack reached the outside, he rolled in the cool earth and tumbled down an incline into a bed of sweet-smelling flowers. A few moments later, Susan knelt beside him and wiped his face with the hem of the dress she was to have worn at her wedding.

"You saved my life," he said.

"Tripod brought down Hosmer," Susan replied. "And the police have arrested him."

Just then, Junius Fane appeared over her shoulder, staring down at Jack. The director wore a bandage jauntily over one ear. "Jack, I'm glad you're all right. Hosmer and his friends did such a good job on our cameras today that I'm afraid we're going to have to do that scene over."

CHAPTER THIRTY-ONE

JACK SAT ON the curb across from the burned build-ings. Susan helped him peel off his padding. It stuck in places where the barbed wire had pierced through and bloodied his skin. Junius Fane came across the road to them, more jauntily than they could have expected, under the circumstances.

"Well, Hosmer's been arrested for attempted murder," said Fane cheerfully. "That ought to pick up your spirits."

"It always seems like we're starting over," said Jack.

"Not so bad as all that," said Fane. "I'd only rented the livery stable, and everything inside was insured."

"But the prints—the negatives," Susan protested. "They're irreplaceable."

"Exactly," said Fane. "That's why I keep copies of everything in my house. They're stacked in the back bedroom, and we can have everything reproduced. In ten days' time, we'll be good as new and in full production again." Fane checked his watch. "Are you two about ready?"

"Ready for what?" asked Jack. "I feel like I'm ready for a nice quiet grave in a cool green graveyard is what I'm ready—*aggggghhh*!"

"Stop bellowing," said Susan. "That's the last of it."

"Ready for what?" Jack repeated as he gasped for breath through gritted teeth.

"For the wedding, you dolt," said Susan.

❀ ❀ ❀

Half an hour later, Junius Fane's Speedking Sixty drew up before a tiny house in the suburb of Culver City, which was as quiet and as sedate as many people wished Hollywood was. Several huge old orange trees surrounded the house and a tangle of roses grew across the front and up on to the roof; the place desperately wanted a coat of paint. A sign on the door read "Justice of the Peace."

The justice of the peace was a pudgy, middle-aged man with pomaded hair, a pursed smile, and eyeglasses with tiny round purple lenses. It was difficult to tell whether the odor inside the house emanated from the roses outside or some powder that the gentleman wore on his skin. He gasped in astonishment when the wedding party entered his parlor.

"It's the Lovers of the Decade!" he exclaimed. "Oh, Lord, I wish Ma was here today. Ma usually acts as my witness, but I was told you were bringing two with you, so she went out to have her hair curled. The Pacific Ocean takes the curl right out of a lady's hair, as I'm sure you have noticed. Wait till she discovers who was here, and who got married today! Miss Conquest, I admire you exceedingly. Mr. Beaumont, there is no other word for it, you are a man's man, I tell Ma that all the time. In *Plunder*, when you was dragged beneath that car, it was the most thrilling thing I ever saw in my life, and I said to Ma, 'Ma,' I said, 'Mr. Beaumont is a man's man.' I have lived in California for eleven years, and Ma has been out here six, and it is a different place, let me tell you, since you movies came in. Miss Conquest, you are very lovely today."

"This is my new frock from *The Crimson Stain Mystery*," Ida said. "It is made from my own sketch, and I chose the bolt of cloth myself."

"And that is *really* your dog," sighed the justice of the peace, seeing Tripod asleep in Ida's arms. "He is very well behaved."

"Gave him a sleeping draft," Ida explained chummily, "else he'd be right at Jack's throat. Jack and Tripod—well, they're not exactly friends of the bosom."

"Oh, Lord," exclaimed the justice, in barely restrained ecstasy, "this is the first time I have ever entertained true stars in my house. Is *Photoplay* going to take a photograph of the rose-covered wedding bower? This used to be an orange grove, but then there was these houses built here, and I moved in and started witnessing documents and marrying people and Ma suggested I plant roses to make it more appropriate. I have a photograph of the place, for couples that wants one for a souvenir, and usually I charge a dollar, but I can let you have it for free, and perhaps I should send one to *Photoplay*? Their address is listed inside, and it wouldn't be no trouble."

"No," Mr. Fane put in quickly. "This is to be a private ceremony. That is why we came here, because it's out of the way. We don't want—"

"But Miss Conquest and Mr. Beaumont are the Lovers of the Decade! All America will want to see a picture of the rose-covered cottage in which they was wed!"

"Ida is not the bride," Susan said dryly. "I am."

The justice of the peace stared at Susan as if she had just risen up out of the floor.

Jack put his arm around Susan. "I'm marrying this woman, Susan Bright," said Jack. "Ida is here as a friend and witness."

"And to hold the damn dog," Ida interjected.

The justice of the peace shook his head ruefully, as if the shenanigans of moving-picture people were quite beyond him.

"Are you sure, Mr. Beaumont?" he asked, casting a doubtful eye at Susan, whose frock was as simple as Ida's getup was ornate.

Jack hesitated a moment, and Susan jabbed him in the ribs. "Quite sure," he said.

❦ ❦ ❦

Jack and Susan's week-long honeymoon was made up of equal parts of their bedroom and the sea. On one afternoon they took Tripod to the zoo, where he was the only animal with three legs. Junius Fane and Ida drove down toward the end of the week, and the two couples had dinner at the hotel together. Their table on the terrace overlooked the cool, sparkling Pacific.

Ida and Fane were celebrating not only Jack and Susan's wedding, but also the fact that Fane's wife in New York had just run off with a partner in Essanay, one of the members of the Patents Trust. So Fane was going to get not only his divorce. He could marry Ida, and—ultimately—he was going to have the satisfaction of seeing his wife's new lover fail.

It was becoming apparent the Trust was on its last legs.

"There are two anti-trust trials coming up this fall, in New York and Washington," Fane said. "Guess who's going to be a star witness? Hosmer Collamore, in return for our dropping a conspiracy charge that was tacked on to his attempted murder. When the Trust brings up how we've stolen their patents, we're going to put Hosmer on the stand to testify how the Trust paid him to steal your invention. *That'll* take a little of the wind out of their sails," said Fane. "We've already instituted a suit to recover your property."

"Property?" echoed Susan.

"That device has already brought in more than thirty thousand dollars," said Fane. "We're suing for that, we're suing for damages—we're suing them for the polish on their shoes."

"Thirty thousand dollars?" Jack exclaimed. "Maybe I should invent something else."

"No," said Fane. "I want you and Ida to go on making pictures. I don't want you tinkering with machinery. That can be dangerous—and the last thing in the world I want is for you to go off and get yourself hurt."

❈ ❈ ❈

Bad fortune never comes singly; in balance, nor does good fortune. When Jack and Susan returned to Jack's cottage on the edge of the oil field, a telegram awaited them. Jack's uncle was forgiving him his former betrayal and begging him to return to New York.

"I know what happened," said Jack. "He discovered that his stepsons knew nothing about the business, and that they were driving a hundred-year-old company right off the track. That's what my uncle found out, and now he wants me back to help him out of his difficulties."

Susan blinked and looked around. "What are you going to do? Are you going back to New York? Or are you going to stay here in California?"

"We're married now," said Jack. "Isn't the question, 'What are we going to do?'"

"Not necessarily," said Susan. "I like it out here."

"That speaks volumes for my capacity to inspire love and devotion. You mean that if I went back to my uncle, you'd remain here with Fane and Ida?"

"And Tripod," said Susan. "I didn't marry a rich

young broker. I didn't marry an impoverished inventor. I married the Lover of the Decade."

Jack read the telegram again. "Uncle says he can hardly wait to meet Ida Conquest. He's seen every one of our pictures, and greatly admires her beauty and her courage in the face of danger."

"What are you going to tell Junius?" Susan demanded, as she unpinned her hat.

Jack considered for a few moments, and then said, "I'm going to tell Fane that I'm moving back to New York."

Susan's face fell, and the light of love fled from her eyes.

Jack grinned. "Then he'll double my salary again, and I'll stay on here, as the Lover of the Century."

Susan hit Jack over the head with her hat, crushing the plumes.

"Bite him, Tripod," Susan commanded.

Tripod stood silently in the door of the room and wagged his stumpy little tail. Tripod had evidently forgiven Jack, possibly because Susan had married the man, and possibly because he was just too well pleased with the new leg—handsomely carved of whalebone ivory—that Jack had commissioned an old retired sailor to carve for him in San Diego.

THE END OF
JACK AND SUSAN'S ADVENTURE
IN 1913